Violets for Sgt. Schiller

Chris Helvey

A Wings ePress, Inc.
Historical Fiction Novel

Wings ePress, Inc.

Edited by: Jeanne Smith
Copy Edited by: Christie Kraemer
Executive Editor: Jeanne Smith
Cover Artist: Trisha FitzGerald-Jung
Cover images: ID 116097812 © Yagorrr | Dreamstime.com
ID 138981622 © Ilkin Guliyev | Dreamstime.com

Wings ePress Books
www.wingsepress.com

ISBN 978-1-61309-570-6
1-61309-570-8

Published In the United States Of America

Wings ePress Inc.
3000 N. Rock Road
Newton, KS 67114

Dedication

For my brother, Andy, and sister, Margaret,
who have put up with me and helped me immeasurably,
all their lives

* * *

One

The Plaza de la Enfants

I am strolling across the Plaza de la Enfants. The sun blazes in a cloudless sky while a band plays a martial tune at the corner.

Before me, a small boy is buying a balloon from the balloon man. He buys a red one, the color of fresh blood, then turns and runs back to an old woman in black who leans on her cane. She is smiling, and they hold hands while a cavalcade of pigeons struts around them. The old woman and the small boy stand in the shadow of the statue of Saint Marguerite. It is a hot day and the winds of Paris have been still all this summer. Under my hat I am sweating and suddenly a longing to be strolling among the thick forests of Bavaria rushes through me.

But I have business to attend to before I can go home. This has been a busy summer for me and I should be grateful. After all, not many poets can claim to have signed three contracts for their books in a single summer.

Over the years, I have noticed that life seems to come at once in cycles, or tides if you will. The tides are coming in now for Karl Ernst

Schiller and gratitude would be appropriate. Yet, I am tired and hot and lonely, and long for home.

As I step among the pigeons, they cry out and rise in a feather whirling mass, obscuring the sun for a moment before they angle above the old woman, the boy, and the statue of Saint Marguerite. Someone, I cannot recall their name at the moment, once told me that she is the patron saint of lost children. But I am a spiritual man and not a religious one, and therefore cannot answer for the veracity of this claim.

The little boy laughs as the birds fly by him and his laughter follows me across the Rue Rampart. The laughter seems to echo in the air. Today the air is not the same as it was yesterday, or the day before, or the week before, or the month before. There is a hollow quality to it and to the day. That quality implies both the air and the day are fragile and that one misstep would shatter the world.

As I reach the far side of the street, I pause to look back. The old woman has turned away, but the little boy still stares at me. At this moment he seems like a younger, more innocent version of myself. In unison, we raise an arm and wave. Somehow it seems that I am saying good-bye to myself.

A bent little man with drooping mustaches has set up his flower cart on the curb. It is a small cart and many of the flowers do not appear particularly fresh. However, he does have a nice pot of violets. Violets have been my favorite flower for as long as I have had memory.

The first I can recall were wild ones in the woods outside of Koblenz. Each summer I would see them, purple and cool looking, on a hot day such as this one. My aunt often took me for long walks in the woods. Beneath the trees it was always dark and cool, and you felt as though you could draw a good breath. Shadows lay on the earth like soft, dark blankets. Under the pines there were violets. I remember laughing when I saw the first patch of violets and running to pick them. I must have been five or six years old.

My aunt followed me. Her name was Berta. We sat among the violets and picked great handfuls of them. We both laughed so loudly that the squirrels scampered up to the tops of the trees. My aunt was a plump woman with a pretty face and bad teeth. Her husband was an old man and she had no children of her own. I recall the tightness of her hugs, and that tears soon replaced the laughter. She said the violets could be our secret. For years I have not thought of that afternoon. I have kept that simple secret well. I am a good keeper of secrets.

Two

Monsieur Aubier

As I climb the stairs, I hear the lilting sounds of a violin. It is being played by a Japanese girl who lives on the second floor. I have seen her twice when visiting Monsieur Aubier. Monsieur Aubier is my publisher. The girl is quite young. She is blind and lives with her grandmother. All the tunes she plays sound blue to me. Colors are very important to me...colors and light. Often I see life solely in those two realms. I recall lines from a poem I wrote last fall:

Blue slowdances up the stairs
In the arms of mauve
as night falls in an uneasy Paris

On the landing of the fourth floor, I lean against the wall to recover my breath. For a man not yet thirty I am in deplorable condition. My days of kicking a football around and hiking the mountain trails seem to belong to a distant past, or to another man. Yet it has been less than ten years since I left the university to strike out on my own. What, I wonder, will another ten years bring?

The clutter of pans and the voice of a woman singing arise from behind the door to apartment 14. She has a pleasant voice, if slightly off key. She is singing a love song that was popular thirty years before.

Behind the door to number 14 live M. Aubier and his wife, Marie. Their daughter Michelle lives there, too, when she is not visiting cousins in Burgundy. For seven years, M. Aubier has been my publisher.

Hand raised; I pause. For the first time I notice that the door is scarred. Someone has kicked it so hard that it has splintered near the bottom and the wood badly needs painting. I glance around me. Today it is obvious that the landing is quite tawdry. Cobwebs drape the corners and fly specks dot the single window. The wallpaper, which must at one time have been a bold blue and gold stripe, is now sadly faded. I wonder.

I knock and the singing ceases. Before I have time to wonder further, I hear the latch being lifted, the door creaks open, and Madame Aubier smiles at me. She has the shy smile of a little girl. At heart, despite her years, I think she is still a little girl. I have noticed it is impossible for some people to truly grow up.

Across the room, M. Aubier struggles to rise from his chair. When he was a boy of nineteen, during the last war, a shell struck the earth near him. Over one hundred fragments lodged in his legs. I am amazed that he does not harbor a burning hatred for all Germans. In those days the doctors were not well trained and his legs have never been right since. He is a remarkable man.

"Ah, Karl, come in, come in. And how is my favorite author? Sit, sit, I know you must be tired. No, exhausted after riding that awful, noisy train. Oh, how I hate loud noises."

There are not many seating choices. The chaise and most of the chairs are covered with books, or newspapers, or what appear to be coffee-stained manuscripts. I sit carefully on the edge of a chair that looks ancient. The spindly legs wobble, but hold.

M. Aubier leans forward and stretches out a hand dusty with age spots. Bones move visibly beneath the blemished skin. His hand touches my knee. With every visit there is the touching. It is as though M. Aubier wants to assure himself that I am real. Or that he is still alive.

"Some tea, M. Schiller? I fixed myself a cup a few moments ago."

"No, no, Marie, Herr Schiller needs something stronger than your chamomile tea. Bring me the wine bottle. Yes, yes, the red. Red is best for cutting the dust. My throat always gets so dry when I travel. It is as though it were coated with dust."

I only smile and nod. When one is around M. Aubier, one does not have to speak often. That is one of the reasons I enjoy visiting his apartment. Certainly, I am a man of words, but I prefer to write mine down.

As Marie Aubier gathers up the wine, I close my eyes. M. is correct. It has been a long day and I am tired. The train was noisy, hot, and full of people with restless eyes. This summer has been decorated with people of restless eyes. All the talk of tension between nations has put the wind up in them. Saber rattling scares the average man. For months I have been afraid. Not since Christmas have I had a really sound night's sleep. Uncle Franz, my father's brother, is in the government, a minister of some minor office. At one time, he was involved with the railroads, but during the winter changes were made. Uncle Franz says the kaiser will not be trifled with. According to my uncle, Wilhelm is volatile. Once, Franz called him a Prussian volcano. I wrote a poem about that, but never summoned the courage to submit it for publication.

Scents of soap and vanilla drift to my nostrils and I open my eyes. Madame Aubier is standing before me smiling. She has taken a moment to dab a drop of vanilla extract behind each ear and her face shines. Without speaking, she offers me a goblet of wine. The goblet is crystal, finely etched. She hands her husband a goblet. It is crystal, too, but the goblets do not match.

M. Aubier raises his glass and clears his throat. He has a marvelous voice...deep, resonant, mellow. Often I have wondered why he never took up the stage or politics. After all, they are much the same.

"A toast, Herr Schiller, a toast to our continued success."

"To success," I echo.

"And to peace," Madame chimes in.

"Of course, my dear." Monsieur leans closer and whispers conspiratorially, "Madame is quite nervous this summer. She is convinced that 1914 will be different than every other year." He laughs and we sip at our wine.

"But the newspapers," she says as her hands tremble faintly, fingers pointing at the papers. Looking around, I can see that newspapers are piled on the floor and on several chairs. Editions are all mixed up. Even a quick glance reveals that several feature prominent articles on the escalating tensions in the Balkans. Headlines reference Serbia and Austria. Such names mean little to me for I read more poems and novels than newspapers. Such behavior may no longer be wise. My uncle would tell me to remain informed. If I were bolder, I would tell him I am well informed, on more important matters.

"All they talk of is war." Madame picks up three newspapers at random. One carries today's date. "War is coming, There May Be War, Can War Be Avoided?"

"Yes, yes, I'll admit the news is glum, Marie. But you must remember, every summer there is talk of war. One year it was Turkey. Another summer, Greece. This year the eye of the world is on Serbia."

Monsieur shakes his head. "A curious place. I visited there once. 1903, I think." He sips his wine. "Have you been to Serbia, Herr Schiller?"

"No, I have not had the pleasure," I say. Frankly, I have little desire to travel anywhere, and no interest whatsoever in going to Serbia. I would far prefer to stay in my room and write. However, Monsieur Aubier is my publisher. Politics are important in the publishing world, too. "In April, however, I journeyed to Austria."

"Ah, Austria, what beautiful snows they have there!" exclaims Madame, and the conversation begins to flow. Now I can safely sip my wine and nod my head and murmur, "oh really" at the appropriate moments. The Aubiers love to talk, most especially when they have an appreciative audience, and I am a good listener.

I sip my wine while their chatter flows over me like a pleasant breeze. It is not a particularly cool one, but pleasant, nonetheless. For weeks the air has been hot and still, and even the thought of the word breeze makes me smile.

After a few minutes, the conversation falters and we all sit in companionable silence, reluctant to move on to the tasks at hand. There are contracts to be discussed and books to be autographed—a pile of them in one corner leans casually against the wall. But there seems no hurry. Nothing monumental ever seems to happen—the days spin on and on, some hot, some cold, children are born and old men die, yet nothing much happens. All of which is fine with me. I am partial to the subtle, the properly placed comma, the color of a ripe persimmon, the unique brushstrokes of a master.

The room grows quiet. So faintly it seems more a dream than reality, the notes of the violin drift into the room. The girl plays well today.

A cart rumbles by outside the window. The horse's hooves ring out against the pavement.

Madame's stomach rumbles and she blushes. When she blushes, she looks suddenly young.

A flicker of movement catches my eye. I wait and then it comes again—just at the edge of vision. Only when it occurs for the third time do I recognize it.

The curtains at the window are fluttering. At first, they move only sporadically, briefly. But soon they are dancing in a breeze that has risen from the hot earth. I glance at M. Aubier. He is looking at me. For a moment, we hold each other's glance. Then he makes caterpillar movements with his massive eyebrows.

I rise, then wander to the window. Across Rue Rampart the flags on the Plaza de la Enfants are flapping in the rising wind. Papers blow down the sidewalk. A man loses his hat and goes chasing after it. People stare at the sky.

Off to the west, clouds are beginning to mass. Purple rims these clouds.

A new sound floats down the street. Around the corner a band has begun to play. The tune is vaguely familiar. After a few notes, I place it. It is a martial tune my local regiment plays on parade days.

"What is going on?"

I can hear the curiosity running through M. Aubier's voice, coloring it. He is a curious man, and that curiosity has served him well over the years in his business. A curious publisher finds the new talent.

"Looks like a parade," I say. Flags are waving from windows across the way and I can no longer hear the blue violin.

"Men are marching," says M. Aubier, "but why?"

"War!" cries Madame, "the war must have come."

"Oh, don't be silly," M. says. "Every summer governments talk of war and every summer passes into autumn and nothing has happened. It is commerce, see. Commerce has tied all of Europe together like threads in a tapestry. These days, businessmen run every country. They don't want war, because war disrupts trade and they certainly do not want their livelihood inconvenienced."

"Oh, Pierre, I do not know. People are not as they were when we were young. No, no, they are not. Oh, I don't know."

I do not know either. M. Aubier is certainly a successful man of business, but this summer has been a strange one and, to me, the atmosphere seems foreboding. But then, I am a poet and often overly sensitive. By now the band has passed and the street grown empty. Across the plaza, the little boy is still standing with the old grandmother. But he has lost his balloon. I feel my line of sight drift up, up, up, until suddenly I see the balloon. The red balloon, a pinprick of blood on a great blue sea.

Three

A Dance at the Embassy

The Austrian Embassy is ablaze with lights as we stroll down the tree-lined avenue. Even for summer, the air is warm—redolent with of scents of night-blooming flowers. Lisa Aubier strolls beside me, her arm linked through mine, and her perfume merges with the floral scents until my head fairly swims. Music floats on the breeze and my ears catch a measure or two. I try to place the song, something Russian, I think.

Lisa is telling me a story about a friend of hers who has danced with the ambassador from Greece. Popopolius, or some such name. I am not paying enough attention. For now, my mind is consumed by the night. Above us the full moon glows while the leaves of the plane trees shift in the wind and throw moving shadows onto the pavement. Sweet scents thread their way through the wind and a pretty girl walks beside me. The night is so fine I would be willing to place a small wager that God himself is drifting across Paris this night. I could stroll like this forever.

"Herr Schiller?"

"Yes, Lisa, I'm sorry, my mind has been adrift on the night winds. What were you saying?"

"I was telling you about Bridget, a friend of mine. Really quite a beautiful girl, red hair and the most gloriously shaped lips. Twice now, she has danced with the Austrian ambassador." She sighs, sounding a little like the evening breeze, "Do you think he will be here tonight?"

"Almost certainly. This is to be a major event. One of the last of the summer, I'm afraid. After tonight, many embassies will be manned only by skeleton crews."

"Yes, but of course, summer vacations." Her head settles against my shoulder and she turns her face up to me. I do not know her well enough yet to kiss her full lips, but I consider it.

"I only wondered, you know, all this talk of war. Do you think such a horrible thing can happen, Herr Schiller?"

I shrug as I rearrange my lips in what I hope is a reassuring smile. "Who can say? Every day one hears rumors, but I am a poet, not a military man."

She lifts her head and we stroll on. Moonlight lies like snow on her dark hair. "I have heard that all German men are soldiers."

"Well, yes, in a way that is true. We all have to serve two years when we finish our basic schooling. Then, every summer, we do have two weeks of drills. So I suppose in that way I am a soldier. But," I say, and then I laugh a little, "I have never fired a gun in anger."

"So you are not a war monger?"

"No, no, of course not."

She squeezes my bicep and I flex it. "But you are not afraid, are you?" Her voice is softer now, deeper too, as though she has tapped into a more substantial emotion.

She has asked a difficult question to answer. What man can answer that question until he has been under fire? For certain, I cannot. I hope I am never placed in such a position. "Who can say?" I murmur as I take her arm. We are at the steps and we climb them together, our backs straight and our heads held high, like young royalty. Moonlight splashes against the back of Lisa's neck and our shadows run on before us.

The hour is not late, but my head is already spinning. Champagne affects me. I am leaning against a wall that slants ever so slightly toward the Seine. Off to my right, two men—one Italian and a Frenchman—argue about whether war will come next spring. To my left, an old man stares across the dance floor with empty eyes. For unknown reasons, I think of my father, and wonder if, perhaps, he is thinking of me as he lies on his back in his big bed with my mother breathing peacefully beside him. Such thoughts are strange for me. I do not often think of home.

Lisa is halfway across the room, whirling in the arms of some Austrian duke. Not significant royalty, only a minor dukedom, but tall, slender, rakishly handsome with a fine dueling scar. The song is ending and I watch Lisa stepping back across the floor on the duke's arm. Her black eyes are sparkling as though lit by candles.

The duke nods, murmurs a few words. My mind is not on the duke, however, and I do not catch what he is saying. Lisa does and laughs. I smile as the duke and I exchange nods.

"I trust you are having a pleasant evening, sir." The duke's voice is deeper than I had expected.

"Very pleasant. And you, sir?"

He looks at Lisa and smiles. "The dancing is wonderful. You must try it."

"Perhaps later."

His smile fades and his eyes narrow to slits. "Take my advice, sir, and do not delay too long." He looks around as though he expects barbarians to be climbing over the embassy walls. "I fear war may be in the offing. Only tonight there have been more rumors."

I feel Lisa shiver against me. "Do you believe such talk?" she asks, her voice pitched higher than normal.

"It is hard to know what to believe. But where there is so much talk..." He shrugs. "I apologize for even mentioning such rumors, but one needs to be prepared."

His face is very dark and his nostrils flare. Then the military and diplomatic training take over and he smiles. "Please excuse me, I see Count Eckert. He was ill much of the spring and I must go and inquire of his health." The duke lifts Lisa's right hand to his lips and kisses the back of it. Such public displays do not appeal to me, but then I am not a duke, or an officer, or on the staff of an embassy.

For a moment, he holds her hand as though he has something more to say. Then he lets it go, yet still he hesitates.

"I do not wish to frighten you two, but you make a lovely couple and I do not want to see you taken by surprise. It may be that all this talk is nothing but annoying thunder and lightning without rain. But I do not think so."

Then, like one of the flashes of lightning he has just mentioned, his smile returns and he nods, turns, and begins to wend his way through the dancers. In his uniform he looks quite dashing. Somewhere on the dance floor, a woman laughs and a man joins in and suddenly the words of the duke seem as verses from some fairy tale.

"What an old worrier," I say. "You must not let him spoil your evening."

"No, no, I will not. Why should silly talk spoil such a wonderful night? However, the duke is a splendid dancer."

"You make a nice couple."

Lisa laughs again. "And what about us, Herr Schiller? Do we not make an attractive couple?"

My checks are suddenly warm. "I suppose we are not too bad. At least you are lovely."

Her smile makes my heart beat a little faster. The orchestra has started another tune, but my legs are not quite steady enough beneath me for dancing. Three glasses of champagne, or is it four, are simply too much, especially on an empty stomach—we had agreed on a late supper. Sweat dampens my forehead and I dab at it with a handkerchief.

"With so many lights and so many bodies, it is rather warm in here," I say. "Shall we go find some cooler air?" I incline my head toward the door. Lisa smiles and slips her arm through mine.

As we step into the night, cool air caresses my face, and I feel profound bliss. Automatically, I reach for my notebook and pen to jot down my swirling emotions, but then I remember where I am and smile at my own foolishness. "Come," I say, "let's walk."

People are moving about in the night: couples strolling, clumps of men talking together as they smoke cigars—the aroma is unmistakable, and here and there single men walk with a more definite purpose.

Lisa and I meander from one shallow pool of light to another, drifting where the wind and our feet take us. Without warning, we come up against a stone balustrade. Shadows are deep here. Lisa is very close and I bend my neck ever so slightly and she lifts her face. Her lips seem like two live creatures of the night. She murmurs something against my chest and I whisper her name in her ear. Lisa has the tiniest ears of any woman I have ever kissed. Her body is soft against me and I close my eyes to imprint the image on my brain. I have no plans to return to Paris soon.

We kiss again as music sweeps out onto the veranda. I lift my head and see men silhouetted against the open door. In the great hall, the dancers whirl and sparkle while the band plays on, but something is different. I can sense the change. My father says I am too sensitive, and that is why I am a poet instead of a good business man or a cavalry officer like Uncle Wilhelm. Whether Papa is right or wrong is not for me to say. Yet there is truth in his words. Often I sense things long before others, and I sense something now. There is a ringing in my ears and a tingling runs up and down my spine. Men shout to one another, but I cannot hear the words above the orchestra. One man turns and begins to run.

Lisa hears the footsteps and her face pivots toward the sound. The night seems suddenly darker and I look up. Clouds have blown in from the west, leaving only a sliver of moon visible.

"What is happening?" Lisa asks. Perhaps it is my imagination, but I seem to hear a thread of fear in her voice.

"I'm not sure," I say.

As if pulled by the same impulse, we turn in tandem and begin walking for the open doorway. One of her hands slips inside one of mine. It feels very small.

Three men separate from a crowd and go down the steps, moving quickly. Another man, older than the rest, turns and walks toward the shadows. When he is no more than a few meters from us, I step forward and touch his arm.

"Excuse me, but I hear excited talk and men have started moving too quickly for this night. Has there been news?"

The man seems surprised to see me step out of the night. His eyes are open quite wide and his teeth nibble at his upper lip. For a moment I do not think he will speak. Then he nods. "Yes," he says with a British accent, "there has been news, definitely. Perhaps quite momentous news."

"And what is that news?"

"What? Oh yes, of course. Why Archduke Franz Ferdinand has been shot in Sarajevo."

The man's words are like cold water flung against my face. I feel stunned, shocked, incapable of coherent thought. Surely this means war. Unless there is a miracle, I tell myself. I am not a man who puts much stock in miracles, however.

Before I can thank him, the man has moved into the shadows. Lisa's left hand crawls on my arm now. Her fingers move like spiders. The night is warm, but I am suddenly chilled. My mind is full of sauerkraut and I cannot marshal my thoughts. She slips an arm through mine and we go down the stairs without talking.

In my mind words are forming...*The fragrance of the autumn night cannot mask the stench of fear that drifts on the suddenly chill winds. An early autumn seems in the offing...*

Four

A Letter at Parting

I look about my room. Although I can't point to anything specific, somehow it has a different feel. But then I feel different, too—somewhat akin to the time my brother, Hans, accidently struck me in the head with a shovel when we were digging a foundation for the new barn. That day the room seemed to spin ever so slowly and there was an ephemeral quality to the light.

Today, I simply stand by the window and gaze down on the street, waiting for my mind to swirl back into focus. This section of Paris is a mixture of commercial and residential. On one side of the street is a line of cafès interspersed with small shops—I can see a pharmacy, a haberdashery, and a place that sells postcards, candy, and cheap souvenirs.

On the other side of the street are small brick or mortar homes—most have porches and tidy yards. People stroll up and down the sidewalk on both sides of the street. Many are talking and laughing, as though they did not have a care in the world. I wonder how long their carefree spirits will survive. Standing there at the window staring down on the innocents, I feel very wise. It makes me feel like I am God, or at least some minor deity. All knowing, but sad.

Exactly how long I stand there I cannot be certain, but when I turn from the window the sky has already begun to darken. My head has cleared and I place my suitcase on the bed and begin to pack. All the time I am packing I am thinking about the telegram I know is coming. It will tell me when to report to my unit and where. Like all healthy German men, I have trained with my reserve unit each summer. By no measure am I a good soldier, but I do know the rudiments of the drills and can load and fire my rifle. I have never trained with the artillery pieces.

I am not sure how I feel about being a soldier. As a loyal subject I must do my duty, but I am not a violent man by nature and have nothing in particular against the French or British people. Actually, I have a number of very good friends in both countries and, of course, there is M. Aubier, my loyal publisher. He has sold my books and I have kissed his daughter, yet soon I may find myself shooting at his friends or family. Perhaps a bullet from my rifle will strike his nephew. I believe the fellow's name is Georges. He lives somewhere in Provence and is a schoolteacher. To think of such an event makes my head hurt.

My stomach rumbles, but I'm not sure if it is hunger or nerves. I should go to one of the cafés I can see from my window and have something to eat, but I want to write a note to M. Aubier. Morning will be too late. There is a knowing inside me that I will be required to take the first train to Berlin. Nothing will ever be the same again—that I can feel in my bones. War is not a thing I know, but I sense I will soon know it all too well.

I sit at the small desk. Above the desk, in a cheap frame, is a photograph of an old man fishing. My guess is he is fishing in the Seine. The Seine is a river I know well, at least from its banks. I have walked them countless times and seen dozens of old men fishing. In retrospect, they all look rather alike. In fact, they resemble the old man in the photograph. It is not a particularly fine photograph, being grainy and slightly out of focus. As I pull my fountain pen from my pocket, I wonder if all the people who stroll the banks of the Seine, or the Thames, or the Rhine, look alike to the fishermen. It occurs to me that perhaps we never really look at anyone—a depressing thought.

I close my eyes as I try to think of the words I want to write. However, this is no good as I keep seeing the faces of my three brothers: Hans, Manfred, Adolph. By now, they may have received their telegrams. I hear footsteps in the hallway and open my eyes. The footsteps pass on and I press the pen to the paper. It is good paper, worthy to convey my farewells.

Dear M. Aubier,

Clouds are gathering on the far horizons. They are purple, dark with blood carrying with them a great storm, and who can say which way we will be blown. I write to thank you for all your hard work on my behalf, for all your kindnesses, and, most of all, for your friendship. Please give my best to Madame Aubier and to Lisa. Remember the good times we have shared. I pray for your safety. Please know I go to do my duty. Until we meet again, or as we say in my country, Bils wir uns wiedersehen.

Dien Freund,
Karl Schiller

I draw seven violets along the bottom of the page and fold the note. I feel as if I am folding away a part of my soul.

Five

A Family Dinner

The feeling is that of Christmas, or a special birthday party. All day my mother and sisters have been cooking. The entire house smells of ham baking and roast goose and cabbage and potatoes and oven-hot bread. Uncle Fritz from Gleshing has come and my cousins Gerta and Trude have just arrived. They are twins, almost identical, with blonde hair that hangs in braids down their backs and eyes more blue than even an October sky. Between them, they also have the brains of a door knob.

The big table in the dining room is crammed with food. Candles glitter and the good china and crystal sparkle. Every chair in the house seems to have been drug in and squeezed around the table. It is hard to see how anyone will have room to eat. I anticipate a few elbows in the ribs.

Off in the parlor, someone, probably one of my sisters, is playing the piano and people are singing. Some have been blessed with good singing voices, Uncle Fritz is a fine baritone who can carry a tune, but others are not so fortunate. Poor Hans, who is quite charming and decidedly handsome, simply cannot carry a tune and while my father sings with vigor, he is always a half a beat slow.

I do not sing, at least not publicly. Without the slightest hesitation I can pour the very heart of my soul out on paper, but always I am reluctant to sing, even speak, in public, especially to strangers, or men who enjoy achieving humor at the expense of another.

The house is full of people. I can hear their footsteps on the stairs and their voices rise and fall from the kitchen and the parlor, even from the porch. The smell of burning tobacco mingles with the scent of roast goose and the perfumes of the women, an incongruous combination, and an unpleasant one.

I stand in the shadows by the big window in the room where my grandfather lived the last years of his life. I suppose one could call it a bedroom, although he never allowed a bed to be brought into the room, not a regular one anyway.

He was of the old Prussian mentality, having served with the famous Steel Brigade for many years. At times he did sleep on an old cot, the kind that officers sometimes have in their tents, and, toward the end, reclined on a daybed that has been in our family for over one hundred years. My grandfather and I were never close during his life—I do not think he respected poets—but tonight, here in the shadows, I sense his presence. Once I feel warm air on the back of my neck as though he were standing just behind me, breathing on me and chills race up and down my arms.

Why do I think of him tonight? No way of knowing for certain, but my suspicion is that the coming war plays a part. Not that we are at war. Not quite yet, although one senses that this time it will surely happen.

I wrote a poem this morning in which I likened this waiting for the blasting of the guns to the sensation of holding your breath. I wrote that as long as you could hold your breath, nothing terrible could happen, and you would hold it and hold it and hold it, until your eyes bulged and your chest felt like it would explode, knowing that it was all useless, that in the end you would have to breathe and when you did the horror would come.

I am not a soldier, not yet, but I have read books enough and heard tales enough from old men with one arm or no legs to know that war is not simply knights in shining armor, banners blowing in the wind, and the muffled beat of drums. In war, there is blood, pain, fear, disease, and death. Deep in my bones, I feel the plague that is war is coming. And, in some way I cannot yet see clearly, I know I will play a part in this horror. The thought of killing sickens me, although I am resolute in my determination to duty my duty to the Fatherland.

Yes, I am afraid. Afraid of being shot and left a cripple for life, afraid of dying, afraid of being a coward. A dark aura seems to surround me tonight, and I wonder if sometime long ago one of my ancestors was a gypsy. Deep in the knowing place, I feel certain something very black is going to happen to me. One of my fears will be realized. Which one I do not know. In fact, I am not certain which I prefer. Perhaps a painless death would be best, but that is only speculation, and I rouse myself from my trance and light up a cigarette. The smoke seems to clear my brain and my breath no longer is an anvil on my chest.

My mother's voice rises above the tumult, calling us to the table. For a reason I cannot name, I am reluctant to go. Today, laughter and talk irritate me and my only desire at the moment is to stay in the shadows.

But in the end, I go. I am a good German and I do my duty. To the Fatherland. To my family.

Except for my mother and my crazy Aunt Klara, I am the last to the table. My brothers Hans and Manfred have saved a seat for me. Adolph, our older brother, sits across the table, smiling as if he knows something no one else does. Actually, it is more of a smirk. There are times when I want to smack it off his face. This is one. I sit down.

Hans elbows me, "Are you ready for the show?" he asks,

"What show?"

"Rumors of war are strong."

"Yes," Manfred says, leaning across my plate, "there is much talk that war is imminent."

Adolph runs his fingers through his hair. "As yet, children, there is only talk of war. Not a single nation has mobilized. This crisis may well blow over."

"They always have," Hans says.

Manfred strokes his chin. He looks very much like the teacher he is. "Nations today, especially in Europe, are too closely bound by economic interests to go to war."

I think of Paris conversations and clear my throat. "I am not so sure of that," I say. "In Paris, there is a sense that Austria desires war in order to teach the Serbs a lesson."

"That would not automatically involve Germany," Adolph says. His smile has faded and he looks older. Older and a bit used up. Last winter he suffered with pneumonia and is still not back to fighting form.

"We will all be called up," Manfred says, "although perhaps not at once." He looks at Adolph. "You are above the age for a first call."

"Then he shall have to volunteer," Hans says. "The Schiller brothers must stick together."

"Hush," my mother says, giving us that look. "Your father is going to say the blessing."

Hans snickers. He is the youngest and almost everything is humorous to him. I love to hear him laugh, though. There is a certain youthful quality in the sound that resonates. I smile at him as we all bow our heads.

I do not close my eyes, however. Instead, I sneak a quick glance at Adolph. His face holds a most somber expression. I wonder what he will do should war come. Then I wonder what I would do were I in his place. War, according to many books, is glorious and the true test of a man. Other books paint a darker picture.

Death is not something I have feared particularly. Yet it is also not a partner I would like to dance with. Volunteering would be moving of your own volition into a dance macabre.

Would I volunteer, I wonder, knowing that such wondering is only an academic process? Should war be declared, I will be recalled to active duty and I will report on time. I will do my duty because I am a good, responsible German and so will fulfill my obligations to the Fatherland.

War has never been something I thought much about. Long have I lived in worlds of words. I wonder if I have done the wrong things all these years. Perhaps I should have lived more, to use a phrase. Well, I think, the world may soon give me a chance to find out. I have to laugh at myself. *Lieber Gott*, but I am full of meaningful thoughts and wonderings tonight. I close my eyes.

"Almighty God," Father begins. I have heard him pray thousands of times. He always prays the same prayer. I close my eyes and think of Helga.

~ * ~

The night is warm and full of the scents of summer: honeysuckle, newly cut hay and freshly turned earth, my own sweat, and the hot, dark aroma of animal droppings. A new scent mingles with the other—burning tobacco. I turn to the scent and, standing there—just at the edge of the light that spills from the open door, is my father. I have been so absorbed in my thoughts I did not hear him step onto the porch.

"Papa."

"Karl."

"I'm sorry, I did not hear you come out."

He takes his pipe out of his mouth. Only half his face is lit by the sallow light falling through the open door. That strange lighting makes my father look like a different man. For the first time, I notice how his face has thinned. "Too much hot air in there for an old man." He stretches and yawns. "What a glorious night," he says.

I look out across the yard and, for the first time, actually see the night. The moon is almost full and it has painted the grass the color of fresh cream. Shadows from the oak tree have flung themselves against the ground in strange and wonderful patterns. Beyond the yard, the road lies white and strangely cool looking. I wonder if I will soon be marching along similar roads. There are those wonderings again. I can feel them trying to arrange themselves into a poem. But now is not the time for writing poetry.

"Yes, it is nice." I turn and face my father. "But you are not old."

"Humph, I thought you were more observant than that. I turned sixty-one in March. Once a man turns sixty, the years begin to wear on him." He looks at me and shakes his head. "Ah, Karl, I see you do not believe."

I start to protest, but before I can speak, he says, "That is all right. Your papa understands. At your age, I would not have believed it either." He jams the pipe between his teeth and begins to puff. The scent of his tobacco is strong and drives me to desire a cigarette. I pull out my case and gaze at the cigarettes. They are Egyptian ones I bought at the tobacconist on Rue Bonaparte in Paris. I extract one and light it. The smoke burns my throat, but it also seems to clear my mind.

"Do you think there will be war, Papa?"

His shoulders shrug. He removes the pipe from between his lips. "That is a difficult question to answer, Karl. So many different countries and leaders are involved. But I have a bad feeling. Only once before have I had this feeling. That was a very long time ago. Just before the other war."

"The war the historians call the Franco-Prussian War?"

"Correct. Even though that was over forty years ago, I remember is as clearly as if it had been only last Sunday. For two weeks before my father, your grandfather, was called up, a strange, dark spirit lived in my body. It affected everything. Food no longer tasted good and sounds were distorted. Even the light was peculiar."

"And then the war came?"

"*Ja*, two weeks to the day after the bad feeling started."

"But Germany won and Grandfather came home."

"True, but there are some nights when I cannot sleep—the years affect a man in many ways—and I lie in bed and listen to your mother breathing and wonder what we really won, and at what cost.

"The cost?"

"Many lives were lost. Many good, strong German boys were killed and those that came home were not the same."

"Even Grandpa?"

"*Ja.*"

"Different in what way?"

"Silences. He was different in his silences. Before the war he was a most talkative man. After the war, there were silences. Not all the time, but they were there. Especially when just the two of us were together. Ya, they grew long then, very long indeed."

"What do you think caused them?"

He puts his pipe back in his mouth and puffs for a moment. A nightingale starts up in the hedges across the road and, as if in response, a dog barks from down the street. I lean against a pillar and smoke and listen. I wonder if Helga will come tonight, then, for just a moment, I wonder what Lisa is doing. As I said, this night I am full of wonderings.

My father removes his pipe, studies it. He studies it quite intently. So intently that I am moved to glance at it. It tells me nothing.

"Truthfully, I cannot say what caused the silences. Always I have thought that something happened during the war that affected him so. But, if there was an event, he never revealed it, and I have never had to go to war. So the cause remains a secret."

He shrugs again. "Too young for the first and now I am too old for this one. If it comes," he adds as he taps his pipe out against one of the wooden pillars that hold up the roof. "I hope you and your brothers never have to discover the secret."

I do not know how to answer him. A man of words and I have none to say. For some time, we simply stand in our own little silence and listen to the night coming alive around us. At first there is only the wind, the twittering of sparrows, and the silken sounds of small creatures slipping through the grass. Then voices and laughter drift out the door to wander around the darkness.

"Time now for a schnapps. Will you join me, son?"

I think of Helga and the path by the stream. "In a moment, perhaps. For now, I think I will take a stroll."

He smiles and one of his hands clasps my shoulder. For a man who claims to be old he has great strength in his hands. “Ah, yes, once I was young, too. Go for your stroll, Karl. Go for your stroll now, while the moon shines and the cannons are silent.”

He gives my shoulder a final squeeze, turns, and walks into the house without looking back. I grind my cigarette beneath my heel and go down the steps and across the yard. I am going to meet Helga, but my mind is on the silences. A poem begins to form:

In the soft silences of the moonbeamed night
are the truths we swear we want to hear.
But do we?
Do we want the truths of life?
Or simply the self-satisfaction of saying so
to others?

Six

Helga

Her face
Is a pale
moon,
rising

The path curls along the stream where the water runs shallow, babbling to itself over smooth rocks. Helga and I pause now and then to listen and to talk softly, and, if she is willing, to kiss. I hope that tonight she is in a giving mood. Passion rises in me like high tide.

"The moon is so bright."

"Yes," I say and nuzzle her neck.

"Oh, Karl, you are a naughty boy."

"*Nein*. It is all your fault, Helga."

"My fault? How is it my fault?"

"Because you look so lovely. I cannot take my eyes off you."

"Ha, you mean you cannot keep your hands off me."

I put my arm around her shoulders and pull her to me. Her body is soft, but not yielding. I whisper, "That is your fault, too."

Helga shrugs my arm off her shoulder and steps away from me. "Karl, please. There are others out tonight."

I look around, but see only shadows shifting in the moonlight, playing hide and seek with the silhouettes of trees and shrubs. Someone with skill has trimmed one of the shrubs so that it looks like an elephant.

"I see no one, Helga. Only you."

"Trust me. They are out. I have heard their footsteps and voices."

"Perhaps that was only the wind. All I hear is the water gurgling to itself."

"Oh, Karl, you hear only what you want to hear. Come, let's walk to the footbridge."

I shrug, then follow. In a way, Helga is correct. About me, and, if one carries the thought on to the end, the world. Every man hears only what he wants to hear, at least to some degree. I feel sure that applies to women, too. Certainly it does to children.

The wind has died and our footsteps sound out clearly. Enough moonlight sifts through the trees so that the narrow path is easily visible. Helga's hair glows like unpolished gold and her braids swing as she walks. I follow a step behind. Perhaps there are others out for a stroll; however, I do not see them. The evening is exquisite, warm without being oppressive, full of summer scents, bathed in moonlight—the way the night was meant to be. At least it seems that way to me. But then, I think, what does that say about God when so many nights are not so pleasant?

We have reached the footbridge and the time for thinking, at least about God, has passed. God is a good subject for four in the morning with a cup of strong coffee and a good Turkish cigarette.

Helga is standing on the bridge, leaning over the railing, staring down into the moving water. I join her.

"What do you see in the water?"

"Only the moonlight dancing on the surface."

"The flow is strong tonight. Hear how it hisses over the rocks."

Helga sighs. "All that water, Karl..."

"Yes."

"Do you ever wonder where it came from, and where it is going?"

"Not particularly, although that is an interesting question. Why?"

"No particular reason. I was just wondering."

I put my arm around her waist. This time she does not resist. "This must be a night for wondering," I say.

"Have you been wondering tonight, Karl?"

"Some," I allow. I hate to admit how much—even to myself.

"Have you been wondering about us?" Helga's fingers slide up and down my arm.

"*Nein*," I say, "I am sure about us."

"Oh, you're sweet tonight. But what about us, Karl? I have been waiting a long time and now there is talk of war."

"Talk is all at the moment. Talk. Just talk. Men are always talking about war. One year it is Turkey, the next year Egypt. Why the Serbs are always threatening war, if not against some other country, then against some of their own people."

"My uncle Gustav says this time Austria may give them war."

"Who can say? So far not a single country has begun mobilization. Until mobilization starts there will be no war."

Helga turns her face up to me. In the moonlight it looks sweet, yet worried. "If Germany mobilizes, will you have to go?"

"Yes. I am a reservist. If Germany mobilizes, I will have to report to my unit within forty-eight hours. "

"But what about us?"

"Us?" I am perplexed. I hear the questioning tone in my voice.

"Oh, Karl, you can be such a *dumkauf*. I have been waiting a long time. I have waited for you, and you are a man who takes many journeys." She turns and looks away. Her back is rigid. "Other men notice me, you know? They ask me to dances and look at me in church."

"Who?" I ask, not sure if am angry or relieved. I like Helga, like her a lot, but I know what she wants. It is what every good German girl wants, but it is not what I want—certainly not with war lurking around the next street corner.

"Henrich Moltz asked me to the town picnic just last month."

"Henrich Moltz? Henrich Moltz is a butcher."

"He makes a good living."

"He is an old man."

"That shows how little you know. He is only thirty-five."

"Fifteen years older than you. How silly."

"Silly? Me? Maybe you are the one who is silly, Karl? Think of what could be."

"Maybe you are the one who needs to think of what could be, Helga."

She pulls away from me and crosses the bridge to the deep shadows on the far side. "Ach," she says, "all you men are all alike. You want only one thing."

I follow after her, but slowly. The night has fallen quiet and I am conscious of the loudness of my footsteps on the old bridge. I am also acutely conscious of my desires. Tonight my passion runs high. However, I am not sure if it is because I am so enamored with Helga, her soft lips and ripe body, or if I am driven by the knowledge that the world teeters on the edge of war. It may come tomorrow, or next week, or next month. But whenever it comes, I will be called, and with that call comes the distinct possibility of death. Death has always seemed so far away. Far away and final. I suppose it is still extremely final.

Shadows envelop me. In their darkness the whiteness of Helga's face is nothing so much as a pale moon rising. She shifts her head and, for a second, her eyes glitter. I step closer and drape my arms around her. At first she is stiff, resistant. Then she softens and comes into my arms. Our lips meet. Her breath is sweet.

"Tonight is ours," I whisper. "Tomorrow, well no man can say. Let's not waste this moment."

"But Karl. It isn't right."

"What? Of course it is. Who can claim love is wrong?"

"But what if—"

I kiss her mouth shut and press myself against her. Certainly she must feel my passion.

"I want to wait."

"You may wait forever. Germany may declare war at any moment, and I will have to go. A soldier's life is hard and lonely. I need something to remember you by. Something special."

"But I want to get married. I am a good girl, a good German girl."

"Of course you are, and yes, we will get married."

Her lips press against my neck. Her breasts push against my chest. "Oh, Karl. When?"

"Soon," I say, "very soon."

I mean what I am saying. At least part of me does. "Before I go, if all the arrangements can be made. If not, when I get my first leave."

"You swear?" Her voice sounds small.

I pull her more tightly against me. I feel very powerful. Never have I felt this way before. Now, even the thought of war seems far away, nothing more than a mirage in a distant desert. Probably there is a poem in that thought, but I am not interested in poems at the moment. Another force drives me tonight.

"I swear," I whisper against her face. She lifts her face and a stray strand of moonlight halos her head. She is lovely beyond words and I want her so much I can taste it. I tilt her chin up and kiss her mouth. She kisses back, harder than ever before. But I know her kisses can merely be promises.

The wind is rising and the rustle of leaves is clearly audible. Shadows dance across the ground as the stream murmurs behind us. I put an arm across her shoulders and we step into the deeper shadows that lie below the ancient chestnut trees. I grow more hopeful.

Seven

All Aboard

The sun is shining so brightly it blinds you to even glance at it. A cool breeze blows. Flags fly from open windows and, at the end of the street, a band plays a marching tune. The entire town seems to line the sidewalk. Old men call out to us, telling us to show the French how Germans can fight. The women all smile and wave handkerchiefs. Little boys run beside us as we march. Our uniforms are new and stiff and scratchy and we are hot in the morning sun, but I have never felt more proud to be a German.

Every man in the squad is someone I know. My three brothers march with me. Adolph just in front, Manfred directly behind me, and young Hans by my left side. Our cousins, Bruno and Erik, are here, too, and many of my friends: Helmut Emmich, Ernst Bowers, even Henrich Goebles—men I have gone to school with and trained with and played football with. All are young and strong. In our uniforms, we look splendid. Our rifles seem mere toys. I pity whomever comes up against us in battle for I do not see how we can lose.

We have reached the platform, and before us a troop train idles on the tracks. The last train I rode brought me home from Paris, now this one will take me off to war. France, I suppose, although you can hear rumors of Russia and Belgium.

Up on the platform, the mayor is making a speech. He is talking about pride and honor and glory and the kaiser and the Fatherland. He rambles on and on. His mustache goes up and down like a small, alive creature. He waves his arms about as though he is conducting the town band. Actually, when he is not serving as mayor, he is our band conductor. Since I last saw him he has grown very fat.

We stand at attention in rows as straight as arrows, precisely as we have been taught. Behind me, someone coughs. Sergeant Gruber gives us the evil eye. We pretend not to notice. Each of the past three summers, Sergeant Gruber has conducted much of our training, under the guidance of Lieutenant Mosel, of course. I cannot see Corporal Schmidt or Corporal Meister. I do not care for Corporal Meister. He is a bit of a sneak. Secretly, I hope he comes down with the shits.

Our uniforms are wool, and I am very hot. Sweat runs down my sides and I can feel it dotting my face. The mayor drones on and on. Never before has he made such a speech. Of course, German has never gone to war while he has been mayor. Even his face is red. He gasps for air, then finishes with a triumphant blast of glory, God, and German greatness. He waves his arms so that he reminds me of a windmill in Holland as the band strikes up a tune for soldiers. A fat woman in a black dress starts to cry. I sweat like a pig being readied for a roasting.

Sergeant Gruber shouts an order. My mind has drifted so far away that I have to jerk it back to the moment. We march onto the platform. Someone calls my name and I look around, but I cannot see them. Helga has said she cannot come—that it would break her heart to see me board the train, but I wonder if she is still mad at me for failing to make the marriage arrangements. Well, she failed me, too, so I am not as hurt as I might be.

Pretty girls surround us, pressing chocolates and roses on us. The son of the village doctor sticks one of the roses down the barrel of his rifle while I twist the stem of one through a buttonhole.

Men pat us on the back. Men of rank and power and privilege. Men such as the mayor and the doctor and Herr Brundt, who owns a munitions factory near Berlin, but who maintains a summer home here. Among the well-wishers are the novelist Hans Bowles, and Herr Levin, who owns the shoe factory, and his cousin, Herr Burkhalter, who is rumored to have sold his banking interests for a fortune. All crowd round and offer us cigars and bottles of schnapps and pat us on the back with vigor and call us "good, brave German fighting men" as they shake our hands with gusto.

The ranks break apart and I am surrounded by pretty girls. One or two of the faces are familiar, but many I do not know. One of them, a dark-haired girl I have seen in town, kisses me on the mouth. No sooner does she turn away than another girl flings her arms around me.

Suddenly my father and mother are standing by my side. My father shakes my hand. His mouth opens, but he cannot say the words that are in his heart. My mother can only cry as she says my name over and over.

All around me families are saying good-bye. Many of the mothers are crying. Even a few of the fathers are struggling to keep their eyes dry. But all my friends are smiling. The praise and the adulation of the town have turned our heads. Deep inside, I know this, but I cannot help but feel invincible. I am young, strong, and full of vigor. No enemy will be safe from me.

Of course, it is easy to think that from the safety of the train platform at Dortburg. Deep inside my brain, I recognize that I may feel differently when I face an armed Frenchie. But for today, for this one glorious sun-soaked morning, we are young and strong and brave and so very proud to be German soldiers.

Without warning, the train whistle blows and Sergeant Gruber and Corporals Schmidt and Meister are shouting at us to board.

Lieutenant Mosel is kissing a very pretty girl and she clings to him like a drowning person clings to a floating log.

We begin to move. We are not marching. Actually, it is more a shuffling, but we are moving nonetheless. I am only two steps away from the train when I hear Helga crying out my name. I turn and there she is, pushing through the crowd to throw her arms around my neck. She is sobbing. Corporal Meister jabs me in the ribs. "Move on, move on," he says.

I pull Helga's arms from around my neck. Her eyes are brimming with tears. Our lips meet, but then Corporal Meister is shoving me along and I stumble into Hans and he laughs as we go up the stairs.

This car is empty and Hans and I both hurry to capture window seats on the platform side of the train. Again, the whistle blows. Sergeant Gruber is shouting, "*Weitergehen, weitergehen.*"

I push the bottom half of the window up. Someone whose face I cannot see thrusts a packet of cigarettes through the opening and I take them. A rose flies through the open window and strikes me across the face. I laugh.

The train rumbles and shakes, then the whistle blows for the third time. Inside the car it sounds louder than it did on the platform. The train jerks forward, jolts to a stop, then jerks forward again.

Now we are moving, slowly, but picking up speed. I thrust my face out the window. I can see my father. "Good-bye, Papa," I shout and he waves, although I do not think he can hear me. The band has started playing again and the mayor is shouting. His face is very red. His lips move, but I cannot hear a word he says. It is a strange moment, vaguely disconcerting.

I look for my mother, but she is lost in the crowd. I look for Helga, and think I see her cap of bright hair. Then the crowd shifts and she disappears. The train is rolling now and, for a moment, the car falls silent. It is good-bye for all of us. Farewell to the little village we know and love. The question that flows through all our minds is will we all come back? Upon reflection, I am not sure the odds favor such an outcome. The tracks begin to bend to the east and Dortburg disappears like a lost dream.

Eight

Goodbye to Germany

The countryside unfolds like a medieval tapestry. This section of Germany is open country, gently rolling with hay fields, orchards, and slender steams so blue they look unreal. The fine hot weather that has been with us for days lingers and the countryside is slathered with sunlight. The scent of freshly mown hay drifts in through the window and birds whirl away in a sky that looks to have been freshly painted.

Cattle graze in the fields, and here and there is a farmhouse flanked by a good solid German barn. Once, on a particularly steep rise, I see a castle rising toward the white clouds. In another time there would have been a poem there, perhaps two or three. But I am no longer a poet. All that urgent need to spill my heart on the white page has vanished. The war is in me now and I, like the rest of the soldiers of Dortburg, long for battle.

As to what has transformed me from poet to warrior, I cannot say, although I freely admit I think often on that matter. Perhaps it was the speeches, or the uniform, or the brass band playing martial tunes, or the old men of the village urging me on. Then again, perhaps it was nothing more than a shifting in my mind, analogous to the shift in the seismic plates beneath the surface of the earth that scientists say causes earthquakes.

Whatever has caused this metamorphosis does not matter. I am quite content to sit by the open window and gaze out at the farms and the cattle, and, now and then, some farmer behind a team or a boy running beside the train for a few yards and waving. I smoke and, when I am hungry, I eat a bite of the chocolate given me by the pretty girls of Dortburg. At times I think of Helga, or my mother and father, and when my mind begins to wander, I read.

I have three books in my bag, although I cannot say why I chose them. They are *Robinson Crusoe,* the *Holy Bible,* and a collection of short stories by De Maupassant. They seem an odd collection. Two written by men from countries with whom Germany may soon be at war, and the other the Holy Word of God Almighty. For some reason which remains stubbornly obscure, it strikes me as faintly blasphemous for a soldier to be carrying the Bible into battle. Still, passages from this glorious book bring me comfort.

Every few miles we come to a town and, at each town big enough to have a railway station, we have to get off the train and stand at attention under a relentless sun while the town's mayor makes a speech praising our bravery, wishing us safe journeys, and urging us to earn great glory for the Fatherland.

We are all heartily sick of speeches and are heavily laden with chocolates, cigarettes, and freshly cut flowers. At every stop we are all kissed by pretty girls and have our hands shaken by the old men of the village. All the young boys stare at us with hungry, envious eyes. By now even the pretty girls are getting to be a bit much, and we all eagerly await the order to march back onto the train.

Once we are inside and the train is moving, we politely wave and smile until we are out of view from the platform. Then we all drift back to our chosen seats. In a strange way it seems as though we have been on this train forever. Each man clings tenaciously to his seat and conversations repeat in familiar patterns.

Some play cards, while others tell jokes and dirty stories. Still others simply sit and smoke as they stare out a window. A few read books, and now and then, one will put pen to paper. I assume they are writing to their family or to the girl they left behind. Suddenly, just as the train runs alongside a streamlined with trees—it is cooler in the shade—it strikes me that there is an inherent loneliness in writing a letter. Loneliness tinged with sadness.

That is, one writes a letter because one is missing another and one feels sad. So they write, at least in part, in an effort to bring forth an image of the person they are writing, and missing—one that is comfortingly familiar. It is as though they think that by writing to this person there is a special connection established, if only on a spiritual level. Or maybe they think that by writing to the one they are missing, they are in some way transporting some basic element of the other person into this hot, dusty, stinking train car. At least it strikes me that way as I ride this troop train. Perhaps I will have a different view when I am in another country.

The tracks bend away from the stream and the trees and now they run straight toward the horizon for as far as a man can see.

Lieutenant Mosel strolls down the aisle. In five miles we will be crossing the border into Belgium, he says. Hans looks at me, his face full of surprise. We all thought we were headed directly for France. No matter, the generals and the kaiser know best. Plans have been made for years. Each summer, when we underwent our training, we heard rumors.

I shrug, shift in my seat, and peer out the open window as Germany begins to fade into the distance. Suddenly I am struck by a thought, or more rightly a question. What I wonder, and amazingly this is the first time I have thought of it, is when I will see Germany again? Then I wonder when I do if I will be the same man. In some fundamental way that seems impossible.

Germany is now no more than a blur of green and gold, bisected by the straight steel rails. Then the rails are only a fine dark line. Then it is Belgium.

Nine

Crossing the Border

The ground falls away from a flat grass ridge into a sloping meadow. The grass looks as though it has not been mown all summer and now is going to seed under a relentless August sun. As we stand on the crest, we are still in German territory. At the bottom of the slope, a narrow bridge spans a small stream. Halfway across that bridge Belgium begins.

Lieutenant Mosel has shaken the squad out and arranged us across the curve of the crest. It is a still morning and our banner hangs limp. The sun is rising in a sky devoid of clouds and the day promises to be yet another hot one. I cannot recall such a splendid stretch of weather.

We are not quite at attention, yet not at ease, either. Our rifles are in our hands and butterflies dance in our stomachs. At least they do in mine.

The reason for this nervousness waits for us on the bridge. There, a small squad of Belgian soldiers has taken up position. At least half a dozen soldiers stand on the bridge itself while ten or fifteen more are scattered along the bank of the stream to the right and left of the bridge. Our squad outnumbers them at least three to one. However, the Belgians have a machine gun. It does not look like one of the newer models and it has been pulled into action by a dog, which strikes me as most strange. Still, dog power or not, a machine gun gives a man pause.

As we stare down at the Belgian soldiers guarding their border, Sergeant Gruber straightens out our line, then goes to confer with Lieutenant Mosel. The lieutenant raises his field glasses and peers across a series of ridges. I follow the line of sight and see, three or four ridges over, a thin gray line. Colonel Weber must be over there. He is the commanding officer in this sector, and a commanding figure, standing well over six feet in height, with a back as straight as a ramrod.

Ernst Kluge is our bugler, and at a sign from the lieutenant, he raises his bugle. The morning has gone astoundingly quiet. Only a small bird hidden in the tall grasses chirps away as if nothing is amiss. Then it too falls silent and the morning grows so still it seems as though the world is holding its breath.

I glance down the slope. The Belgian soldiers stand at the ready. From the crest they look small, but I know that is merely a trick of light and distance. Sunlight glints off the barrels of their guns and they lean ever so slightly forward as if they are preparing for the charge.

My chest is beginning to hurt and I realize, with a tough of chagrin, that I have been holding my breath. I let it out and the sound is loud in my ears. The earth seems to tremble ever so faintly, but, after a moment, I figure out it is only my legs quivering. Always in my imagination I had pictured myself as a brave man. Now even my hands tremble.

A bugle blast shakes me from my reverie and Sergeant Gruber windmills his arm as he shouts, "Forward!" For a second, perhaps two, the line stands unmoving. Then, with a throaty roar, we all rush forward, running and shouting like wild men. The Belgians raise their rifles and sharp cracks of sound puncture the morning.

Now our line is firing back, a ragged volley. Corporal Meister curses us, for what I cannot make out. I pause, raise my rifle, and fire. Whether I hit anything more than air I cannot say. Corporal Schmidt taps me on the shoulder and we charge down the hill once again, our bayonets fixed, sunlight glittering off the steel.

My breath is ragged in my throat, but I charge on with the others. My legs are moving smoothly now, pistoning like a well-oiled machine. My helmet is too big and slips down over one eye while the bridge seems to tilt and sway.

More rifle shots from both sides and then the machine guns start up: tat tat tat tat tat tat. Suddenly the machine gunner flings up his arms and sprawls on his back. Another Belgian falls heavily against the railing of the bridge, then tumbles over. He seems to fall in slow motion. Beneath his helmet, his face looks very white.

Our cheers ring out, accompanied by more rifle shots. Within a few seconds the Belgians turn and run for the rear. Somehow, they have hooked the dog back up to the machine gun and it jolts up the slope behind him.

Belgium is now only twenty yards before us and then we are on the bridge. The good Sergeant Gruber leads the way and we pound after him. For a big man, he runs fast. My breath comes in great gasps, but I can feel my mouth grinning and a rising wind blesses my face. I cannot remember being happier.

I am pounding across the bridge and I can see the Belgian soldier floating face down in the water. I run by the fallen soldier on the bridge. His arms are above his head so that he looks like he is trying to surrender. His chest, however, is a pool of blood. His face is very youthful and he looks quite innocent lying there.

Quite innocent and quite dead.

I am halfway up the slope before I realize that we have crossed the border and are now in the land of our enemies. In that moment, the thought does not bother me in the least. We have won our first victory without a single causality. On that August morning, even God seems to be smiling on us. I feel invincible.

Ten

Out of the Mist

There are mysteries
floating in the mists,
half-realized visions
that beckon to us
with silvered fingers
and hollowed whispers

It is not yet daylight and Sergeant Gruber and the corporals are kicking us awake. Only they are doing it quietly, speaking in words scarcely more than whispers. "Up, up," they say. "We go forward in ten minutes."

I rub sleep out of my eyes and sit up. I have been dreaming about Lisa and wonder how the Aubiers have taken the official declaration of war. It seems quite strange, and vaguely wrong, to be fighting against a country where such good people live. Besides, my books have always sold well in France. But all that seems a long time ago. A very long time, when I was a different man.

Hans touches my shoulder. "What is going on?"

"Corporal Schmidt says we move out in a few minutes."

"Yes, but move out where?"

I shrug. "Guess we will find out."

Hans begins to button his uniform. "Fat lot of help you are."

"Hey now. I have never been a soldier before, either. Not in a wartime."

Hans mumbles something under his breath, but I am not listening. I am pulling on my boots. Manfred catches my eye and grins. Adolph puffs on his pipe as he studiously ignores us.

"Up, up now. Move along, move along." Corporal Meister strides among us, his long thin nose twitching like some small, alive creature. His blue eyes are small and have a certain hard-boiled look. However, they do not miss much.

We stagger to our feet. My stomach growls. If we are to fight, surely we will get breakfast first. But already Sergeant Gruber is shaking us out in a line. Three lines actually. Two long lines, one directly behind the other and a third line, smaller, some forty yards to the right. My brothers and I are in this third line.

I can see the lieutenant. He is resplendent in his uniform and he stands very straight. Word is whispered down the line that he has just been to see the colonel. I assume to receive his orders.

Sergeant Gruber takes the first of the longer lines and Corporal Schmidt the second. We get Meister. Aren't we the lucky ones? He motions us to gather around.

"All right, men," he says. "Just across that field," he half turns and points to the east, "is a small woods. In that woods are Belgian soldiers. They are going to try to stop us from moving forward and connecting with the Seventh Division. Our job is to destroy them. Here is how it will work. Gather in closely. I do not want to have to shout. In this mist they cannot be certain where we are, and I don't want to be the one to tell them."

We all huddle round Corporal Meister. I make sure to stand behind him, so I do not see his face. He looks like a wharf rat. Hans is beside me and Manfred is on the far side of the ring. I cannot see Adolph, but he is surely close by.

Meister rambles on for a few minutes. He is not a great leader, but I gather the plan is for the first line to creep as close as they can to the woods without being noticed and then rush the Belgians. The second line will swing left and stand by in case the Belgians try to retreat down the road. Our little line is the hammer. We are supposed to swing right, then attack through the woods, catching the Belgians, whose attention will be occupied elsewhere, by surprise and smash them on the anvil of the first line. This morning there is a thick low-hanging mist that should give us good cover. My stomach growls again and I can feel a sheen of sweat forming on the palms of my hands. I wipe them on my trousers.

Suddenly, before any of us is quite ready, the order is given to advance and we begin to move to our right. Peering through the mist, I can barely make out the front line of trees in the woods the corporal was describing. They remind me of the totem poles carved by Indians of the Pacific Coast in America I have seen in books.

Here, the ground is unbroken and covered with grasses that brush damply against our trousers. We crouch low to the ground, moving forward in imitation of wild animals. My stomach gurgles again and my mouth waters at the thought of hot coffee. The wind shifts and I can smell the warm, thick smell of animal hides. Cattle, to the south of the woods. I would like to see a cow. Funny what a man thinks off as he goes into battle.

"To the left," Corporal Meister calls out, his voice a raspy whisper, "to the left and double quick."

We are going double time now, almost a run. The woods must be no more than forty or fifty yards ahead. Belgian soldiers are clearly visible moving among the trees but they have not seen us. For a second, I see Helga's face in my mind and wonder if I will ever see her again.

Suddenly there is the chatter of guns. The Belgians have seen our first line. Flashes of fire flicker among the trees. Shouts ring out and someone screams. We are only twenty yards from the trees.

"Fire!" screams Corporal Meister and we pause and aim, at least in the general direction of a Belgian soldier. I squeeze the trigger and the roar fills my ears. The butt kicks against my shoulder and I wince. If I hit anyone, I cannot tell. Corporal Meister is waving us forward and we thrust our rifles before us, bayonets glittering. We are in amongst the trees. Everybody is shouting and I feel my own throat vibrating. A branch slashes against my face.

The Belgians see us and some turn and fire. A bullet whines by my head. I fix my eyes on a tall Belgian whose helmet sits askew and run for him with the bayonet before me. Ten yards away, he whirls and takes to his heels. I chase after him, but a vine catches my ankle and I stumble forward. By the time I recover my balance, the tall Belgian is gone. Only his helmet is left, lying on the ground where it fell. I give it a good kick as I catch my breath.

The skirmish is over. It could not have lasted more than ten minutes. Two Belgians lie on the ground. One has a very neat hole in the precise middle of his forehead. The other one's throat has been smashed. They are very dead and the woods have been taken. A sense of pride surges inside.

My ears have cleared and I hear voices. We have captured three Belgians and Lieutenant Mosel is assigning two men to take them to the rear. The rest of us will move out soon. Well, not quite all of us. One of the Brecht twins is lying on his back. His face is very calm, only the mouth twists to one side. A few strands of his hair peek out from beneath his helmet. It is red. The twins are a year older than I am, but I know their sister from school. I look around for his brother. I cannot see him, but there is no time to look further. We are moving out.

"What about Rudy?" someone asks.

"Others will bury him," says Sergeant Gruber. "We must keep moving. We are the advance of the division. Now, form up by twos, then move out."

As we pass, all look down at our fallen comrade. He is our first casualty, but we have pushed the Belgians back again. There is a sense among us that we can march all the way to Paris—that nothing can stop us.

Eleven

A Small Town in Belgium

The air has gone purple and still. Dust puffs around our boots with every step. Birds chirp from a thin line of trees beside the road. Directly ahead a few lights begin to flicker on.

Since well before dawn we have been marching. Sergeant Gruber drives us forward. The Belgian forts at the border have fallen and we are now in a race to get around the French flank. If we can accomplish that, nothing will stand between us and Paris. I think back to the train we rode out of Germany. Someone had painted on the side of one car: *Meet You at the Arc De Triomphe.* At that time, I thought the message whimsical. Now it seems a prophecy.

Our boots are going to pieces and our feet are blistered and sore. Food has become something we snatch when the opportunity presents itself. We have outmarched the soup kitchen and the artillery, and are off on our own, rambling loose in the heart of France. We are tired and thirsty and hungry. For two days we have no hot coffee and no hot meals. We have begun to forage and no home or café is safe. At first I felt bad when we took bread and meat and wine. Now it is a habit, a necessary one—a German soldier must not be denied.

Today we have been on the road almost continually. Only two short breaks and no real chance to find food or wine. All I have eaten since dawn are a few crusts of dry bread, washed down with water from a well at an abandoned farm house. My stomach feels hollow and my head throbs.

We have been marching since before good daylight and all through the long afternoon. Now the shadows have grown long and dark and wrapped their arms around one another. This is the time of day my mind turns to home and I wonder what my mother and father are doing. We have had no mail since we got on the train and I worry about them. If we ever stop for more than a few hours, I will write and let them know all their sons are safe. I am confident they would be very proud of us.

More lights flicker on in the gathering dusk and we can see that we are coming to a town. I do not know the name. Not that it would make any difference. In the past two days we have marched through a dozen. They run together in my memory until they are a blur.

Faintly I hear the crackle of gunfire. Rifles only. No machine guns or artillery. Since noon we have heard rumors of civilian resistance, of snipers. All around me heads come up, looking for the enemy.

The road begins to bend south. We trudge up a rise, then down the slope and across a narrow bridge. A stone wall runs along the right side of the road. The air has gone almost dark. Something in the town is burning and the smell of smoke hangs in the air.

Almost hidden by the coming darkness, a German soldier sits with his back against the wall. I might not have noticed him except for the bandage on his left arm. It is white against the dark, although I can see a dark smear running through it. Blood, I think. The wounded soldier stares at us. I nod.

"Watch yourself," he says. "This town is full of partisans. They have killed two of our soldiers, including my sergeant. The Twenty-seventh is rounding them up now. I heard the captain say they will be shot."

"Are you hurt badly?" I ask. For some reason we have halted and at least a brief conversation is possible.

"Just a flesh wound, but it keeps on bleeding and it burns like hell when I move it."

"You need medical attention."

"They will be along. What I need now is a drink. Have you any wine, friend?"

"No, sorry. I do not even have any water. It has been a dry day."

The man nods. "It has been a hard day. I'm ready for the division to come up, and for some wine."

Hans nudges me. We are moving again. "Good luck," I call out.

"Watch yourself," the man responds and bows his head. His helmet is off and he pulls his knees up and presses his face against them.

I am out of step and hurry to catch up. We are inside the town. There was a sign, but I did not catch the name, only the first letter "L." Buildings rise from both sides of the street. Many look like shops on the lower level, with living quarters above. Ahead I can see German soldiers running in the street and there is much shouting.

"Can you tell what is going on?" I ask Hans.

"*Nein*, just a lot of our men running back and forth in the street."

"I see fire," shouts someone behind us. I cannot tell who spoke. A rifle shot rings out.

"Snipers," someone calls out.

"*Nein*, that was one of ours," says Corporal Schmidt. "Keep moving, keep moving."

The sharp, clear sound of glass breaking punctures the night. Our men have broken into a store down the street. I wonder what is in there. Before we get to the building, I see two territorials come running, a bottle of wine in each hand.

Manfred twists his head around. "By God, I could use some of that."

'Yes," I shout back, "my throat is like dust."

Before either of us can say any more, we grind to a halt. A piece of field artillery has broken a wheel and turned over on its side. Furthermore, reservists are pouring into the square from a side street. In the faint light from the shops and flats, I can see their uniforms are brand new. Surely they have never seen action.

On the far side of the artillery piece, a few Jaegers shout orders. The horse pulling the field gun has gone lame and the Jaegers are ordering some soldiers to pull it out of the way. The soldiers, who look like infantry, pay them no heed. They have been in battle—several sport bandages—and they are more interested in the wine shops.

Our lines have broken apart in the square. I can hear Sergeant Gruber shouting, but I cannot see him. Corporal Meister goes by, running hard. Hans gouges an elbow into my side.

"Come on, Karl, let's grab us a bottle."

"But..."

"Oh, come on. In all this chaos no one will know."

A great shout goes up and we turn. Flames shoot toward the sky. A building, perhaps three stories high, has gone up in flames. An officer shouts for his unit to put out the fire. Three or four start in that direction, but just then a rifle rings out and we all scatter like wild birds. Another shot, and some of the soldiers start shooting back, although I can see no targets. At best, they are shooting at lamp-lighted windows. I hear the tinkle of breaking glass.

Someone grabs my arm. "Come on, brother, let's get out of the street. It is not a healthy place."

It is Adolph and Manfred is with him. "Where's Hans?" I ask.

Adolph nods at a building. "In that wine shop. Come on, let's go before the sergeant finds us."

We all take off on the double across the street. Soldiers are pouring into all the stores. Some are grabbing bottles of wine, others sausages, shirts, even pocket watches. The store we have entered is a wine store. Across the room, Hans already has a bottle to his lips. Someone jams a bottle into my hands and I take it and worry the cork out. Adolph has disappeared in the crowd. I can hear Manfred, but cannot see him. Suddenly I realize how thirsty I am and tilt my head back and raise the bottle.

The wine hits my stomach like a sledge hammer. I have not eaten all day and there has been no water since noon. I can feel the wine sluicing in my veins. I drink again and again. It is not great wine, but already I sense its potency.

Some soldiers have started singing. They have their arms around each other's shoulders and are arrayed in a line. There must be nine or ten of them singing a German drinking song. I drink more wine. The bottle is half empty and the room seems to be tilting ever so slightly. Someone puts a bottle of schnapps in my hand and I jam it down in a trouser pocket.

I can hear more gunshots and a corporal bursts through the door. "They are shooting our men. The bastards of this town are shooting our men. They gut shot Sergeant Grimolski. He is badly hurt."

A great roar goes up from the men and we pour into the street. I have never heard of this Sergeant Grimolski. I think the corporal is from a Dusseldorf regiment. Gunfire blasts in the square and another building catches fire. Shadows dance like demons possessed before the flames. A bullet pings off the wall close to my head and I duck and start running down the street.

Someone has shot the horse and it lies dead in the middle of the road. Soldiers run wildly in all directions. Discipline has totally broken down. A young lieutenant is trying to restore order and someone hits him in the head with a baguette.

Half a block away, I see Hans and some of the fellows and run toward them. A woman screams and I look toward the sound. A large soldier has a woman slung over his shoulder and is trotting down an alley. The woman is screaming and kicking and pounding at the soldier with her fists, but he trots on.

"Come on, let's go," shouts one of my squad. It is hard to see in the flickering lights, but I think it is Gregor Platz, who helps his father run a butcher shop. Hans windmills his arms and I follow. We are running hard now, going down a side street.

Suddenly one of my companions stumbles, then falls. At first I think he is drunk, or clumsy. Then another building flares up and in the firelight I can see he has been shot. Blood gushes from his shoulder. Two inches higher and the bullet would have ripped his neck apart.

Anger surges through me and I slug down the rest of the wine and throw the bottle into the darkness. Seconds later I hear a satisfying smash. Before I realize it, my rifle is in my hands and I whirl and aim at a patch of lamplight on the second floor. I squeeze the trigger and more glass smashes.

"Damn civilians," someone shouts.

"Bastards," another cries. "They deserve to die."

"Kill them."

"Kill the men, and have your way with the women."

Another shot rings out and we all dive for cover. To tell the truth, I cannot distinguish between our rifles and theirs. Then another shot sounds and this one is a blast from a shotgun. It is true then about the civilians. We have no shotguns.

"I'm hit," cries a voice as I pick myself up and look around for a target. A line of our soldiers moves down the street and I tear off after them. My running is clumsy for the wine has hit my poor stomach hard. I stop and take a swallow of schnapps to counteract the wine. I know I am not thinking straight, but between the wine and my anger, who can blame me? I jam the schnapps back in my pocket.

I snatch a quick breath then start running again. Some of our men, they look like reservists, are breaking down a door to a house and I push past them. A bullet pings off the wall in front of me and I stop and fire at the building across the street. Then I take off again, although I have no clear idea where I am going. Behind me the flames rise toward the heavens and my shadow runs before me. I am screaming.

Twelve

A Night to Remember

Darkness is an overloaded wagon
carrying more than light can bear:
mercy and relief and absolution,
and chance and fear and death

The night has gathered around me. The town lies a few dozen yards off to my left and I am wandering down what appears to be a quiet lane. Ahead, lights swim, miniscule against the immense darkness. Behind me is a roar of noise and flames that light up the night. The whole town seems to be ablaze, although I do not think that is so. At least I think that as well as I can think. My brain is besotted. I don't handle strong drink well, and, between the wine and the schnapps, I am unclear in my mind and unsteady on my feet.

Now and then a rifle or pistol shot rings out and once a grenade explodes only a short distance away. German soldiers from various regiments seem to be everywhere, even out here in the countryside. At least the privates and corporals and occasional sergeant. I have not seen an officer in an hour.

The road bends and I bend with it. A farmhouse rises out of the darkness. Two corporals, pioneers, pass me arm-in-arm, singing. They look quite drunk and I wonder how I look to them.

I feel sure I look different than when I boarded the train on this fateful journey. Life happens so quickly in war. Without question I am not the same man I was in those early August days in Paris when I visited the Aubiers. I have watched my comrades die and fired a gun in anger, perhaps even taken a life. The pace of life seems to have accelerated so rapidly I no longer control my own destiny. I am simply a gear in a machine far greater than anything I ever imagined.

A low moan drifts across the night and I peer off into the fields by the side of the road. I hear a grunt and then another moan. The moon is up and stars are sprinkled across the sky like confectioners' sugar. In the feeble light cast by a lantern, I can just make out a group of men. They are arranged in a semicircle and are intent on what is in front of them. I stumble to the side of the road for a better look.

It takes a moment while my eyes adjust. Then I wish I had not looked. Three civilians are sitting with their backs to a stone wall. They look like farmers. As I watch, a tall soldier steps forward and rams his bayonet into the body of one of the men. A scream rips apart the night.

Another soldier shouts "Partisans!" and thrusts his bayonet. I whirl away from the screams and start jogging down the road. So, I think, it has come to this—the killing of civilians. But then, only a few moments ago, I was shooting at houses where innocent people, likely women and children, live. I am no better than any other solider.

Never have I felt as I feel now. I am drunk, yes, I admit that. But it is more than that. My mind reels at the noise, the violence, the blood, the grossness. Without my company I feel lost. I wonder where Hans and Manfred and Adolph are. I tell myself I should turn around and head back to town and try to find them. At least find Sergeant Gruber. Even Corporal Meister would be a welcome sight at the moment. But my legs do not turn. They carry me forward toward the farmhouse.

I am at the gate and can see three or four of our men running about the yard. They are running, laughing, falling down and getting up, only to laugh again. I cannot imagine what they are doing. They must be very drunk indeed. Then, as I step closer, I hear the clucking of a hen and can see the men are trying to catch chickens. Actually, they have caught one and are trying to catch others.

I step through the gate and wander down the path. A private from the pioneers lies by the side of the path. His face points at the moon and he is snoring. Singing and cursing come from inside the house as I step into the light.

I am in the kitchen and it is full of German soldiers. They are sitting in every chair and some have flung their jackboots up on the table. A corporal is trying to get the stove going and a rather chubby private is very slowly and methodically emptying everything from the cupboards he can find onto the floor: flour and sugar and potatoes.

I wander through the house. In every room I find soldiers who have made themselves at home. All appear drunk. One man has found a good coat, such as a man might wear to church, and has put it on, only backwards. A fusilier has become sick in one corner. A soldier, without his blouse and helmet, urinates unashamedly against a wall. Pictures have been pulled down and smashed and a corporal is stuffing silver spoons into his knapsack. Is this what German soldiers do, I ask myself. Were I a braver man, I would ask it of them. Instead, I turn and clomp back out through the house and into the night. I am disgusted at the soldiers I have just seen, and at myself.

I should go back to town. I should find my brothers. I should find my company. But the day and the wine have caught up with me and I long for sleep. I stumble toward the barn. A pallet of good clean straw sounds most inviting. Surely the cows or horses won't mind.

Thirteen

Man or Beast

The barn rises out of the darkness like a medieval castle on the Rhine, and in my woozy state, they seem much the same.

My head still spins gently, but the stomach churning I experienced outside the gate is easing. The barn appears to be a fine one, with stone walls, two stout doors, and a pitched roof. I lean against the barn partly because I am tired and partly to steady myself, and piss away a fair portion of what I've drunk. I wipe my hands on the sides of my trousers and give one of the doors a good pull.

To my surprise it swings open. I don't quite know what I'd been expecting. Perhaps that a squad of Belgium's finest had barricaded itself inside. But all that greets me are scents of straw, grain, earth, and, more faintly, the warmish scent of animals. A cow perhaps, or one of those massive Belgian horses. A good farmer could probably sniff out which one had been there most recently, but I am a man of towns and cities. Still, the mingled scents are not unpleasant. In fact, they create, in some strange way, a sense of peace inside my mind. I stand for a moment just inside the door, as though getting my bearings, although certainly I have never seen this place.

Behind me are the raucous sounds of drunken men and now and then the sharp report of a rifle. I pivot and gaze back toward town. Flames are still visible, although somewhat reduced. I wonder if the fires have begun to burn themselves out or if wine and distance have conspired to confuse me.

Suddenly it strikes me that I do not want to be part of this violent night any longer, so I turn and push the big barn door closed. The closing click brings a certain satisfaction to my mind and a tension I had not known was there begins to drift from my body.

With the doors closed, it is dark inside the barn, although stray bands of light, or at least a lesser darkness, drift in through fissures in the walls. I begin to walk slowly, feeling my way. Straw rustles as my feet slog along and I can hear mice in the feed trough. In some way I can't explain, I want there to be animals in the barn: horses, cattle, even chickens. It is not so much that I am lonely. It is more that I am, for the moment, tired of mankind.

Another sound, different from the rest, catches my ear. The flesh on my arms puckers and I am grateful for the comforting weight of the rifle in my hands.

I stand very still for several seconds but do not hear the sound again. My eyes grow accustomed to the dimness and I can make out stalls and feed troughs, even scythes and hoes and shovels hanging from the wall. They are neatly arranged and the barn seems clean and tidy, as good as any German barn I have ever seen and I realize, with some surprise, that I would like to meet the farmer who has cared so well for his property. Such a man is to be admired.

My head is clearing and hunger gnaws at my insides. I walk, more smoothly than before, to a pile of straw and ease down. It feels wonderful to lie back in the straw and close my eyes, even if only for a moment.

Sleep would seem to be the order of the moment, but when my eyes are closed the room gently spins. I open them again and, just then, I hear the sound again. My head whips toward the sound and at the edge of vision I catch a glimpse of movement.

I ease up to a sitting position and raise my rifle. Something, or more likely someone, is in the barn with me. Perhaps it is the farmer caught here doing some late chore. Or, maybe it is a Belgian soldier who has come seeking shelter. It could even be one of my fellow Germans who has wandered here much as I have. I place my finger on the trigger. It is not that I particularly want to shoot anyone; it is more that I have no desire to die in this fine barn.

I will myself to stillness and silence and the night slowly comes back alive. I can hear the mice again and a sparrow chirps sleepily high in the rafters. Without moving my head, I allow my eyes to traverse the darkness, not focusing on anything, but rather scanning for movement or the glint of metal. I breathe as shallowly as possible. Fear creeps up my spine, sobering me wonderfully.

My mouth is terribly dry. After all I have drunk that doesn't seem possible, but cheap wine can have that effect. Sweat forms under my uniform and dampens my chest, yet I feel chilled. That must be the fear.

One splendid aspect of fear is that it heightens one's senses sharply. Never have I heard so many small sounds, and my eyes are like those of a cat, piercing the darkness.

There, by the old wagon, I see something, not quite movement, more a shifting of shadows. I smell something, too. It rises above the stench of my own sweat and the sourness of the wine I have spilled on my clothes. I smell fear. Inch by inch, I rise. Whatever is out there shifts in the darkness and my scalp constricts. I raise the gun to my shoulder and my finger tightens on the trigger.

Out of the darkness comes a sharp intake of breath, and then a figure is running.

"Halt!" I shout, but the figure keeps moving. The figure stumbles, falls, then scrambles to its feet. I am running now, my strides double that of my prey. They are closer to the door, though and it is a mad dash.

Now they are tugging the door open, but it is heavy, and they are not strong. I toss my rifle aside and fling myself at the figure. My aim is good and I hear them grunt as my weight forces us down.

A shriek assaults my ears. Never have I heard a man make such a noise. In reflex, I smash a fist against his jaw and he goes limp. I peer through the darkness at his face.

Something does not look right. Two feet away a patch of moonlight about the size of a dinner plate splatters on the earthen floor of the barn. I drag the body over to the light and tilt the head so the light strikes it squarely.

My breath catches in my throat.

The man is not a man at all, but a woman. At least it appears that way from the face. I fumble with her clothes and, yes, she is wearing a dress. Against the darkness her legs are white, smooth to the touch. It has been a long time, and what is that old saying about to the victor...? But no, I am better than that—at least I tell myself so.

She stirs, then moans like a hurt animal. I force myself to scoot against the wall. She moans again and then her eyes flicker open. In the splash of light the fear is easy to see.

"Who are you?" she asks, in heavily accented French. I wondered what language she would speak. Three languages are spoken here: Dutch, French, and German. From my travels I know many Belgians speak at least two of the languages.

"My name is Karl Schiller," I say in French. "Do you speak German?"

She nods.

"Good. My German is better than my French."

I study her face, what I can see of it. Her hair hangs down and across much of it, but one eyes glistens. She gives no clue what she is thinking, although I can imagine.

"As you can see, I am a German soldier."

She shrugs.

"I mean you no harm."

"That is easy for you to say. Look at what you and your friends have done. You have burned the town and now you're destroying our farms. You are killing the livestock and trampling the vineyards. You Germans are going to ruin us, and we have never done anything to you."

"Your soldiers and partisans are shooting us."

The woman sits up and glares at me. "What? What are you saying? You are the ones who invaded us. You are nothing but animals."

"We are only crossing Belgium to attack France. Your country should not be our enemy. France is our enemy. They are the ones who started this war. Germany only mobilized because we were forced to."

She jerks her head back and her hair swirls around her face like a dark curtain. "Ha. You are even more stupid than you look."

I am tired and quite willing to acknowledge that I am not the smartest man in Belgium. Probably I am not even the smartest poet in Belgium. But I don't wish to argue with this woman—her anger is too intense. So I work up a smile and pull the bottle of schnapps out.

"Would you like a drink?"

"Why? So you can get me drunk and have your way with me?"

I shrug. "I was only asking. You do not have to drink any."

"It's probably poison."

I uncork the bottle and lift it to my lips. I do not need more to drink, but I want to show the woman the schnapps is safe to drink. I swallow a small amount, lower the bottle and smile. "See, it is safe." I extend the bottle toward the woman.

For a moment she eyes both the bottle and me with great suspicion. Then she scoots across the floor and takes the bottle from me. She lifts it to her lips and takes a long drink. Then makes a monkey face. "Nasty."

"It will help calm your nerves."

Shots ring out from what can be only a few meters outside the barn. The woman rolls her eyes. "Ha, as if anything could calm nerves with that insanity going on."

"Take another drink...it seems to be a night for drinking."

"A night for death, you mean."

She is correct—it has been a night for death. But I want to ease her fears so I say, "I only hit you because I thought you were a man who wanted to hurt me. No one else has touched you, have they?"

She glares at me. “Not yet.” Even in her anger, I can see that she has a face that deserves to be painted. Her lips are full, and they look soft and inviting. I would like to kiss them, but...

“No one will hurt you while I am here. I will protect you.”

“Ha. And who are you, a lost medieval knight in shining armor?”

“No, I’m no knight in armor, shining or rusty. As I told you my name is Karl Schiller, and I am a private in the German Army. Before the war I was a poet.”

She lifts the bottle and takes another drink. I watch her slender throat work. She swallows. “I have never heard of you.”

“Nor has most of the world. Nevertheless, I am a published poet and my books sell well, or so I am told. At least for poetry.”

“Hmm.” She studies my face then takes another sip. I cannot read her expression but I sense she is less angry. I wonder where her father or husband is. Desultory chatter drifts through the cracks in the barn—two men are talking about how tired they are. One has heard that tomorrow we will get a day of rest. That, I doubt. A small bird flutters in the rafters. In the distance there is more gunfire.

For a few minutes we sit quietly, listening to sounds rising from the night, thinking our own thoughts. I wonder how many of my brothers and the other men of my regiment will make the next formation.

Something heavy thuds against the side of the barn where I sit and a man moans in pain. The woman is indeed right...it is a night for dying, or at least for pain and suffering.

I stretch my legs. *Lieber Gott*, but I am tired. “You are quiet.”

“I have nothing to say.”

I nod. “Moments of silence can be golden.”

She cocks her head, stares at me. “You’re a strange one, Herr Schiller.”

“We’re all strange, in our own way.”

She takes another drink, longer this time. “Your companions are wrecking my house.”

I nod. “They are not doing it any good. But in the morning we can tell more.”

"If we live to see morning."

"You will live to see tomorrow. As long as I am here, no one will hurt you."

"Ah, yes, the good poet knight in his rusty armor." For the first time, she smiles.

"Tell me something about yourself."

"Why?"

It is my turn to smile. "If I am your knight, I should know something about you."

She shifts position, but remains silent. I listen to the voices rising and falling in the outer darkness. They seem fainter now, as though the speakers are growing tired. I wonder if the woman will speak; I wonder what she will say.

She takes another drink, sighs. "What do you want to know Herr Schiller, the great German poet?"

I consider her question. What can I ask that would not arouse her ire? Ah, yes, family—always a safe subject, I think.

"Do you have children?"

She shakes her head.

"A husband?"

Her eyes blink again and her lower lip quivers for a second. "No, he died in the spring."

I am not off to a promising start. At least our army did not kill her husband.

"Brothers?"

"One. He has been called up. He serves at Liege."

"Father?"

"Yes," she says, brushing the hair from her face. "His farm is next to this one. He and my mother are old, but in good health." She smiles again, wider this time, and I breathe easier, having moved the conversation to less contentious grounds.

More gunfire erupts outside the barn and, from some miles away, the thicker, heavier cough of artillery. I cannot be certain, but it sounds like German guns. We must have encountered stiff resistance. Out of the corners of my eyes I see the woman shiver. It is August, but perhaps she has experienced a chill.

"Are you cold?"

"No." She shivers again. "I am afraid." She raises her chin. "Afraid of the guns." She lifts the bottle and takes a long drink.

I watch her throat work. It is lovely and I am lonely. I tell myself to get a grip on my emotions, but that is easier said than done, especially in the presence of such an attractive woman. Surely there are comforting words I should say, but I cannot think of any.

The woman cocks her head so that her hair falls across her eyes. She peers at me through the curtain. "Tell me, German solider, are you ever scared?"

I smile and nod. "Every day."

"Good," she says, tossing back her hair. "That is what you deserve for invading my country."

There are arguments I could raise, but I find myself strangely attracted to this woman and I do not want to make her mad again, so I nod agreement and say, "All soldiers are scared at some time."

She takes another drink and stares into my eyes. I wonder what she is seeing, or perhaps it is more what she thinks she is seeing.

"Do you think you will die?"

I shrug my shoulders. "Everyone dies at some point."

"No, I mean in the war?"

"I have never really thought about it."

"Are you ready to die?"

"No."

"If my brother was here he would kill you."

"Then it is a good thing he is not here," I say with a smile. Perhaps a smile flickers across her lips. I could like this woman, I think. I could like this woman a great deal.

Artillery hammers the night again. The big guns sound closer. Outside the barn a man is crying. I am not surprised. All soldiers feel like crying at times. At least I have.

The woman sighs, "Will those guns never cease?"

"Eventually," I say. "All things cease eventually." I am trying to be clever and comforting, but to my ears my words sound like grandiose pontifications.

For some time, we sit in silence, listening to the faint krump of artillery, the restless stirring of barn swallows in the rafters, and the murmuring voices in the darkness outside. I wonder why no other soldiers have come into the barn, but decide the others must be drunk, or tired, or wounded, or dead. This night has been long and bloody.

I glance at the woman, but her face has slipped into the shadows. I wonder what she is thinking. Sitting up straighter, I ask her a question that has been on my mind. "What is your name?"

"Sorry, what?" she says softly.

"What is your name? I have told you mine."

She glances at me, then turns her head away. "My name is Sanne, Sanne Desmet." She lifts the bottle and drinks once more. Suddenly I want the bottle and stretch out a hand. She scoots closer and passes me the bottle. I take a short sip, then a longer one. Schnapps mingles with the remnants of the wine I drank in town. It is difficult to believe so much has transpired in a single night.

"You are very pretty, you know."

Out of the corner of my left eye, I see the swinging curtain of Sanne's hair as she turns toward me. I turn my face to her. Her face is still wreathed in shadows.

"What did you say?"

I swallow and smile, although I doubt she can see it. "I said you are very pretty."

"Ah, you are just lonely."

"Yes, I am lonely, but you are indeed pretty."

"You honestly think so, or is that a line all you German soldiers use?"

"It is no line. I truly think you are pretty."

"No one has told me that in a long time, a very long time."

She hiccups and I wonder if she is not growing slightly drunk.

"You are not bad looking yourself, for a German. Let me have another drink."

I pass her the bottle and watch as she lifts it to her lips. A stray shaft of moonlight drifts through a crack in the wall of the barn and paints her face, highlighting her lips. As she lowers the bottle, I scoot closer to her and incline my face toward hers.

She doesn't speak, but her breath is warm against my face. Then, as if by mutual accord, our lips meet and I feel her body press against mine. I curl an arm around her shoulders and pull her to me.

"I don't know you," she whispers against my neck.

I am unsure how to respond, so I do not speak. My heart beats strongly in my chest and I feel my pulse throbbing in my temples.

"But you don't seem a bad sort, although I have never known a poet."

"Poets are fine fellows, full of truth and love."

She sighs and runs the fingers of one hand across my face. "I am lonely. For months I have been lonely."

I think of her dead husband as I run the fingers of my right hand through her hair. The woman is lovely and full of life. Loneliness is only to be expected. I feel a desire for her, to be with her, to be one with her.

"You do not have to be lonely tonight, Sanne Desmet."

"No," she whispers, "I do not."

Again her lips press against mine and her hands trace secret patterns on my back. Longing rises in my throat like a storm surge and I pull us to the floor of the old barn. She comes willingly. Moonlight brands our faces as our hands grow busy.

Fourteen

A Farewell and a Promise

Something soft tickles my face and I blink awake. A lovely face looms above mine and I push off the floor of the old barn and kiss the lips that smile at me. They are very soft and I feel my mind shifting. The morning feels young and sweet and I wonder if a certain soldier poet is falling in love.

"Oh," she moans, "my head is cracking open. Oh."

I smile as I realize my brain is throbbing. "Believe me, I understand." My fingers search through the straw until they locate the schnapps bottle. Our luck is in—a small pool of the liquor sloshes around the bottom. I lift the bottle.

"Here, take a drink to counteract the poison. Only save me a swallow."

Sanne holds her head in her hands and groans. "I never want to drink again."

"Go on, just a sip. It will help, I promise."

She gives me a look that seems to question my sanity, but dutifully takes the bottle and downs about half of the remaining schnapps. Her hand trembles faintly as she hands the bottle back.

I finish it in one long swallow, then ease my head back to the straw. The barn seems to be slowly spinning. Not since my student days have I have been this hung over.

Above us, barn swallows are already flying their morning missions and I can hear the sounds a military company makes as it wakes up in the morning. For a few hours I had forgotten about the war, but it has not forgotten about me.

Sanne snuggles her naked body against mine. "Is it really morning?"

"Afraid so, and I will soon have to find my regiment."

"Must you go? Surely, the mighty German army could spare one soldier."

"If only."

She sighs and rolls away. After a moment, she sits up. Her body is lovely in the pale morning light.

"You are even more beautiful than I imagined."

She snorts like a horse. "What I am is hung over." She glances at her body. "And naked." She sighs. "I had better get dressed."

Sanne turns and looks at me. "Now, my good German solider, if you are a gentleman you will not watch." She begins to gather her clothes and I decide it would be a wise move to do the same.

I struggle into my underclothes and uniform, sneaking peeks at her whenever I think she might not be looking. Once she catches me and smiles. "Ah, I see you are not a gentleman. After last night I was most suspicious, anyway." She ducks her head, but not before I see her lips beginning to form a smile.

"No, I am not a gentleman, and have never made formal claim of being one. Actually I am a lost poet."

"I thought you were a soldier."

"Well, that too, but hopefully not for long. In a week, maybe two, we will be in Paris and then the war will be over."

"Perhaps," she says, frowning, "but I am not so sure it will be that easy. You have not even taken Belgium yet and we were not really your enemy. Then you still have to face the French. Countries do not mean much to a simple farm woman like me, but to some men they mean a great deal, more than life itself, as I am afraid your army will soon find out."

I pull on my trousers. She is right, I know, but I do not want to think about it. I have never liked to think of unpleasant things.

"He was drunk, too, you know?"

Her words take me by surprise and I am confused. "Who was drunk?"

"My husband, Jean. He was drunk when he died. He had gone to help a neighbor work on the roof of his barn that had been damaged by a storm and he got blind drunk and fell off the roof." Sanne turns away and peers across the floor of the old barn. "He was a drunk, my husband, a nice, sweet, lovable drunk who couldn't stay sober for even one day that we were married."

She turns to face me, smiles and shrugs. "And now I have gotten drunk and gone to bed with a strange German soldier who claims he is a poet. Ah, perhaps now I will fall off a roof, or down a well, or—"

"Hush, Sanne." Her name sounds sweet to me. "Yes, we were a little drunk last night, but you are lovely and I don't regret a moment of our interlude."

"*Ja*. Our sin, you mean. I hope I don't regret it in a month or two."

"A month or two, what do you mean?"

Using her hands, she traces a rounded shape in the air around her stomach.

"*Ja*, I see," I say as I feel a faint blush steal up my cheeks. I look more closely at her face. She is a few years older than I thought. Closer to thirty, closer to my age. But, oh, she is lovely in the holy morning light.

Sanne reaches out and presses the fingertips of her right hand against my left cheek. "Shall I go fix us some breakfast?"

"That would be wonderful, but, alas, I must go and find my regiment." I glance around the barn. Daylight pours in through the cracks. "Already I am late."

"So soon?"

"Unfortunately."

I hear voices calling. One of them is Corporal Meister and I know I must go.

"They are calling now. That is my corporal."

Sanne cocks her head to one side and peers at me out of the corners of her eyes. "I fear you will soon forget me."

"Never."

She smiles. "We shall see. Time always reveals the truth. However, perhaps you are an honorable man. Perhaps."

I hear Corporal Meister call my name, my brothers' names. I hope we are all alive to face the day.

"I must go...can I write you?"

"If you like. My name, in case you have forgotten, is Sanne Desmet. I live in Hasstend." She presses the palm of her right hand against my face.

"May you remember your sin every time you think of my name. I hope my name haunts you."

"I will never forget. That is my solemn vow, Sanne Desmet. And my name is Karl Schiller. I am with the Forty-second. I will write."

She kisses my left cheek then pulls away. "We shall see, Herr Schiller, poet, soldier, despoiler of innocent Belgian women."

She smiles briefly, then quickly unclasps a chain from her neck. A small cross dangles from the chain. "Here," she says, laying the chain in my palm. "I am no longer pure enough to wear it. Take it so that it may remind you of our sin."

"Our night together."

She smiles again. "All right, my honorable German solder, our night together."

I return her smile, then embrace her quickly, brushing my chapped lips across her soft ones. "Be safe," I whisper, then turn and swoop my helmet up from the straw. I grab my rifle and start jogging across the barn. At the door, I pause, turn, and lift one hand. She lifts one in return.

I say her name again and again as I hurry back to the war. Sanne Desmet, Sanne Desmet, Sanne Desmet.

Fifteen

Cross of Stones

Build an altar of stones,
pile up a memorial to the dead,
stack the stones one on another
the way the dead lie on the road
to Paris.
Raise the altar high enough
so God will be sure to see it,
although I have heard rumors that
He has gone blind in one eye
and can see only angels
out of the other
Yes, Mon Frere,
raise that altar
to the sky,
to the sun,
to wherever it is
our fallen comrades
have gone

We are a pretty lot as we slog through the morning mist. Our powerful marching strides of earlier days have been replaced by a slow, laborious plodding, one foot before another, then do it again. No longer do we march erect with our chins thrusting forward. Instead, we stumble along with queasy stomachs and heads swinging low.

I am certain the officers plan to teach us a lesson. Last night we lost control and I understand that discipline is crucial in war. Still, we have had our moments and they cannot take that away from us.

From the scraps of conversation I hear between Lieutenant Mosel and Sergeant Gruber, I know that the time it took to round us up in the town square and shake us out into lines of march has put us hours behind schedule. There has been much talk of this schedule, known more formally as the Schlieffen Plan. The intricacies of it are beyond me, but I understand our objective is to capture Paris and crush the French army before Russia can fully mobilize. Numbers dictate that we cannot fight on both the eastern and western fronts at the same time and expect to win. Forty days is what I keep hearing. Forty days to capture Paris and force the French to surrender.

It is mid-morning and we are only now back on the road and moving. Perhaps we are not moving quickly, but we are moving. After the night before, this is an accomplishment.

"Move along, move along. Step lively, men," chant the corporals. Corporal Schmidt looks a bit the worse for wear himself, but he manfully sticks to his post. My stomach has settled and the pounding in my head has eased and I am moving better.

I lift my head and look around and the landscape looks familiar, yet different. This puzzles me until I see a break in the fence and a lane running back to a farmhouse and I realize this is where I was last night. I wonder if Sanne is watching us pass and if she is if she is thinking of me. I would like to stop and talk more now that the pain in my head has eased, but Corporal Meister shoves us along and there is no chance. The road goes up a slight rise and then down and then up again.

Suddenly we come to a crossroads. Ahead I can see the backs of other German soldiers. I glance back at the men behind me and catch Adolph's eye. He winks. This makes me feel better and I step with greater vigor.

Just at the crossroads, to the right of the road we march down, someone has built a magnificent cross of stones. The cross stands twenty feet high and it had to have taken hundreds of hours to construct. Stones gleam like alabaster in the morning light so that it looks as though the very eye of God is shining directly on it.

The sight is beautiful, yet frightening. I wonder if it tells our future. For some, I suppose it does, for what is war without death. Even with a hangover from Hell, I do not feel as if I will die this year and surely the war will not last longer than a few months. After all, Paris in forty days and then we turn and crush the Russian hordes. I will admit, however, to being a bit intimidated by mounted Cossacks. They are supposed to be both brutal and fearless.

Surely Sanne has seen this magnificent cross of stones. It cannot be more than a mile from the entrance to her farm. If she were here, she could undoubtedly explain how it came to be placed here and what it symbolizes. Perhaps her brother marched by it only weeks ago. I wonder what he looks like. I do not even know his name, yet I have lain with his sister. Soon, at some yet unnamed battlefield, it is conceivable that we may kill each other. To consider that spooks me and I shudder and elbow Hans in the ribs. He snorts and elbows me back and we march through the shadow of the cross, moving resolutely toward Paris.

Fifteen

Out of the Mist

The mists hide the trees and the
trenches and the shell holes and the
mud that has no foundation
and the horses writhing in the throes of death
and the broken fences and broken houses
and broken men,
but the mists cannot hide my broken mind

It is quite early, not yet good daylight, and we lie on our stomachs staring into a silver mist that shimmers like lace curtains in a gentle breeze.

The mist is thick, making it difficult to make out objects more than a few feet away. All I can tell is that we are in a field of plowed ground and before us is a short stretch of open ground that rolls gently to a dark woods. Trees rise up from the mist like sentinels. Beyond the trees are our enemies. A scouting party came across their camp just before dark yesterday and we have lain here all night so that we can attack at dawn.

If anyone were to ask me, I would admit to being afraid. A man would be a fool not to fear death and it seems likely to me that some of us will die this August morning. An hour ago they brought up coffee and what I drank sits cooling in my stomach like a stone. I glance at my hands and they are faintly trembling. I grip my rifle tighter.

Hans lies beside me on my left and I turn my head and grin at him. He shows me his teeth. He does not look afraid. I am quite proud of him. Down the line, three or four men, is Adolph. I can just make out the familiar line of his jaw. Yesterday, I spoke to Manfred at twilight, but he had sentry duty and I have not seen him since.

Sergeant Gruber is on my right and I wonder what runs through his mind. He is a career man and has been in the army for a dozen years but like the rest of us, has never been in a real battle. Today will be a first for all of us. The few actions we have had before have all been little more than skirmishes. Today promises to be something altogether different.

Someone sneezes and then I can hear my stomach gurgle. Strange, but I think I could eat if food were available. What I would like is plate of sausage and eggs. Such hunger seems odd. My mouth waters.

Out of nowhere, I think of my mother and father, and I long to see them. Then I think of Helga. Finally, I think of Sanne. Her face hangs in my mind like a polished cameo, and I would like to kiss her once more before Death claims me. Sergeant Gruber nudges me with his elbow and jerks his head toward the woods. I nudge Hans and we rise up from the ground like ghosts in the mist.

We move forward in a low crouch. It seems as though we are only creeping along, but the woods grow rapidly nearer, and then we are in them. Branches snap and leaves rustle and I wonder that the French do not hear us. I glance about and see lines of men in gray on both sides of me. They move among the trees like the American Indians I read about as a boy. Above the snapping of our footfalls comes the dull sound of artillery firing in the distance. The sound seems to come from the north; I would guess the field pieces are at least two miles away. I cannot tell if it is our guns firing, or the enemy's.

I trip over a vine, but only stumble. I am a couple of steps behind the rest and hurry to catch up. Among the trees the mist is very thick and limbs scratch my face and snag my uniform. Someone calls out, but I cannot catch the words.

Before I am quite ready, we are out of the trees. The ground slopes away before us and the grass grows as tall as a man's waist. A flock of larks whirls up out of the mist and wings skyward. Before us is a line of hedgerows. I take one step, two, then gunfire erupts.

We run down the slope, firing on the move. The charge down the slope to the bridge as we crossed into Belgium flashes across my mind. But far more than a handful of Belgian soldiers with one machine gun pulled along by a dog awaits us. Flashes of gunfire flare up all along the hedgerow and off to my right I hear one of my comrades cry out. The taste of fear fills my mouth and my legs seem far away and suddenly limber.

I cannot seem to run and fire my rifle at the same time, so I halt for a second, aim at the hedgerow and squeeze the trigger. The report is louder and sharper than I expected and the recoil jars my shoulder. I do not have even the faintest idea if I have hit anyone.

A machine gun opens up from the hedgerow and right away, I hear one of our men cry, "I'm hit." As if by mutual consent, we all fall to the ground and begin firing from a prone position.

"Look out!" Hans cries. "Off to the right."

I turn my head and catch a glimpse of a thin line of men moving through the swirling mists. They look to be dressed in khaki rather than the blue uniform of the French and I wonder what army we face. It is obvious they are trying to flank us and many of us begin firing on them. I see one man fall, then another. A bugle blows and the entire line turns and legs it for the hedgerow. We fire after them and two more men fall.

Artillery begins crashing from behind us, just beyond the woods. They are trying to hone in on the hedgerow. The first shot goes long and the second, while closer, also crashes thirty or forty meters beyond the hedgerow. Our spotters are very good, however, and I feel my confidence rise.

The third shot falls only meters short, sending a mountain of earth into the air and cascading down on the hedgerow. From the hedgerow, the machine guns hammer at us and I hear a bullet whiz by inches above my head. Our artillery has them bracketed and I press my helmet against the earth and wait.

Our artillery roars again and shells scream over our heads. I lift my head just in time to see a shell smash into the hedgerow. The explosion is terrific and hedge and earth and men are flung into the air. A great gaping hole has been torn in the hedge and Sergeant Gruber is on his feet, waving his arms and shouting at us to charge. I push off the ground and stumble forward, sprawling on the ground. I am not hurt, only my pride. My legs are simply limp, like overcooked noodles.

I push up again. As I stand, I notice a man a few yards to my left is still lying on the ground. His arms stretch out before him as though he flung them there and was then unable to use them. I hurry over and kneel by his side. He is not moving and I shake him. He does not move and I get a sick feeling in the pit of my stomach.

I toss my rifle on the grass and turn him over. Half of his jaw has been shot away and all around his head is a pool of blood. I know this man. His name is Kleist and when he was in school he was our fastest runner. I look at his face and my stomach revolts. I turn my head and vomit in the grass.

The sergeant is shouting at me to leave Kleist and move forward, so I give the man a final look, grab my rifle, and hurry after the others. I can hear them shouting and shooting and, before our onslaught, the enemy has turned and is running up the next slope. Thanks to the artillery, we have broken their nerve and I shout and run after the others. My cheeks are flush with victory and my heart hammers like something gone mad in my chest.

At the hedgerow we pause and regroup. Hans and Manfred stand together off to one side and I join them. After a moment,

Adolph saunters over and we all clasp hands and pound each other on the back.

The soldiers we have routed wear the uniform of the British Expeditionary Force. This comes as a shock. We understood the British were at least two weeks away from being on the continent.

Still, they have proven to be only a little more trouble than the Belgians and seven or eight of their number lie dead. In addition, we have captured another six who were injured too badly to retreat.

The sun is coming out and the mist is burning off. I am suddenly ravenous. I try not to think about Kleist, or what awaits us over the next rise.

Sixteen

A Good Cup of Coffee

Dawn is a faint blue slash on the eastern horizon. My brothers and I crouch around a campfire. For August the early morning is cool. In the flickers of the flames I can see my brothers' faces. They look tired—for good reason. For the past five days we have marched virtually without ceasing. The soles are coming off our boots and blisters dot our feet. My legs ache like they have been beaten by a stout hickory stick.

Manfred sips from his tin cup. "Ugh, what lousy coffee. How can it taste sickeningly sweet and bitter at the same time?"

Adolph makes a face. He has not shaved in days and his chin bristles with stubble. It is coming in gray and I am tempted to call him an old man. "The fools have scorched it then added too much sugar."

Hans tosses another branch on the fire. "At least it is warm," he says. Then he lifts his face and grins at us evilly. "Although perhaps not as warm as where we will be going."

"Yes," Manfred says, "where are the French? We have been marching for days and haven't seen a one. At this rate we'll be in Paris before the week is out."

I chime in. "If our boots don't wear out first."

"There is that," Adolph says.

"I wonder how Mama and Papa are doing." Hans is such a good, sweet boy. I attribute that to him being the youngest.

Adolph shrugs. "Worrying about us, probably."

"And with good cause."

"Yes, I have heard artillery fire on our right and left flanks."

"I heard Von Kluge's army is within sixty miles of Paris."

"On to Montmartre."

"No, the Moulin Rouge."

"Now you're talking."

"Better to think about such than what faces us."

I nod. "Agreed. The French will retreat, yes, but only so far. They will give up ground, but not Paris. Not without a fight."

"A brutal one," Adolph says.

Manfred spits into the fire. "Yesterday I heard the Russians were on the move."

Adolph gives him that big brother look. "Better worry about the French."

"Let the French worry about me."

"At least we are still unhurt," Hans says. "And only three men from our regiment have been injured."

"Yes," Adolph says, "but two of them are dead."

Memory pictures flash across my mind like summer lightning. "Yes, I saw Kleist."

Hans makes the sort of face you make when you bite into a rotten apple. "They say his face was shot off."

"His jaw," I say.

Manfred shifts uneasily and looks off toward the east. The smear of blue is bigger and the air is two shades less dark. He looks east for so long that I wonder what he is searching for. Finally, he turns and gives us each a long, cool look as his upper teeth gnaw on his lower lip.

"I've got a bad feeling about today," he says.

"What sort of a bad feeling?"

Manfred is silent for some time. Then he shifts his feet and stretches his hands out to the fire. "The sort of feeling I awoke with the morning Uncle Henk died."

Adolph snorts down his long nose. "You act like you are part gypsy."

"No," Manfred says, drawing the word out, "but at times I sense things."

"Visions?" I ask.

"More a sense of something happening, or a feeling that it will.

I sip at my coffee. Manfred is right—it is awful. Still, as Hans says, it is hot and who knows when we get anything hot to eat or drink again? Days ago we outmarched the soup kitchen, then the artillery. Yesterday even the cavalry had to rest their horses. We have marched like no army in history.

Manfred is talking again. My mind has drifted down the dusty French roads and I struggle to catch up.

"My point is," he says, "that we must stick together. Once the fighting begins, we must be brother with brother. No matter what the officers say."

Adolph punches Manfred on the shoulder, and not lightly. "Sergeant Gruber will tell you where to go."

"And I'm telling you not to listen to Gruber, not today. The Schiller brothers must stick together. Together we can watch out for each other. If we are separated, disaster looms."

"You always were a worrier."

"Perhaps, but I am truly a prophet."

I laugh a little, vaguely remembering a passage from the Holy Bible. "And without honor in his own country," I say.

"And in France," Hans spouts, and we all laugh.

Around us the air is growing brighter and the eastern sky is streaked with pinks and oranges. The morning is coming alive with the sound of one massive army preparing to meet another. Men cough and spit and laugh and curse. Metal clangs and screeches. And through it all, my ears catch the sharp call of an unseen bird. His song is particularly piercing this morning and I ask myself how many of my comrades will be around to hear it tomorrow. Manfred's premonition has cast a pall over the morning and I shiver as I lean closer to the fire.

"Ah," Manfred says, "what I wouldn't give for one really good cup of coffee."

"Yes," Hans says, "a good cup of coffee before dying."

Nobody laughs. The bird trills on. Daylight streaks the face of the earth.

Seventeen

Forty Kilometers

I have made an amazing
discovery,
truly amazing!
Forget, my friend, all you have
read about hell fire and damnation,
forget about the painting of the flames
of fire,
and the forked-tongued devil.
Hell is none of those things;
it is merely having to take one more step,
and one more step, and one more step,
and one more
and one
and
a...

Even though it no longer seems possible, still we march. Artillery rumbles off to our left and, not an hour ago, half-hidden in a stand of oaks, we saw an English cavalry detachment.

At that moment Hans had mumbled, "We are marching into a trap."

Although I had been inclined to agree with him, I had murmured back, "No, we are marching to Paris." At the time I had the energy, and it had seemed important to keep his spirits up. Being five years younger, Hans is inclined to be emotional.

But now it is well past noon, and still we plod on, heads drooping, willing our legs to move. I summon my reserve and look around me. We look like a defeated army in full retreat. Instead, we are surely closing in on Paris. Never in history have men marched so long, so fast, so well. At least that is the story Lieutenant Mosel tells us. My head drops of its own accord and I plod on, staring at the puffs of dust that rise around my ankles with each step.

Suddenly a great shout goes up and I hear elation in the men's voices.

"What is it?" I ask. "What has happened?"

A hard-eyed blacksmith named Heinson who is marching beside me, cocks his head to one side.

"Up ahead they have seen a sign. Paris is only forty kilometers."

"What? Only forty?"

"Yes, can you believe it?" Heinson smacks his lips. "I can almost taste those women of Paris."

My heart lightens and my head swims at the thought of Paris. Only forty kilometers and it will be ours. Will any victory ever have tasted as sweet? New life funnels into my legs and I feel I can walk eighty kilometers. Forty is mere child's play.

A ragged cheer goes up and, to a man, backs straighten, necks stiffen, and eyes glitter. Only forty kilometers—it seems like a dream.

Men laugh and talk and even the NCOs don't chastise them. Our pace quickens until we are almost running. My breath rasps in my throat and the muscles in my legs burn, but I drive myself forward. All we have to do is make it to Paris before the French army can retreat and block our path. Every day we hear rumors of

German victories and advances and wonder if they are true (armies are wonderful places for rumors). Now we know. The road bends gently to the north and climbs a rise in the ground. Before us the road is white in the sun, and I can almost taste the wines in the cafès of Paris.

Eighteen

An Army Whose Hour Has Come

Sunlight spreads across the earth, turning everything golden. We stand along a treeless ridge, gazing down at a green and fertile valley. A narrow road cuts between fields of oats and wheat and potatoes. We haven't had any good vegetables in a week and only the dreaded iron rations the past two days, and a desire for peas and cabbage and Brussels sprouts almost overwhelms me.

At the mouth of the valley lies a small town. From our vantage point the houses and stores and churches look like doll furniture. To the east of the town is a heavily wooded area. Even in middle of the morning it looks dark and foreboding. A thin blue line curls around the western edge of the town and suddenly, I long for a drink of fresh water.

A staff car pulls up and several officers get out. Colonel Burkhoff strides out before our lines. He is tall, square shouldered, and reputed to be a brave man. Sunlight glitters off his helmet.

A captain I do not know shouts "*Achtung!*" and we all snap to. The colonel allows his gaze to run up and down our ranks. He draws himself up even straighter.

"Men, our advance parties report a large contingent of French soldiers in and around the wooded area just outside the town you see before you. They may be all that stands between the German army and Paris. It is our job to probe their lines for weakness. If we can break through, it may be the end for France in this sector. General Von Hinkle's divisions are only two hours behind us and closing fast. In precisely twelve minutes we will attack. Follow the commands of your officers and do your duty as good German soldiers and as loyal subjects of the kaiser. You are an integral part of a great army whose time has come. Our artillery barrage will commence in one minute. Good hunting."

As though he were a statue, Colonel Burkhoff stands straight and tall and still, the sunlight playing on his rugged face. He is every inch the soldier and his speech has honed my nerves to the point where I can hardly maintain position.

The colonel goes on standing as though he means to stand there forever. Then, as if in response to some signal that only he can hear, he salutes, whirls on his heels, and marches off toward the staff car.

Our artillery erupts in a thunderous applause, firing again and again until the earth quakes beneath our feet. Shells rise high above the earth and begin to descend, their trajectory a surprisingly graceful arc. There is a certain sense of choreography to the barrage, a ballet for iron and steel.

The first shell explodes in a field short of the town and a plume of earth shoots skyward. More shells shriek overhead and a hand taps me on the shoulder. I turn to face my brothers. Their faces have turned hard against the coming fury and we grasp one another's hand in turn. This is not a time for words. Our eyes speak volumes.

I can feel a trembling in my legs and pray it does not show. While I was watching the shelling, fear wormed its way into my brain. I struggle to choke down the lump in my throat. Lieutenant Mosel shouts a command as he waves an arm and we start down the slope, going slowly, almost hesitantly at first, then picking up speed. Shells whiz over our heads sounding like speeding trains while down below pyramids of earth rise and fall. Manfred shouts something, but the artillery has temporarily deafened me, so I smile at him and whirl my hand.

~ * ~

There are swales in the slope and as we come out of one, the French are visible for the first time. I can see their blue uniforms and the glint of the sunlight off the barrels of their rifles.

"Artillery!" Hans shouts and I turn my head and follow his pointing finger. Yes, a line of the French 77s are unlimbering just at the edge of town. One of our shells lands short and a geyser of dirt rises. A few grains sprinkle down on us, stinging our hands and faces.

Rifle fire from the front and a line of French infantry rises from the far side of an upslope, close enough to make out their faces. I grip my rifle tighter and begin to zigzag across the open ground.

"I'm hit!" someone cries off to my right. I do not recognize the voice; anyway, I am too busy pressing my face to the good earth. The 77s have opened up and the shells smash our lines.

"Fire!" shouts a voice I know well. Old reliable Sergeant Gruber, calm as a Lutheran church steeple, duck walks behind us, tapping us on the leg, urging us to shoot. Keeping my head as close to the ground as possible, I aim at a blue uniform and squeeze the trigger. Grass tickles my chin and I wonder if this is the last earthly sensation I will know. For a second, from some lost corner of my mind, I think of Sanne and finger the chain she gave me.

Our artillery is finding the range now. Shells smash into the line of infantry and into the artillery, even into the town. The roof of a house goes flying off. Screams ring out all up and down the line and I know that this is no one-sided battle. I fire again, reload then squeeze the trigger once more.

"Up, up, move forward," Sergeant Gruber shouts, and I struggle to my feet on trembling legs. I look around for my brothers and my eyes lock with Hans' and he waves. I wave back and then Corporal Meister is whacking the backs of my legs with the nasty little stick he carries. I despise the man, but start trotting forward. In my look around I did not see Manfred or Adolph and hope they are all right.

The French infantry is indeed retreating, but they are going in good order, firing as they fall back. Off to the left, their artillery, what is left of it, is pulling back. Quickly I reconnoiter. Many of my company still lie on the ground. Some writhe in pain, others cry out for a medic, or water, or mother, or mercy. More than a few make no sound at all. They are still as death, and one can only assume that death has indeed claimed them.

But there is no time now to grieve for the dead, nor tend to the dying. And, in the end, aren't we all dying? Some have just gone to an early grave and it seems clear many others will soon join them.

As for me, I am unscratched. My uniform is not even stained, only dusty. I am very thirsty and take a quick drink from my canteen as we jog on. The man on my right shouts something, but I cannot understand him, so I only nod and keep walking. A moment later it strikes me that I do not know the man and that his company patch is new to me. Glancing around, I can see that different companies, even regiments, have mingled together in the charge. The NCOs are rushing about trying to straighten out the lines. But the French reserves have come up and they fire into us like wild men. Our lines dissolve like snow on a warm April afternoon.

Hans and I curl off to the right. The firing seems less intense from that direction, and, besides, I see Sergeant Gruber and Corporal Schmidt running hard in that direction. I shout to Hans and he nods with vigor as we pound off in pursuit.

At the bottom of the hill is a shallow draw, really nothing more than a natural depression in the earth, scarcely more than a ditch. We gather there, Gruber's little flock. Hans is there, and a boy who grew up down the street, and four or five others I recognize. Joining us are a half dozen men from a Saxon regiment who have been separated from their companions. We gather around the sergeant. I stand next to Corporal Schmidt who is bleeding from his arm. "Only a flesh wound," he says. However, his face is drawn and pale.

"Our task is to take this town, then hold on. Reinforcements are coming. Lieutenant Mosel heard that from the colonel." He pauses and looks around. His eyes stop on me. "Karl Schiller, you and your brother and the Saxons will go with Corporal Schmidt. Your object is that church just ahead."

He points and we follow his finger. All I can see along that line is a white steeple rising above the rest of the town. It appears to be in the very middle of the town. A huge shell screams overhead and smashes into the side of a building maybe fifty yards away. Splinters rise and fall like elongated confetti.

"Make sure you know where your hand grenades are. Also, your bayonet. Within the town we may meet the enemy face-to-face. In close quarters, certainly. Aiming and firing your rifle will take too long."

The corporal gives all of us the steel look, takes a deep breath, whirls, and starts up the draw. We swallow hard and follow after him, Indian file. In spite of the sunlight, I shiver. The prospect of hand-to-hand combat has a way of chilling a man's blood.

Nineteen

A Holy Place to Die

We move up the defile, each man keeping his eyes on the helmet of the man in front of him. A hundred sounds of battle rise and fall around us. At any given moment a man can hear the whine of bullets, the scream of shells, the thud of a dud smacking into the earth, punctuated by the tremendous roar as a shell explodes against a building, and, piecing through the din, the cries of men. Cries for ammunition, artillery, water, reserves, medics, grenades, and mercy.

Our move is made without speaking and it seems that so long as we can stay in this sunken passage we are in a safe place, one where no bullet or shell or grenade can go. I find myself holding my breath, as if that alone keeps me safe.

The man ahead of me slows and I bump against him. The man behind me bumps into me and, in a moment, we are all gathered in a bunch, ready to storm the town on the signal of Sergeant Gruber. He gives each of us an individual, piercing look, directly in the eyes.

"You heard Colonel Burkhoff. We are an army whose hour has come. Follow me and make for the steeple. We will reconnoiter there and hold it against all attacks. If a man falls, you must leave him for the medical corp. Our only goal must be to capture the church. From there we have the high spot and can control the town. Understand?"

Around me heads nod.

"Any questions?"

"Good, then we attack. Follow me."

Without waiting for a response, our sergeant charges up out of the defile and starts down a street with Corporal Schmidt only a stride behind. They do not look back. Someone raises a cheer and we all join in as we clamber out of the low ground. This is the first French town we have attacked and it seems strange to pound down the street knowing there might be a Frenchman behind any window. I wonder where Adolph and Manfred are, and how they are faring.

We move as a mass and the sound of our boots striking the earth echoes off the walls. We seem an unstoppable force. Hot pride surges through me.

For a block, two, there are no shots. It is as though we have slipped through some secret passage and are taking the enemy completely by surprise. Then we round a corner and race headlong into a hail of bullets.

They scream by our ears and one rips through my tunic without even scratching me. Up ahead, Grinkle, who always wanted to own a beer hall, spins and falls, grasping his left shoulder. His rifle clatters to the ground and, as I run by, I see blood oozing between his fingers.

Another man cries out and then up ahead, maybe thirty yards, a squad of French infantry dashes out from between two buildings, firing as they run. Without any need for orders we aim our rifles and return fire.

A Frenchman falls, his forehead blown away. Two others are wounded and the little band scurries back to shelter. A shout goes up from our men and we pound on. We turn another corner and there is the steeple straight ahead. Only four blocks to go.

Hans runs beside me and we pound each other on the back as we charge. The thrill of battle that we have heard so much about is on me now and I feel invincible. A quick look at any of our men and I can tell they feel the same. Paris seems almost within our grasp.

Then, from a distant place, the French artillery starts up. Shells smash into the buildings, sending pieces of brick and splinters of wood flying. I had never considered that the French would shell one of their own towns. To do so speaks of their desperation.

A shell smashes high into a building immediately to our left and bricks and mortar rain down on us. Private Lindeman goes down. We pound on. The church is only two blocks away.

A bullet pings off of Hans' helmet and he spins like a top. I catch him as he starts to fall, but he is only dazed and, after a few seconds, he begins to laugh. We run hard after the others.

Suddenly the men in front of us fall to the ground and begin firing. Hans and I do the same. At first, I am firing blind. Then I see a squad of French, bigger than the other, arrayed along the steps of the church. They are shooting down into us and I hear Ekes cry out, then Freidsbacher. I steady my elbows against the ground and aim at a bearded French soldier who stands on the third step. A second later he throws up his arms, spins halfway around, then falls like an uprooted beech. I see Sergeant Gruber fling one of our stick grenades and I hurry to do the same.

Half a dozen grenades explode into the French lines and men fall like wheat before the scythe. Every German seems to be firing at once and the noise is tremendous. More French fall and then Gruber rises and waves us forward. We spring up from the earth roaring like wild beasts and charge for the steps. The remaining French fire a final, ragged volley as they fall back.

We pound up the steps, cheering. Corporal Schmidt pounds my back. Hans is grinning so that it seems his face must split. The fighting force is strong in me and I long to go after the French, but Sergeant Gruber is shouting for us to set up the machine gun and form a defensive line all along the top row of steps.

Now that we have captured our objective, it seems to me to be the time to attack and I cannot fathom why the sergeant has ordered us to go on the defensive. Then Hans taps me on the shoulder and points up the street. I turn and look and my blood instantly runs cold.

Down the street come a mass of French soldiers, a hundred of them, maybe more. A shell smashes into one of the pillars that holds up the portico of the church and chips of mortar and stone prick the back of my neck.

"Fire!" screams Sergeant Gruber and we let loose a wicked volley. The front ranks of the Frenchmen fall like October leaves. Still they come on, firing on the move and some of their bullets strike home. Dietrich, who has a wonderful baritone, grabs his stomach and falls on his face. A bullet smashes into Corporal Schmidt's right leg and he falls heavily against me. Other men cry out, but there is no time to even see who has been hit. The French are only thirty yards away and I aim and fire and aim and fire, and aim and fire. Here and there a Frenchman falls, but still they come on, the brave bastards.

Now it is hand to hand combat, and the world is nothing but a blur. The French are right in amongst us on the steps. We retreat to the top step and still they come. They attack us from the front and the left and right. Only the massive stone church itself protects our rear. For a wild second, I wonder what the good Lord thinks of such fighting, and bloodshed, on his sanctified ground.

Hans and I stand back to back and knowing he is there gives me some small comfort. If I die this day, and the odds are looking good, my passing will not go unremarked. I say a quick, silent prayer that if I fall Hans be spared.

Sergeant Gruber shouts something, but all I can hear is one word, "Germany." At my feet, Corporal Schmidt, in spite of his shattered leg, coolly fires his pistol. I see a Frenchman fall, then another. Ultimately, the sheer force of their numbers sweeps up the steps and over the fallen, German and French, and they are in our ranks.

They are too close to fire at with the rifle and I think I am out of bullets anyway. It is bayonets now; bayonets and fists. A Frenchie lunges at me and I lean to the right and let his bayonet go by. Before he can recover, I lunge and drive my bayonet deep into his side. He screams and his rifle flies from his hands. I jerk my rifle, but the bayonet is stuck; it must have lodged between the poor bastard's ribs. I put the boot to him and shove and he goes flying down the steps, taking one of his cohorts with him.

There is no time for rejoicing. Another Frenchman is upon me, a great bearded fellow, a head taller than I am, trying to smash my head with his rifle butt. I get a hand on his arm and we dance across the steps, cursing and spitting, twisting and shoving for any advantage. He is stronger than I am. Desperation fills me and I fight like a mad man, but the Frenchie outweighs me by forty pounds and I find myself gradually giving way,

Muscles in my arms burn and I feel myself growing tired and weak. During the struggle his arm has grown sweaty and my grip is beginning to slip. I curse and then I pray, but neither does one damn bit of good. With a mighty roar, he jerks free and swings the rifle high. I step back.

Without any warning I feel something firm at my ankles and then I am falling backwards. The rifle butt swings so close to my face that I feel the breeze against my cheek.

I land hard on my back and gasp for air, unable to move. The bearded giant towers over me. I look up into his face. He is grinning, and I notice he is missing a tooth in the front uppers. It strikes me as a terrible shame that this will be my last sight on this good earth.

For a second the tableau is frozen—the grinning French giant, his stick of death poised at the top of the swing, the poor fallen German gasping for air he will never use. I close my eyes and commend my soul to God.

Screams and shouts and curses and gunfire fill the air. I clench my teeth and wait. Surely my death blow will fall any second now. But it does not, and I suck in a lungful of air and open my eyes.

The French soldier is slowly pirouetting, like some mechanical toy winding down. The stick has fallen to the stone steeps while his hands grasp a gaping hole in his abdomen. I look down and Corporal Schmidt smiles weakly at me, then falls back, the pistol still clenched tightly in his fingers.

As quickly as I can I scramble to my feet and turn to look for Hans. But another Frenchman is slashing at me with his bayonet.

I jerk my head back, but not quickly enough. The tip of his bayonet rips across one cheek, and I scream at the pain.

He draws it back to try again and, for lack of any other weapon, I rush forward and butt my head against his chest. The rifle spins out of his hands and he goes flying back down the steps.

I stoop and pick up the Frenchie's rifle. I whirl and look around me. Everywhere German and French soldiers are engaged in private death struggles. I cannot see Hans. But I do see Sergeant Gruber. He smashes a French corporal head with the butt of his rifle and turns to meet the next foe. But two men come at him with bayonets glittering, one from each side. Instinctively, I raise the rifle and fire at the man closest to me. I have no way of knowing if there are even any bullets in the chamber. But the rifle crackles in my ear, and the enemy arches back, then falls dead at Sergeant Gruber's feet.

Suddenly a great shout goes up, and a squad of Hessians charges down the street and up the steps. Before I can accept the fact of their presence, they have routed the French, who leave many comrades dead or dying on the steps.

Blood drips from the slash on my face. It feels like a warm slug crawling down my cheek. I turn to search for Hans. My search is over almost as soon as it starts.

The young boy, my baby brother, sits with his back against a holy pillar of the church. His face is unmarked, but a crimson flower blooms in his chest.

I step over and on bodies in a mad rush to get to him, crying for a medic. But even though my heart holds hope, my eyes tell the bitter truth. Even now life is draining from his face. I kneel and cradle him in my arms. He turns his beautiful face up to mine and I see the flicker of recognition in his eyes. They are blue as the Danube.

His lips part and his throat works, but no sound emerges. I cry out his name and his eyes flicker. Then his body shudders and I am holding only skin and bones. My tears mingle with the blood from my wound and I close my eyes. I want to say a prayer for his soul, but in this moment I can think only of our parents.

I say his name as a benediction then ease his head back gently until it rests against the wall of the holy church. Now is not the moment to mourn. My wounded comrades need me. So I blink at the tears and stumble to my feet.

Twenty

The Breakthrough

Four-thirty in the morning and Sergeant Gruber is rousting the vestiges of sleep from our brains. My brain feels thick as porridge. I rub at my eyes, sit up, then glance around. Our squad is smaller than when we boarded the train. When we crossed the Belgian border, we had one hundred and fifty men. Now there are 96, and seventeen of those are replacements from another decimated squad. Twenty-four of our originals are known dead, the rest wounded, captured, or missing. Instinctively, I rub at the scar forming on my cheek. In a way it gives me status, especially as it resembles a good dueling scar. No regulation states I have to tell that it was made by a French bayonet.

I think of those who are gone, like my brother, Hans, and of those whose injuries have taken them out of the war. Good Corporal Schmidt, whose timely pistol shot undoubtedly saved my life, heads the list. I miss them all and recognize Germany has lost many fine soldiers. Others have lost, too. Parents and wives and sweethearts, and, saddest of all, the little kinder who have lost their fathers.

"Up, up!" cries the sergeant, and little Corporal Meister strides around whacking the slow movers on the soles of their feet, or their shoulders, or their backside. I struggle to my feet. I hate that little pissant more every day. If shrapnel were to slice his head off, I would not shed a single tear.

There is no moon, and the air is black as pitch. I wander off into a stand of trees and answer nature's call. A breeze arose in the night and it is pleasant to stand in the dark listening to the whispers of the leaves. I think of Sanne and wonder if she sleeps well these days. Or perhaps she lies awake worrying about her brother and her farm and what will become of her. Some days I wonder if she thinks of me. It is foolish I know, but I hope she does. I finger her chain around my neck. Even in the dark I tell myself, I could see that huge cross of white stones that stands less than a mile from the lane to her house.

"At least it's too dark for the French bastards to see us." Gerhard Klopmann has walked up and stands just off to my right. Lost in memories, I had not heard him approach and his voice startles me. My body jerks involuntarily. I button up.

"Yes, but that means we can't see them either."

"Not to worry, Schiller. I can smell the animals. Smell their fear." Klopmann laughs. Actually, it is more of a braying sound, putting me in mind of a donkey. Even though I don't believe him, I join in the laughter. For a brief moment it takes my mind off what awaits us. We start back toward the squad.

"Gather round, men," calls Gruber. We push together around our sergeant.

"Listen up. I have just been talking to the lieutenant. Our advance parties have been probing the French lines for over twenty-four hours and have found a soft spot. Along with the Seventy-ninth and the Eighty-third, we have been given the honor of making the breakthrough. Our job is simple, and I always like simple. We are to smash the weak point like a hammer. Open the gates, in a manner of speaking, so that our armies can flow through. Paris is almost within our reach. Today we will make the kaiser proud. "

Out in the darkness someone snickers, then tries to cover it with a cough. My eyes have grown accustomed to the darkness and I can make out the line of Sergeant Gruber's jaw. It looks as hard as steel.

"Pay attention. You must hear the orders to follow them. And believe it or else, they may save your life."

The men grow so quiet I can hear the wind. Then, far away, probably outside some lonely farmhouse, a dog howls. Hairs on the back of my neck rise in response.

"Just off to our left, no more than fifty yards, is the beginning of a low spot. It is not deep, but it runs all the way to the French lines where they occupy the high ground about a mile away. Our artillery has not come up. I do not know why not. But the lieutenant has checked and the attack is to go on regardless. We have the great honor of leading the attack and it will be made where this depression intersects the French lines. Watch for my flare. That will be the signal to spread out and charge the lines. The lazy French will still be asleep or fixing their breakfast and we will smash into them like a sledge hammer and shatter their lines. Two regiments of General Von Hinkle's men are in the second line and they will exploit our opening."

The sergeant pauses and I sense, more than see, his eyes making the rounds. "Now listen, because this is important. Visibility will be limited and it will be difficult to get a clear target. So go in with grenades and bayonets. We have the element of surprise on our side. Total surprise will be ours and a complete victory is anticipated. Once we break through their lines, keep going. According to our scouting parties, the French reserve lines are very thin here. One powerful blow and we can push all the way to Paris."

He pauses again. "Any questions?"

No one answers. My stomach gurgles. Klopmann passes gas and, on the other side of the ring, a man coughs. It is a nasty sound, damp and deep in the chest.

"All right then, we go now. Follow me. If any man falls, do not stop. I repeat, do not stop. Keep going. The attack is paramount. We must have a breakthrough before the French can bring in reinforcements.

If I go down, the command goes to Sergeant Baedeker of the Eighty-third. Lieutenant Mosel is going forward with the colonel."

For a second I think he is going to say something else. But he whirls on his heel then strides off into the dark. With a collective shuffle and shifting of guns and gear, we start off after him. Darkness surrounds us. The only light is a faint blue line on the eastern horizon no wider than the mark of a pencil. The dull thud of marching boots fills the night and I feel a nerve in my face twitch. I need to piss again.

But there is no time...already we are in no-man's-land. I sense an uneasiness among the men. Perhaps, though, it is only tiredness, or should I say exhaustion. For twenty some days we have marched, twenty kilometers, thirty, forty a day, who can say? There are moments when we feel we have marched so far and so fast that no one, not even General Grau, knows where we are.

But that is only the way exhaustion plays with the mind. A chance to fling our aching bodies down for a few hours' sleep, a bowl of soup, a hunk of bread, a good cigar or pipe, and we are ready to go again. After all, Paris is achingly close. For a week we have been told it is only been one good march away. I have begun to suspect that Paris is exactly like that pony a boy wants—it will always come next Christmas.

This morning we have the element of surprise, at least I hope so. If the French can see through this inky blackness, then I am sore afraid, as it says in the Bible.

Darkness seems to amplify sound. I can hear the footfalls of my companions and the huff of their breathing. A twig snaps and it pings in my ears like a rifle shot. Off to my right a bird tweets sleepily and, in the distance, that same lonely dog howls again. Metal clangs on metal until the night threatens to become an orchestra.

Still, I suppose the dog, the bird, and the faint whispers of the wind are good cover for our advance. The French have heard them all their lives. I search the eastern sky. The thin blue line looks no larger, but the quality of the air around me seems changed. They are faint, but I can vaguely make out the silhouettes of my comrades creeping forward in the dark.

The ground has begun to slope up and the shifting wind carries the scent of wood smoke to us. We must be very close to the French lines and our approach slows.

At first I think it is only my whirling mind imagining things, but then, yes, I truly do hear the murmur of French voices in conversation. Two men are talking, discussing a café they frequented in Paris before the war. No, they are discussing the merits of two different cafès. The Select and the Dome. If I recall my Parisian excursions correctly, both are in Montparnasse. I prefer the Dome.

I can smell coffee and bacon. My mouth waters. I try to remember when I last had a good meal. The final dinner at home flashes to my mind, and I think of my parents and wonder if they have been informed of Hans' death. To lose a child must be a foretaste of death to a parent. Then, my mind shifts and I think of Helga and wonder if she thinks of me. We left things quite unsettled at our bittersweet parting.

Off to my left, someone stumbles and falls with a great clatter. "Halt!" cries the French sentry. "Who goes there? What is the password?"

Out of the darkness a figure rises up. By its bulk and height, I know it is our good Sergeant Gruber. There is a blur of motion, followed by a flash of light, then I hear the bark of his sidearm. A great roar goes up from the squad as we charge.

Seven strides and I am in the French lines on the crest of the ridge. Beyond are a half-dozen smoldering campfires. Everywhere French soldiers are running for their guns. We stand at the crest and pour fire down on them. It is like shooting rabbits and they fall in waves. Screams and curses mingle with gunfire and the night is a madhouse of sound. A few French soldiers stand and fire, but we mow them down like so much wheat. The rest, those who can still maneuver, race off down the hill. "After them!" the good Gruber shouts and we tear off down the hill. A few stop to grab a loaf of bread, or a tin of peaches, or a bottle of *vin ordinaire*.

I am tempted, but I am a good German soldier, at least in my mind, and so I pound down the hill. I am still no good at shooting on the run, and not a marksman even in the prone position, but I fumble at my belt and pull out a stick grenade and fling it at a handful of Frenchies who have decided to stand and fight. The explosion is terrific.

We press on, waving our free hands, shouting like madmen. We have broken through the frontline and there is only a thin line of reserves between us and Paris. At least that is what we have been told. A tiny kernel of doubt gnaws at the back of my mind. To state it in diplomatic terms, our intelligence has yet to achieve perfection.

As we run down the slope, we race by abandoned helmets, blankets, and rifles. Here and there a body sprawls upon the earth. I even see a bugle, brass gleaming faintly in the first blush of day.

The eastern sky has gone from blue to a pale rose that strikes me as extraordinarily beautiful. Such beauty makes it seem that it would not be such a bad day to die, although I doubt the French soldiers who have fallen share my view.

The light is better and I can see faces. Manfred runs maybe a dozen meters to my right, and, off to my left, I can see Adolph's elongated head bobbing along at the front of the pack. If only Hans were here. Somehow his absence makes me think of Sanne and I marvel at the untamed wildness of my mind.

The ground levels off and then begins to slope upward again. We have run what seems like a long way and my legs ache while my breath rasps in my throat. Above the pounding of boots and heavy breathing, I hear a crack and then a ping. Suddenly bullets whiz by our heads like hornets. We fling ourselves to the earth, gasping for air and searching the landscape for the French.

"There they are!" shouts Eitmann. He is pointing up the slope to our right. Seconds later I can see the breastworks they have thrown up. Earth and timbers have been mounded together and French soldiers stand behind them, firing down on us with near impunity.

A man crawls up beside me and digs his elbow into my ribs. It is Manfred.

"Well, brother, so much for the thin line of reserves, eh?"

"If they are thin, they are wonderfully enthusiastic."

A machine gun has opened up and the tat-tat-tat chills my blood. Down the line a man cries out, then another.

"Look," Manfred shouts in my ear. "Up ahead is a fallen tree. It isn't large, but it should serve us well. Let's try for it."

"Yes," I say and start crawling, slithering forward on my belly like a snake. High above us, the French are blasting away like maniacs. Manfred crawls by my side and I find comfort in his presence. This lovely morning no longer seems like a good time to die.

Men are shouting, crying out for medics and water. Here and there a man snaps off a shot, but most of the squad cling to the ground. If they are like me, they are praying.

The fallen tree is maybe twenty meters ahead and we crawl on through a hail of bullets. I can hear them singing by my head, then thumping into the earth. It has not rained since the invasion began and everywhere a bullet strikes the earth a puff of dust is raised.

As if in a nightmare, we crawl on. Sweat is running down my chest and back and legs. Dust coats my face. I want to cry. Finally we reach the fallen tree. It was massive, a giant sycamore that has fallen of its own accord, and fairly recently; clods of earth still cling to the gnarly roots. We press our bodies to the fallen giant and then we are breathing again, luxuriating in the sweat rolling down our backs, grinning foolish, dusty grins. To be alive feels wonderful. I glance at Manfred and have to laugh. His face is coated in dust, except where drops of sweat have carved tiny trails.

He laughs, too. "So much for our vaunted intelligence corp. Those reserve lines don't look so damn thin to me."

"No, I'd say they are rather stout." As if to lend credence to our comments, a machine gun rakes the tree trunk. Bullets made a dull thudding sound when they strike the wood and splinters fly like a dozen woodsmen were furiously chopping.

"It's too far to fling a grenade."

"Yes, we're pinned down here, but good. If we try to raise up and get off a shot, some marksman will shoot our eyes out."

Manfred grimaces. "Unpleasant thought, brother."

"This is an unpleasant situation."

"To say the least." Another round of machine gun bullets hammers at the tree. I close my eyes and press myself so tightly against the pale smoothness I feel almost one with the fallen giant. I am afraid of death, yes, but to die by a fallen tree seems rather anti-climactic. A huge thump fills the air and a giant shell screams overhead, headed toward our lines.

Manfred groans, "Oh, good. That's just what we need, the French artillery." He twists his head around and peers back down the slope. "Speaking of artillery, where the hell is ours? They haven't been keeping up with us, the lazy sods."

"Gruber said they were only a few hours behind."

"Well, I wish they would get a move on."

Before I can say anything, the French artillery really opens up. The noise is incredible. I do not understand how any artillery man keeps from going stone deaf. Sticking a bit of cotton in one's ears isn't going to block out much. We listen to the scream of shells overhead and, moments later the earth itself trembles. Dirt flies up in huge fountains, and it is easy to imagine the damage even one of those shells can cause.

But what can a man do? That is the question, and a very important one. I look all around. If any of our squad is out there, I cannot see them. Only one German soldier is visible and he is face down in the dirt with his arms flung forward. His helmet has fallen off and his neck is twisted at a funny angle. From this vantage point I cannot see his face, but I would be willing to bet he is dead.

"Got any water?"

I shake my canteen. "About half. You?"

"A few swallows, but I did liberate a bottle of wine last night."

I smile. "That should make our life more pleasant."

"Indeed." Manfred twists around, reaches in his knapsack, and pulls out a tin. "Here, open us some iron rations and I'll uncork the wine. It looks like this will be a long day and we might as well enjoy ourselves." Another barrage of artillery from the French and a shell falls short. Dirt rains down on us. Manfred is right. It is going to be a very long day.

Twenty-one

A Home Away From Home

Tonight a sweet breeze blows gently down the trench line, carrying with it the smell of something sweet and green and fresh. After the long winter, such an aroma is like a blessing from heaven. Manfred, Adolph, and I hunker around a small fire in our trench. We keep it burning low, so no smoke escapes. Well, only a little, and anyway, the French know exactly where our trenches are by now. We have been in this line since the snow started falling back in the late fall. The day has been warm, the warmest in weeks, but with darkness the temperatures have started to fall again and I shiver inside my greatcoat. It is going to be a chilly night, and I have sentry duty.

"Damn, that wind has a bite in it. Must be blowing straight out of Siberia." Adolph hunches his shoulders as he peers down the trench. Never heavy, he has lost weight, looking more each day like some Romanian refugee.

Manfred squats as he pokes at the dirt at his feet. "We have been here too long. Even the rats are starting to feel like family. If we stay here much longer, I will name them."

"I heard we move out next week."

Adolph snorts like a horse. "Rumors are the only thing there are more of than lice in this place."

"But it has been so quiet. There haven't been any trench raids for a month."

Off to the south, shots ring out as if on cue. But it is only sniper fire—eager beavers anxious to take headshots. Dusk and dawn are the most popular times. Something to do with the lighting, I understand. Not being a marksman, I merely nod and listen when others tell their tales.

Footsteps thud down the trench. It is Corporal Kerr. He is new to our line, coming from another outfight that got shot to pieces last fall. Not many of the old squads remain even close to intact. We have fared better than most. Adolph counted it up the other day and we have fifty-seven percent of our originals still in the line. It is easy to tell the veterans from the newcomers. Of course all men age quickly up here. Some days I feel one hundred.

Kerr comes up and hunkers down beside us. He reaches inside his coat and tugs out a loaf of bread. He hands it to me. I tear off a hunk and pass it on to Adolph. The bread is not warm, but it is fresher than most loaves the field kitchen brings up when they bother.

"*Danke.*"

"*Bitte.* I was over visiting my cousin. He is with the Twenty-first. And their field kitchen paid them a visit. Thought I'd grab a little something for my mates."

"It tastes good. Better than most," I say.

"*Ja,*" Manfred says and grins, showing his teeth. "Tasty."

Adolph nods. Of late he has grown quiet. Moody, our mother would say. I worry about him. But what good does that do? Days pass when I wonder if anything does any good. I try to think of pleasant things on those days; of home and my mother and father, Helga, and the Aubiers, even a few of my better poems. Other days, when I'm in a different mood, I recall Sanne and the night in the barn. Of late, however, none of them brings me peace.

Days also pass when I wonder if I will ever write poems again. If I do, I know the poems will not resemble my work before the war. They could not be the same, for I am not the same man. I have seen too much—too much death and disease and destruction. I need only think of Hans, Corporal Schmidt, and a Belgian farm widow named Sanne to I know I am not the same man, and can never be again.

"Eat up," Kerr says. "Our field kitchen is slow tonight." He gazes at the sky. Darkness has not quite come, a faint afterglow lingers. The corporal glances at me. "Well, Karl, I saw on the roster where you are on sentry tonight. Hate to rush you, but Strench is waiting."

"All right," I say and push up, stuffing the rest of my bread in a pocket. Sentry duty makes for long nights where hunger is a frequent companion. "See all you men in the morning," I say and fling up a hand.

Without waiting for a response, I turn and start off down the trench, keeping my head low. Someone will relieve me at midnight, if nothing happens, but the rest will all be asleep by the time I stumble back. I hate sentry duty. After an hour or two, loneliness grabs you by the balls and hangs on with a fervent vigor.

~ * ~

Tonight the rats are out. I can hear them scurrying before me as I trudge down the trench. When walking in a trench, one has to take care where they step. Men sit with backs to the earthen walls and stretch their legs out into the passage so that it is easy to trip and find yourself sprawling. Plus, of course, there are the rats. They feed on the corpses that come up out of the ground after every hard rain. French and English and German all have fallen across this fought-over ground. You can actually step on a corpse if the light is bad, or if you are very tired, or simply not paying attention.

I pass by a young soldier sound asleep with his head on his arms. He came up to the front line only three days ago, arriving with five others. Already two of the new arrivals are dead. I don't even know the fellow's name, although I heard that he is from Mannheim.

Two veterans stand quietly against the side of the trench smoking their pipes. They speak as I pass and, when I tell them I am on my way to sentry duty, one of them tells me to keep my head down. We all chuckle. Gallows humor, one could call it. Or maybe trench humor is a better name. We have been in these trenches for eight days and are due to be relieved any day. Our commanders have discovered that after a week men get so used to the way of the trenches that they become careless. And a careless man is soon a dead man.

~ * ~

Strench is tall, three or four inches over six feet, and he has to crouch rather severely when on the parapet to keep his head from getting blown off by a sniper. Although now that the French are back in the trenches on the far side of no-man's-land, the danger is not quite so great. Back in February when the British occupied the line, we really found out about snipers—the hard way. British soldiers are extremely zealous snipers.

"That you, Karl?"

"Yes. How goes it?"

"So far it has been quiet, but you know what that usually means."

"Unfortunately," I say, and Strench chuckles as he begins to climb down. Actually, it is more of an unfolding. I am not a short man and he towers over me. I have misjudged. He has to be at least six inches over six foot.

"Did the field kitchen come up?"

"Not yet. They are running late tonight."

"Ha," Strench snorts. "What do you mean tonight? We haven't had food on time in a week."

"Maybe they are busy."

He snorts again. "Too many officers."

"Perhaps," I say as I climb the ladder. It has only three rungs. Our trench is not a deep one. Rumor has it that some around Reims are over twenty feet deep.

"Well," Strench says, "I'm off. Good luck."

"*Danke.*"

"Keep your head down."

"Mind the rats."

"Ha," he replies and starts off down the trench. Still working the kinks out of his muscles, he moves slowly. In addition to being taller than most, Strench is also older. Thirty-two, I believe. He was an early volunteer. I understand his wife died last summer.

Ah, last summer. Those warm sunny days seem a lifetime ago. Trench life numbs a man's brain. Some days I have trouble remembering crossing the Belgian border.

Sanne, though, I remember. In the trenches, a man thinks first of surviving, then of food, and then of women. Not being a great lover, I do not have a storehouse of romantic memories like Becker and Ewalt. A few kisses with Helga seem fairy tales told by a child. And promises seem to have been made to be broken, especially in war time.

One drunken night in a Belgian barn is not much to brag about, though it was special to me, so I keep Sanne to myself. I have not even told Manfred or Adolph.

The moon is up now, a half moon, waning. Moonlight splatters across the barren ground and glitters on the barbed wire. We only have a single strand strung before our trenches, but more is scheduled to arrive next week. Barbed wire is often more effective than rifles, as barbed wire never has a case of the nerves.

The same moon that blesses the battlefield also shines over Belgium and I wonder if Sanne is peering out her kitchen window at the night sky. I wonder also if she ever thinks of me and, if she does, is it with fondness? Part of me feels bad for what we did that night, but, if I were to tell the truth, not all of me feels that way. I ought to write her, tell her again of my feelings. Letters can't compare to being with her, but I do not know what else I can do. Perhaps I will write when we are pulled out of the trenches.

Considering writing a letter makes me think about my mother and father. I have not had a letter from them in over a month. Of course, mail delivery at the front is very much a hit and miss situation. A man can go six weeks with receiving a single piece of mail then one day he receives four letters.

I need to write them, however. Manfred, Adolph and I all wrote them about Hans. Lieutenant Mosel also wrote, commenting on the bravery Hans showed. Bravery is all right, I suppose, but staying alive is better. Still, my parents are getting old and I need to be more conscientious about writing to them.

Helga, yes, I should write Helga. But then, I have not heard from her in weeks. Perhaps she has found someone else. Or maybe it is only the lousy mail delivery at the front. Some nights I have trouble remembering her face. The faces of the dead, however, I cannot forget.

I ease one eye over the lip of the trench and peer out through the barbed wire across mutilated ground. Even the afterglow has gone and I cannot make out the French trenches. I scan the ground for movement.

Just as we do, the French send out night patrols to probe for weaknesses in our lines and try to determine our strength. Some nights they even send raiding parties. Company K lost four men to one raid only a week ago.

The wind is down and the night grows so still I can hear the rise and fall of my own breath. Nothing moves before our lines and I listen to see if I can hear underground sounds. Last fall, before the ground froze, the British went on a tunneling binge. One of their tunnels reached all the way to our lines near Dubois before an alert sentry heard them digging. Another week and they would have been in our trenches.

Tonight the moon shines brightly. The air must be very clear. Even though it is only a half-moon, I believe I could read a newspaper by that light. In that way, I am lucky. Such moonlight makes the night too bright for much activity from the French. I doubt we will send out any patrols either, although our new captain is a proponent of the offensive.

Bright as it is, the moonlight feels cool. Night has a way of chilling a man's blood. I wish I had a cup of coffee, a cigarette, someone to hold. Sentry duty is lonely. I ease back against the cold, hard earth and stretch my legs out, hoping midnight will hurry. War is not at all what I expected. Gallant charges with flags flying are apparently no longer in vogue. Books with war themes are misleading at best. Some are ludicrous. Words like glory, valor, and honor are only hollow collections of wandering letters.

A rifle shot rings out across the night. Another answers. Fun and games—trench warfare style. I am not at all sure I will ever grow accustomed to such activities. A longing for the Fatherland rises up in me until I almost choke. Tearing my mind back to this slice of France that God has forgotten, at least temporarily, I finger the chain around my neck as I peer out across land that belongs to no man.

Twenty-two

A Vacation at the Seashore

I have made a great discovery. One I doubt seriously anyone has ever found before me. It is beautiful in its simplicity. And to think I found it in a barn in France. What is it? I laugh as I ask myself the question.

Why it is nothing more, nor less, than being able to luxuriate in a bed of clean straw in a warm, dry barn where there are no prospects of a French 77 blowing your arse off.

Ha! I am a great comedian. Maybe I will go on a cabaret tour when I return to Germany.

I stretch, yawn, and open my eyes. For the first time in what seems like years I feel truly rested. It is our third day out of the line and I suppose I have begun to catch up on my sleep. For some time I do nothing more than lie on my back and stare at the rafters. Sparrows twitter up there and barn swallows swoop about. I can see a hay loft and a ladder nailed to a wall that leads to that loft and, for a moment, I allow my imagination to run wild; I see myself climbing the ladder behind Sanne and thoughts of what we will do when we reach that hayloft race through my mind.

Something sharp jabs me in the ribs. I turn my head and see Manfred's left boot.

"What are you grinning about?"

"Just thinking about how pleasant it is to lie on clean, dry straw."

"*Ja*, and back home we would moan we were being abused."

I laugh. "As if we really knew something back then."

"Ha," Adolph says from my other side. "As if you two ever knew anything."

"Oh, listen to the old man," Manfred says. "You always did think you were smarter than everyone else."

Adolph scratches at his chin, creating a rustling sound, the sound a dog makes trotting through dry leaves. None of the squad has shaved since we came off the line. Heintz says he is going to keep his beard. My guess is Sergeant Gruber will have something to say about that. As for myself, I have begun to consider a mustache. I fancy it would make me look more dashing.

"Damn, but this is the life." Manfred stretches until it seems the muscles in his arms must tear.

"Better than a vacation at the seashore," Adolph says. Manfred snickers. He is the only grown man I know who snickers.

I sit up. "Think I'll go scrounge up a cup of coffee. You two want to come along?"

"Not me," Manfred says, "I'm going to roll back over and go to sleep, and when I get up I am going to find something stronger than coffee."

Adolph shakes his head. "I've already had two cups. I woke early and decided to be kind and let you two youngsters sleep in."

"Kind, my ass," Manfred says. "You just were being your usual selfish self."

"I choose to ignore that remark, coming as it does from an imbecile. No, I shall stay here and write a letter to the folks. Later, I plan to hit the delousing station and see if I can find someone who knows barbering. Never has my hair been so long."

"Are you sure you want to do that?" Manfred says. "Maybe your long hair is what is giving you strength, like Sampson."

"If only yours would give you wisdom."

"Ha, what would you know about wisdom?"

Adolph replies, but I am no longer listening. At least not to them. The wind calls from the far side of the wooden doors and the sunlight slicing through the cracks in the planks looks warm and inviting. This is an invitation I shall accept.

I step gently into the morning. Daybreak is long past, but the air is still cool. Spring has finally come to France and, while the days are warm, the nights are chilly. Yet there is nothing like a cool morning breeze to get the blood flowing.

Away from the barn, I can smell rashers of bacon frying and loaves of bread being baked. Even the wondrous aroma of coffee boiling. I wander toward the scents.

Our field kitchen has set up just outside the town of Merced. This part of France has yet to be touched by the war, and it is easy to imagine that I am nothing more than a tourist on holiday. An old man tips his beret, and the old woman on his arm blesses me with a gap-toothed smile. Not for a minute do I believe they are pleased to see me. No, they are only worried about what I might do. They are old and fragile and I am young and strong, full of life. At least, I suspect I appear that way to them. If they knew how this war has aged me, changed me, their nerves would be better. I nod and stride on.

After a good night's sleep and without the constant wear of the nerves that being in the trenches creates, I feel like a new man. Or maybe it is more like my old self, whatever that means. My leg muscles feel strong and my energy is high as I cover the ground in great loping strides. I can see breakfast fires and dozens of my fellow German soldiers who have gathered round them.

A private is handing out tin mugs of coffee and he offers one to me. Steam rises above the cup. I take it and carry it over to a group of men standing in a patch of sunlight. I can tell by their shoulder patches that they come from different regiments. A couple of them nod at me. I sip at my coffee and listen to their conversation.

"For France, this is not a bad place."

"Better than where I have been.'

"And where was that?

"East of here about twelve kilometers where there is a double-backed ridge. We hold one crest, the French the other."

"Better the French than the English."

A tall sergeant nods. "It is best never to charge the English directly. Their rifles are as bad as machine guns."

"No, no," cries a corporal from a Saxon regiment. "The French artillery is the worst. I have been out of the line for five days and every night, I have nightmares about that artillery."

The man who nodded leans forward and speaks to me. His left arm is bandaged. "What about you? Haven't seen you around before. You just out of the trenches?"

I swallow my coffee. "This is my third day out of the line. We were stationed just up the road. Maybe five kilometers."

"Active?"

"Not especially. Snipers, of course."

"French?"

"Yes."

The sergeant leans in. "Well, I hear that is all about to change."

A hare-lipped private sniffs. "What have you heard?"

The sergeant motions us closer. He has a conspiratorial look on his face. "Keep this to yourselves, now. But last night after supper, when I went to report to receive today's orders, I heard my lieutenant talking to our captain about a breakout. Don't know exactly where, but somewhere south of here."

The man who spoke to me asks, "Did they say when?"

The sergeant shakes his head. "No specific date was mentioned. I heard only a few sentences as I was rearranging my tunic outside the lieutenant's tent, you understand. But I got the distinct impression that it will be a major push and it will launch soon. Within a fortnight is my guess."

The hare-lipped private grins. "Good. I have a few days left for wine and women."

"In your dreams," says a short, squatty corporal, who vaguely resembles a tree stump.

We all laugh and I wander on. It is too lovely a morning to grow depressed hearing about breakouts and assaults. Plenty of time for that later. A few of the group call out good-byes and good-luck. I lift a hand, but keep moving. I hand my cup back to the same private who gave it to me. He grunts. I laugh and stroll on. Some people don't know when they have it good. Send that coffee boob up to the line for a month and see if he doesn't enjoy kitchen detail more.

I shrug my shoulders, determined not to let a grouch spoil my good mood. A kilometer down the road is Merced. I haven't seen a real town in months. At least not one untouched by the artillery. I start in that direction; it is a pleasant morning for a stroll.

Merced is a pleasant looking village. The road curves as it enters the town, creating a sense that you are entering some place different than you had been before. That is a pleasant sensation, one I turn it over in my mind as I wander down the main street of the village.

Shops line both sides of the street. In the summer, dust from the street would make it almost impossible to keep the shop windows clean, but it has rained in the last week and the sun has dried the surface until it is almost as good as macadam.

The shops are all small. Each one seems to specialize. A women's hat shop is followed by a tobacco shop, which in turn is followed by a greengrocer. French ladies are out doing their morning shopping and it is very fine to see them in their pretty dresses and hats. Not that I am a connoisseur of women's fashion, but their hats seemed quite stylish to me.

At the end of the first block there is a café on the corner and I cross the street and sit down at a small table. I sit quietly, gazing at the sunlit street. A small boy rolls a hoop along, a small dog barking after him. A horse pulling a farm cart clops by. A man calls out to another across the street and the second man hellos back and waves. Change the language to German and I could be in any of a thousand villages back in the Fatherland. The people all seem nice and they look all right and I grow a bit unclear on why we are fighting them. But then, I am merely a private.

After a moment a waiter appears. He looks young and I wonder why he has not been called up. He nods. "What will monsieur have this morning?"

"A coffee and a brioche."

"Very good." He keeps his face blank. I wonder what his emotions are. It is easy to imagine what mine would be were our situations reversed. He turns and limps away. As he walks away I can see one boot is built up in the heel. The poor fellow would be no good at marching. If the French have to call him up their armed forces will indeed be in sad shape.

Even though I enjoyed a good night's sleep, I grow drowsy in the sunlight. I jerk when the waiter clears his throat. He sets down my coffee and brioche. I say "*Merci*" and he nods, turns, and hobbles off. At this rate we are never going to become pals.

The coffee is hot and bitter, but the brioche tastes wonderful after weeks of dried beef, soft potatoes, and soups of dubious origin. I eat slowly, thinking of my parents and Helga, whom I have not heard from in weeks. I wonder why she hasn't written. Perhaps she has forgotten me. That last night together seems so long ago.

I shake Helga's hazy image from my mind and new thoughts drift in to replace it. Thoughts about my brothers back in the barn, and all the men in the trenches, and all the men who have died. That makes me think of Hans and the coffee is suddenly too bitter to drink.

Four young women stroll by, chattering like magpies. One is taller than the rest and something in the way she carries herself reminds me of Sanne. I turn my head and watch the women until they are nothing more than tiny, dark marks in the street.

Twenty-three

Writing a Letter

Dear Sanne,

Perhaps I should not begin this letter with such a greeting. However, that is the way I was taught in school. Ah, school seems long ago and far away, as if I were referring to some ancient medieval days, or to the Teutonic Knights, or even the times of the Goths and Visigoths. In any case, those carefree days as a student more properly belong to another man, for I am not the same man who crossed into Belgium with a happy heart and a smile on his lips. None of the men in my old regiment are the same. Some are dead and buried and some have gone home to fight no more. Others of us remain on the battlefield, awaiting the next order. But we are not the same. This war has changed us all.

Some of the changes are for the good (I am stronger, tougher, more durable, and more disciplined), while others are, perhaps, not for the best (killing another human being no longer particularly bothers me, for example). But, without question, we are changed.

Many factors, of course, have helped create these changes, and, there can be no doubt, our night together was one of the most powerful. I know what I did that night was not right in society's eyes. Many is the night I have lain awake asking myself why I acted in such a manner. Part of it was obviously the wine. Wine and fatigue are a most potent combination. Also, you were very beautiful, and seemed to like me—at least a little, and I had been without a woman for a long time. Now, I know that is not an answer society would accept, but then a year ago shooting another man to death would have been abhorrent to me.

Actually, now that I reflect on the words I have written, I realize they are not entirely true, or it may be more accurate to say only partially true. For you see, part of me remembers you that night as something wonderful, and, when I lie awake at night in the trenches with the shells falling around me like falling stars, I treasure those memories.

Enough romanticizing. I meant this to be a chatty letter bringing you up to date on my travels. Since I left you that morning, I have marched many miles and fought dozens of engagements large and small. I do not know your sympathies for certain, but I imagine that they do not rest favorably upon Germany.

The hard fighting for this year ended with the snow and ice of winter and, since then, we have been living in what are called trenches, but are actually little more than hastily dug, rudely reinforced ditches. French soldiers live in trenches a few dozen meters away and we take turns shooting at each other, or lobbing grenades at the other's trenches. Most days the big guns fire huge shells across the lines, and, occasionally at night a few men will venture across the land between the trenches, known as no-man's land (an apt term if I ever heard one), in order to conduct what are called trench raids.

Death is a constant companion in the trenches, along with many rats, hunger, mud, dysentery, homesickness, fever, and a nasty disease of the feet, caused by going too long without changing to clean dry socks, called trench-foot. Snipers usually kill a man or two a week and trench raids can easily kill or maim a dozen.

Speaking of death, my younger brother, Hans, was killed in street fighting not long after I left your farm. My other two brothers, Adolph and Manfred, still fight by my side. I trust you and brother are safe. According to what we hear, not much fighting takes place in Belgium these days.

Life in the trenches is no fun, not that I imagine you are having much, either. Between sniper's bullets, grenades, artillery shells, the rats, the cold, the mud, the lousy food, and very little sleep, our days are rather gruesome.

Fortunately, every week or so, we are rotated out of the lines. Sometimes, we only go to a reserve status a few kilometers behind the trenches, but occasionally we are afforded a real rest and sent deep in the rear (the High Command knows we would crack like rotten sticks if we were forced to stay in the trenches for weeks at a time). Four days ago they pulled my unit out and brought us back to a town named Merced, which is at least five kilometers behind the front lines.

Merced is no resort town (my brothers and I sleep in a barn that, while not as nice as yours, is relatively clean and warm), but it is so pleasant to be away from the constant threat of death that it seems quite nice to us. Just yesterday I wandered into town and had a coffee and a brioche at a quaint little cafe on a corner. It felt wonderful to sit quietly, drinking coffee and watching the town's people pass. Merced reminded me of certain small towns in Germany. I feel sure you have similar ones in Belgium.

Sleep is one of the things one never gets enough of in the trenches and I have been a real slug since arriving in Merced. My brothers and I sleep till midmorning, then take a nap in the afternoon. Before our week is out we shall be quite spoilt by such a life. But then they will round us up and march us back to the front and that will be the end of such laziness.

But for now I am away from the trenches and I count my blessings. A good warm, safe place to sleep, a chance to properly bathe, hot and nutritious food for a change. All that is wonderful, but I suppose it is the absence of the guns, the sudden lack of death that is the most wonderful thing of all. I deeply regret that the war came to your quiet farm, and I trust that it has moved on.

Speaking of moving on, I suppose I had better close. If you have read this far I hope I haven't been too big a bother. Also, I hope that you are feeling well and as happy as possible. Again, to some degree I regret my actions that night, but, as my father says, what's done is done, so what more can I say. If I could only ever see you again, I would do my best to tell you of my deepest feelings, but I doubt that such a thing can ever be. Still, one hears and reads of miracles. Perhaps the miracle will be that I survive this war. But now I am only tempting fate, so I will close by wishing you peace and happiness.

Your German soldier,
Karl Ernst Schiller

P.S. Mail delivery is very spotty, but if you should ever decide you would like to write to me, the best address is: Private Karl Schiller, Forty-second division, Company...

Twenty-four

Offensive

Never did I dream that in war so many great events start in the dark hour just before dawn. It is four o'clock in the morning and I hunker down in the trench between Adolph and Manfred. I wish for a cigarette, but no smoking is allowed immediately before an attack. If I smoked a pipe like Adolph, I could at least gnaw on the stem while waiting.

We got our briefing last evening after supper. Not that it came as a surprise. All requests for leave have been denied for a week and every day more artillery has been brought up. The generals have decided that an artillery barrage should precede our attack. They believe that, at the least, it will destroy the barbed wire in front of the French trenches and perhaps wipe out the front line. Apparently, the English had some success with this approach near the Belgian border.

"I wish they would start," Manfred whispers. We are supposed to be quiet, but you can hear whispering all down the trench.

"Yes," I say, "let's get this over."

Adolph snorts. "Don't wish your life away, little brother."

"I'll be all right once we start."

Manfred grunts. "Yes, it is the waiting that is so hard. Once the shelling starts it is as though some force overtakes my body and I simply react to the moment."

"Quiet down the line," Sergeant Gruber orders. I feel bad for Gruber. He had two weeks of leave scheduled to begin tomorrow. Like heat lightning, a question flashes across my mind—how many of us will even be here tomorrow?

Wham! Wham! Wham! Off to our east the artillery starts up. It rolls our way like thunder as the night seems to split apart. The barrage is deafening. Huge blasts of the mortars and field pieces are punctuated by shrieking shells. Their shrill sound makes me want to scream, but I pull my tunic up and sink my teeth into it as I press my face against the wall of the trench. Soon we will be going over the top and I can only hope the artillery has done its job.

Manfred shouts something, but the screaming shells drown him out. Without warning the very earth itself shakes and dirt spills down onto our helmets, sounding like hard rain. The French artillery is firing back.

The next shell lands behind us. They are trying to get the range. A shell smashes into the trench twenty yards away and earth spews forth like dark vomit. There is no explosion and I know we have caught a dud.

Wham! Wham! Wham! Our artillery answers back. I open my eyes. The air is a few degrees lighter. Daylight is coming. Wham! Wham! Wham! Shells scream overhead. It won't be long now. Already this barrage has gone on longer than any I can recall. Any moment and Sergeant Gruber will come along tapping us on the shoulder, shouting at us to attack.

Our objective is the point where the French trenches bow out. I have often wondered why the line formed that way. Perhaps certain features of the ground, like a stream or a cavern, forced them to dig it in such a fashion. Other platoons have their own objectives. We are fresh and rested, having come back from Merced only two days ago. It seems a shame to die so soon after such a pleasant interlude, but undoubtedly, many on both sides will not see the sun set.

Speaking of the sun, the eastern horizon is rimmed in blue. The blue hour is supposed to be romantic. This morning it prophesizes death. Still, if we can break the French lines this stalemate can be lifted. Paris is only a few days' march. I would like to see Paris. I would like to see my parents. I would like to see Sanne again. I would like to see Hans, but that will only be in heaven.

My stomach churns and my legs quiver beneath me. The iron taste of fear is in my mouth. Only a fool would not be afraid. Especially after what we have been through since we boarded the first train. That day seems a lifetime ago.

I find it challenging to remember the faces of the people of my hometown. In certain ways they seem unreal, like actors in a movie. I feel as if I am an actor in a movie. Only I seem to have forgotten all my lines.

Something strange has happened. I cannot think what it is. Then I know. The guns have gone silent. I feel a tap on my shoulder. "Over the top," is the cry. "Attack!"

I finger the cross around my neck as my legs push up of their own accord and I climb the ladder. God, how I wish there was a mist this morning. No-man's land lies naked before us and we will make fine targets for the French. Adolph and Manfred are beside me. As one, we start to run for the French trenches, zigging and zagging as the notion strikes. The air grows lighter and I can see the barbed wire. Rifle fire breaks out en masse along the French lines. A man screams.

Maybe I am screaming—my throat seems raw. But no, I am too scared to scream. Adolph, Manfred, and I run, keeping as low to the ground as we can. The French have got a machine gun up and firing and the ta-ta-ta-ta-ta is ripping our lines. Out of the corner of my left eye, I see Manfred sling a grenade, and I grab one from my belt and throw it on the run. I dive to the ground and let the dirt and shrapnel and whatever else is flying through the air go over my head.

There is a comfort in clinging to the earth and a part of me wants to stay where I am. But that is only foolishness, not to mention conduct unbecoming a soldier of the kaiser. In the first place, I am lying out in the open in no-man's-land. If a Frenchman doesn't shoot me intentionally, I may very well be hit by a stray shot or the shrapnel that seems to be extra heavy this morning. In the second place, Adolph and Manfred and most of the other members of my platoon who are still able to move have gone on forward. In the third place, to lie here is to be a coward. I get to my hands and knees, take a deep breath, then push myself upright and lunge forward.

No more than thirty meters away are the first French trenches. The artillery barrage didn't blast all the barbed wire apart, but there are sections where a man can pass. I pound after the others.

I see Sergeant Gruber fall, but he has only tripped over the wire and, in an instant he is up. Muller spins and falls, blood pouring from his shoulder. Grossman doubles up and sinks to his knees—gut shot. A Frenchman pops his head over the lip of the trench and I fling another grenade at him.

This time I keep moving. Mother Earth is too tempting. I angle for the trenches. Our objective is merely meters away. Already our soldiers are in the French lines. A giant Frenchman smashes a corporal in the head with the butt of his rifle. The corporal collapses and another good German soldier steps up into his place. I stand at the edge of the trench, waiting.

Before me, the two men are locked in mortal combat. Then, with an oath, the giant flings my comrade against the side of the trench and, before I can react, thrusts his bayonet home.

I aim down the barrel of my rifle and squeeze the trigger. The giant's mouth flies open and he spins and falls. I leap into the trench.

A few feet away, a French and a German soldier have each other around the throat. I turn my rifle around and smash the butt of my rifle into the Frenchie's spine. His arms fly up and he sinks to his knees. My comrade thrusts a knife into his throat. Blood spurts as though the man were a hog being butchered. I have forgotten how warm fresh blood is.

Orders are being shouted. My ears ring and I cannot hear. I shake my head and they clear. “Charge,” is the cry. “Charge! Forward! Attack!” This trench is now ours, but we clamber out of it and rush toward the next line. Our hope is that the reserves are thin here.

Great holes have been gouged in the earth by our artillery. If the gunner officers had the proper range, surely no one could live through such a barrage. I dodge one hole and almost fall into another. Sporadic rifle fire comes from the French lines. I can no longer see either of my brothers. In the mad charge, I have gotten amongst a platoon of Hessians. They are good soldiers, but they are all strangers. I do not want to die among strangers.

Here and there a man falls, but there are not many of the enemy before us and we charge on. Off to the right the French are in headlong retreat. A great shout goes up, and I feel my heart lift, and my blood runs hot. I stop, aim and pull the trigger. A French soldier falls.

“Victory,” a man on my left shouts and it seems that it surely must be in our grasp. I am swept up in a mass of gray uniforms and I run with them.

A thin man is on my left and a short fellow on my right. I do not know them, but I feel a warm sense of camaraderie. A smile breaks out across my face. The second line of the French trenches is visible and already our vanguard is leaping into them. Very few French soldiers occupy this line. Everywhere they are tossing their rifles aside and throwing up their hands. The entire French flank must be in collapse. Perhaps, after all, Paris is more than a pipe dream.

Twenty meters to go and I will be in the second line. My legs are strong and I feel as if I could run for an hour. I leap over a dead French soldier, knowing the next leap will be into the trench. My heart is aflame with our great attack. I gather myself for the leap.

Only the ground explodes and I feel my body being flung into the air. I cannot breathe and the morning has gone dark. I feel myself turning end over end while a streak of fire burns up my right side. Some thought is trying to break through to the surface of my brain, but it will not quite come. I sense that it is important, but my head is spinning as consciousness slips away.

The ground rises up and smacks my head and everything goes black. I see a shower of sparks. Then a single fine white light. I stare at that light until it is only a pinpoint. Pain courses through my body, a wall of pain so strong I cannot breathe. All I can see is the tiny pinpoint of pure white light.

Almost idly, in some remote corner of my poor brain, I wonder if that white light is God.

If is it, I must be dying.

I stare at the white light.

It fades to the deepest darkness I have ever seen. Is this death?

Twenty-five

A Swinging Light

A white light swings before me. It moves slowly, to and fro, smoothly for a while, then with a vigorous jerk. Now and then it is still. I know I am looking at the light, but what I do not know is if I am dreaming or even if I am alive. If this were a dream surely I would wake up. Perhaps I am dead—although I do not feel dead. But then I have never been dead and perhaps this is how being dead feels.

The light swings again and this time I feel my body rocking. The rocking is not an unpleasant sensation. Not that it is exactly gentle, but...It seems to me I have felt such a rocking before, however I am badly confused.

My head has begun to ache and I squinch my eyes shut and focus on the rocking. The light swings slowly. It begins to fade. The rocking is somehow comforting. The light swings and swings, growing dimmer, dimmer, dimmer.

~ * ~

My head throbs. Or do I mean my brain? Finally, I decide it is my brain that is throbbing and my skull that is cracking. The right side of my body burns and it hurts to breathe. Inside my mind, it is as though I am swimming underwater. Through the water I can see the sun, but it seems to be swaying back and forth, probably due to the distortion made by the water.

Sounds drift to me, muffled and dim, but definitely sounds. I realize, with some degree of surprise, that I have been wrapped in silence. Silence like a thick blanket, smothering all sound. This I do not understand at all.

I realize my eyes are closed. This seems strange and I decide to open them. Surely, I must be dreaming and waking up, only very slowly.

However, they don't open. Not at first, anyway. My brain is working slowly. On the third try, my eyes open.

I am lying on a blanket on the floor of a train car. All my life I have ridden trains and I instantly recognize the interior walls. I can feel the rhythmic rocking that only a train makes. However, I can tell I am not in a sleeper car. Rather, I seem to be in some sort of converted box car. Why am I here? I have no memory of getting on a train. The last thing I remember is...

I sit up. Or at least I start to. The throbbing in my head and a tremendous jab of pain in my right side drives me back to the blanket. Nervously I feel my head. It is bandaged in gauze. I am totally confused. I hear myself groan.

I am starting to remember. The offensive. Almost to the second line of French trenches. Why the hell am I on a train, and why does my head hurt so badly?

I hear voices. They are close, but not distinct. It sounds like two men talking. I wonder if they were talking about me. I listen more intently.

"I thought I heard him moan."

"He's been unconscious all the way."

"Still, I'm sure I heard him make some sound."

I try to open my eyes. After a few seconds, they flutter open.

"Ah, he is with us after all."

"So it seems."

I can see two soldiers are crouched down staring at me. They are wearing the same uniform I wear, so that is comforting. Questions flood my mind and I try to ask one, only my voice isn't working satisfactorily. Words come out together in a jumbled croak. I swallow, lick my lips. Then try again.

"Where am I?"

"Ah, the same first question every time," says the soldier on the right. He is a youngish man with pinkish skin and a faint mustache.

"You are on a hospital train," says the other man. He is older and darker complected. "We are headed to Dusseldorf where they have a large hospital for soldiers injured on the Western Front." He smiles, but it looks like a practiced smile. I hear a man groan and I ease my head up and look around the car.

My vision is almost clear and I can see that I am one of a dozen men, all lying on blankets like me.

"How badly am I hurt?"

"That will be for the doctors to say," says the dark-haired man. "You were concussed, a bad one. They couldn't wake you at the aid station. Plus, you've got a few broken ribs, and, of course, the assorted scrapes and bruises that always occur."

He turns his head and coughs. Then he looks back. "I'd say in your case, Private, since there are no bullet holes, that a grenade smashed you. If it had been an artillery shell, they'd have been picking up the pieces and dropping them in a picnic basket. Shrapnel would have sliced you like an onion being prepared for a stew." Both men think this is a very clever line. Their laughter makes my head hurt.

"How long was I unconscious?"

The pinkish fellow rubs his face. "Can't rightly say. Don't know how long you were at the aid station, see. Also, it could have been some time before the stretcher bearers got you to the station." He tilts his head to one side, somehow managing to look like a bemused owl. "Do you remember anything?"

"*Nein*. Last thing I remember is starting to jump into a French trench."

The darker man presses very gently against the bandages swathing my head. He lifts the blanket and inspects my right side. "I'm no doctor, but I'd say whatever smashed into you gave you a real pasting. You were lucky."

The train jolts down the tracks. I wish for a window. Something to take my mind off the pain. Every time I try to draw a deep breath, my broken ribs stab me. My skull feels like it has cracked open—I think of the Liberty Bell in America—and, I suppose, in a matter of speaking, it has.

"Mother," a man cries out. He sounds terribly young.

"Give him something to shut him up," another man mumbles.

I wouldn't mind a little something myself, I think. The two medical orderlies are standing. "Can I have a bit of something for my head," I say. "It feels like it is cracking wide open."

Dark man snorts. "It has, dummy." He jerks his head at Pinky. "Get him something."

"Okay."

"What are you giving me?"

Dark man curls his lips. The look is not flattering. "You're getting what the rest of these wretches get, a shot of whiskey." The train rocks and clatters to itself. A man moans, and then I hear somebody start to cry. I feel like crying myself, but what would that accomplish? I stare at the roof of the boxcar and wait for what passes for medicine in the German army.

Twenty-six

Hospital

I am in a huge room. Before the war it must have been a warehouse, perhaps a factory. Certainly, it was not a hospital, for there are no private rooms. For privacy, the nurses wheel in a curtain. There are simply rows of wounded soldiers arranged like parked automobiles in this huge room.

While it is a big room, it is most assuredly not a quiet one. All day and all night men groan and moan and talk and sing and whistle and cough and sneeze and curse and cry out for their mother, father, brother, girlfriend, wife, comrade, even their sergeant or lieutenant or captain. Late in the night, a number of them simply cry.

Crying is understandable. Even the strongest man feels pain, and when you come out of the operation with a leg or an arm gone, or you are blind, or your nose is gone, well, I, for one, am not going to criticize a few tears.

Dying is probably the reason most men cry. They say a man knows when he is dying, unless it happens in an instant on the battlefield. Even then, I wonder if in that last second before death a man who has stopped a bullet isn't somehow aware that he is dying. Unless, as in my case, the brain is the first thing smashed. Perhaps they will come to me later—memories are tricky things—but at the moment, I have no memories beyond that instant when I was preparing to leap into that trench. I can't remember the blast or being carried to the aid station; I don't even remember the pain. Before coming back to consciousness on the train, I have no memories after beginning my leap into the French trench.

For a week I have lain on my cot, hearing the sounds of pain and death and wondering about my brothers and my platoon. No one here seems to have any information. I have asked the doctors, the nurses, and the other patients. The doctors and nurses are simply too busy with the wounded to have even the vaguest idea of what is happening on either the Western or Eastern Front. Most of the wounded soldiers are more than willing to talk, but they have come here from all across the Western Front (apparently, there are other hospitals, too, including at least one for the Eastern Front), and none of them have news of my regiment. What factors determine who goes where are beyond me. I have met one man, a corporal named Otto Henne, whose platoon was posted no more than a quarter mile from mine, but he was struck by shrapnel before the attack began and knows nothing. So I am forced to lie here and wonder.

Still, it is not a bad life, at least while I heal. All doctors and nurses have been most kind. My bandages are changed daily and I have had two sponge baths. Already my ribs are mending. My brain still throbs at times, and apparently I will have some scarring. Fortunately, if I wear my hair long it will cover most of those reminders.

They had to shave my head—in order to get all the fragments out—and now my hair is starting to grow back in and my incisions are healing and they itch. My skin there is too tender to scratch and when I do rub it gently with the tips of my fingers my hair feels like wheat stubble.

In addition to doctors and nurses, there are volunteers. These women come as often as they can to help the wounded in various ways. Some bring candy or cigarettes; others bring newspapers or magazines. A few bring religious pamphlets. Few men are truly glad to receive those.

Some of the volunteers enjoy sitting and talking to the wounded and that does provide some comfort. One woman spoke to me yesterday for a long time about her son. He is on the Eastern Front and is doing well, except for a minor wound to his foot which has him on light duty. This woman was quite the talker and I had to do little more than nod and say, "Oh really" from time to time.

Other volunteers help the wounded write letters. Three days ago I felt well enough to write my mother and father. The day before yesterday I wrote Helga, although I have not heard from her in well over a year.

Today, if a volunteer comes, I will ask her to help me write a letter to Sanne. If circumstances were different, I would write the Aubiers.

During the night the man across from me died. I am not surprised. When I first arrived he kept me up with his moaning. Yesterday he was silent. I don't understand his wounding. Apparently a shell smashed so close to him that, although it did not strike him, the sheer force of the projectile passing crushed much of his insides, damaging his brain and heart.

While I knew him, he was never quite conscious or unconscious, existing in a twilight zone. Now he has moved on to some other zone. When I was a boy I believed quite strongly in heaven and hell. As I grew older I began to have my doubts. Certain passages, such as the story of Jonah, seemed nothing more than religious fiction. Once doubt seeps in, believing becomes more challenging. No longer do I believe. Surely, if there were a God, he would long ago have stopped this insanity. Too many young men, starting with that Belgian boy on the bridge, have died for me to believe. Hans was the final straw. Now, the only thing I know about the hereafter is that I know nothing. From a certain perspective that is not so bad; at least one has hope of a better world. On the other hand, maybe this is all there is. Dying with your face shot off in a strange country seems a bitter end to life.

They are bringing lunch now. I can smell the food cart. I watch it roll slowly down the aisle. Certainly the food is better than at the front. It even smells good. Today, for the first time, I am truly hungry.

"Good day, soldier. Are you hungry this fine day?"

"Ravenous."

"Ah, a good sign, always." The man smiles. He is an older fellow, nearly bald. He holds a ladle in one hand.

"We have soup today. It is pretty good, for a change." He laughs. I hope he is right about the soup. I feel like I could empty the kettle for him.

"What sort of soup?"

"Potato."

"With real potatoes?"

"Some."

"And?"

He shrugs. "*Ja*, there are a few Swedes."

"Just as I thought." Swedes are what we call turnips. Not many care for them, but the potato crop was not good last year. "Oh well, give me a bowl, anyway. And some bread. You have some bread?"

"*Ja*, and it is pretty fresh. Baked just yesterday."

"All right, give me a big hunk then." I prop myself up against the wall as best I can. The pain is there, but not as bad as it has been. I reach for the bowl. The balding man wraps a piece of newspaper around my chunk of bread and places it on the bed within my reach.

"*Danke*."

He nods. "Eat in good health. Get well and they will send you back to the front." He laughs as he turns and pushes the cart on down the line. He thinks he is a funny man, but what he is really is short, fat, balding, and forty. In the trenches he would not last a week. If I were stronger I would get up and push his face in his lousy turnip soup.

But I am not well, and he is probably correct about sending me back to the front. In a hospital there is always gossip. It seems our losses have been heavy, especially on the Western Front. Already they have called up two more classes. Fresh troops are always welcome, but an experienced man is so much more valuable.

I spoon soup into my mouth. I have tasted worse. At least this is warm and somebody did sprinkle salt in it. I think old Baldy lied about the bread. Maybe it was baked last week. I break off a chunk and dunk it in my soup. That helps the bread and certainly does no harm to the soup. I long for some of my mother's homemade bread, hot and fresh from her oven. An urge to see my parents swells through me and I jam soggy bread in my mouth to take the desire to see home off my mind.

Down at the far end of the room, there is some commotion. I spoon more soup into my mouth as I turn to see what is going on. Stretcher bearers are bringing in more wounded. I gnaw on the bread.

Stretcher bearers lay one man on an empty cot. Another pair carries a wounded man down the next row. He is moaning softly. I look down my row and can see three empty cots. Before the food cart came, there were two.

The three empty cots are actually close to me. One is just three cots down from mine. The other two vacant spots are in the row across the aisle. They are within easy grenade range. I smile at how the war has become so imbedded in my brain. Here in this hospital room, hundreds of miles away from the front, it is not difficult to see that the war has changed everyone. No person in Germany, or France, or England is unaffected.

No doubt some are affected more than others. Some are dead, or, like the men in this room, seriously wounded. Others are forever maimed. Mothers and fathers have lost sons. Sisters have lost brothers. Hell, brothers have lost brothers. Those without a family have undoubtedly lost a friend, or at least an acquaintance. Postmen are dead. Teachers are dead. Farmers are dead. Lorry drivers are dead. And all of them, every last one of them, has died before their time. I have not died, but I am old before my time. Before the war I was not young, true, but I was not old. Now I have an old man's point of view. Now I have an old man's fears.

Stretcher bearers bring in another wounded man. His head is swathed in white bandages and they put me in mind of an Indian fakir. One of the bearers calls the turbaned man lieutenant. This war is very democratic. Officers are killed and wounded just the same as enlisted men.

I spoon up more soup, then jam the last crust of bread in my mouth. The man in the cot to my left groans. He has a bad stomach wound. Twice we have talked, about nothing. That was the day before yesterday. Last time the doctor made his rounds his face was very grave as he examined the man. I do not know the wounded man's name, but I do not think that will matter. Wartime friendships tend to be brief. I have discovered that, among other things, most of which will not do me a great deal of good after the war.

It is funny, but I have never thought about what might happen after the war, and I rest my empty soup bowl on my stomach and consider what I will do when I am no longer a soldier. I have no plans. Planning seems foolish, or is futile the better word? I draw in a long breath, and there is a sharp stabbing pain along my broken ribs.

Stretcher bearers are coming down the aisle again. I wondered what happened to this poor wretch. He lies quietly on the stretcher. I cannot see his face, but he is extraordinarily quiet. Perhaps he passed out, or maybe he has taken a vow of silence, like certain monks do. War makes men do things they otherwise would not dream of doing.

The stretcher bearers ease the wounded man down on the vacant cot. His body is covered in a sheet and from the way the sheet collapses midway down his left leg I know he is an amputee. One of the stretcher bearers mumbles a few words and the two men turn and walk back toward the entrance, the empty stretcher between them. It looks rather symbolic, but I am not sure what it is supposed to symbolize. Whatever poetic graces blessed me before the war have fled. Still, there are moments when I long to see violets. Violets have always been my favorite flower.

The wounded man turns his head. My pulse hammers in my brain like something gone mad. I blink and look again, even though

I know I could not be mistaken about such a thing. Hope makes men do foolish things.

The man with half his left leg gone is my brother Manfred.

I have to wonder
you know,
if it truly is better
to see so clearly.
For then the truth
becomes as clear as
polished glass,
but the pain,
oh the pain...

Twenty-seven

Reunion

He comes to consciousness in stages. First his eyes flicker, then his lips twitch, then he lets out a low, shuddering moan. I lie still and watch him closely. In a rather strange way, he puts me in mind of a baby being born. He is in the cot next to me; I talked two medical orderlies into switching out his cot with that of a Bavarian sergeant who simply lies on his back with his eyes glazed over all day. The poor wretch never spoke the entire time he was in the cot next to me.

Manfred blinks again, then moans. His body shudders and then his eyes flick open. For several seconds I do not believe he is seeing anything. Then he blinks, once, twice, three times and his eyes clear. Moving with deliberate slowness, he raises his head a few inches.

"Karl? Karl, is that you?"

His voice is very soft, and I strain to hear. He sounds so weak my heart cracks. I feel a lump in my throat and I have to swallow hard to clear it. "Yes, Manfred, it's Karl. Your brother, Karl."

"Am I dead, Karl? Have I died and gone to Heaven?" One of our neighbors cries out in a dream and I see Manfred's eyes change. "Or is this Hell?"

"No, you haven't died. Only gotten yourself wounded. We are in a hospital back in Dusseldorf."

"*Gott im Himmel*, but my leg hurts. What have they done to me?" He closes his eyes against the pain.

"It really is what have the French done to you? Your left leg was badly damaged by a shell or a grenade. They had to amputate."

His eyes open. They are open very wide. He looks directly at me and it is easy to see the fear on his face and in his eyes. "You mean I am a cripple, a one-legged cripple?"

"The doctors had no choice if they wanted to save your life. They amputated your leg just below the knee."

"Ach," he moans as he turns his face away. His shoulders begun to convulse. When the room falls quiet, I can hear him crying. I cry a little myself. Then I stare at the ceiling. The volunteers have not come today and the afternoon grows long. My eyes feel hot and tired and I close them. These days I tire easily. Most of all I tire of the war. I am very tired of the war.

~ * ~

I come awake to the sound of his voice. He is talking to me. "What?" I say.

"I said, we thought you were dead, Adolph and I. Out of the corners of our eyes we saw the explosion and you went up in the air and when you came back down your body was as limp as a rag doll. We jumped in the trench then and, when we had gotten out the other side, Adolph said to me, "He's gone, you know. Dead as a mackerel." I thought he was right.

Manfred turns his head and looks straight at me and smiles. It is only a small smile, but much better than the tears.

"I never knew a thing till I woke up on the train bringing the wounded back to Germany. What happened to the attack? Did we make Paris?" I can hear the excitement in my voice. If our armies have made Paris, then the French will surely surrender. Oh, to have the war over.

"No," he laughs a phony laugh. "We did not make Paris. We did not even get close. The French brought up their 75's, and the entire attack bogged down less than two hundred meters from where you fell. We made it to the woods shaped like Spain. You remember that on the map?

I nod.

"We made it there and regrouped, then, before we could move out again, those damn 75's open up and ripped hell out of us. Splinters from the trees were flying everywhere. Muller caught one in the eye. Never have I heard anyone scream like that. Then that Henkel boy, the bigger one, caught one directly in the throat." Manfred shakes his head. "Dead before he hit the ground." He sighs.

"It was pure hell. Units were thoroughly mixed up and men were dying all around. A man would fall on your left and before you could move to help him, the comrade on your right would go down. We kept trying to advance. All afternoon we tried, but we never even made it out of the wood."

"Gruber? Meister? The lieutenant? Adolph? What about the rest?"

"Last I saw, the sergeant and Meister were still there. They were a few yards ahead and off to my right, hunkered down at the base of a little rise of ground. Lieutenant Mosel took a bullet in the arm. Remember seeing him being helped to the rear by one of the Wentz brothers. He was bleeding like a stuck hog."

"And Adolph, our brother? You did not mention him."

"I cannot say. When the shelling started, we got separated. I had not seen him in over an hour. As for the others..." He shrugs.

"Bogged down, you say the attack bogged down."

"*Ja*. Just like the others. It went nowhere. The whole line didn't move three hundred meters."

"All those men," I say. "All those men for three hundred lousy meters?"

"Yes, all those men for three hundred stinking, worthless meters." Manfred closes his eyes, and I watch the pain spasm across his face. Compared to his loss, my wounds seem insignificant. He presses his lips tightly together, but it does not work. In a few seconds a groan escapes. Across the aisle, another man moans. On the other side of Manfred a young one cries. He does not look old enough to be dying. Suddenly a man screams, "Shrapnel!" My brain throbs. This place is straight out of Dante's *Inferno*. Manfred moans, then cries out.

"Nurse!" I shout. "Nurse! Doctor! Orderly!"

Twenty-eight

Return to France

"Well, we know at least one of us will survive this war." Adolph scratches at his scraggly beard.

"Yes," I say. "Manfred will be safe now."

"What's left of him."

I shrug. What is there to say? Manfred is no longer the man he was. But then, neither is Adolph. Nor am I.

Intermittent gunfire breaks out a few meters to the south. Merely sniping between our trenches and the English who moved in a week ago and are considerably more aggressive than the French.

Adolph sighs. "I don't care for the English. They make it hard for a man to sleep."

"Ha," I exclaim. As if any of us sleeps much. Trench life is not for those needing a rest. 'Go to the spas if you want to sleep,' is what the men say.

Two privates hustle up. By their clean uniforms and the fearful expressions on their faces, I can tell they have not been soldiers for long. After a few weeks, we all start to look alike.

"We are supposed to report to Captain Erskine. Can you direct us, sir?" one of them asks. He is trying to grow a mustache. It is coming in very fair and fuzzy.

I am taken aback by the "sir." Then I remember I am now a corporal. For one week I have been a corporal. Why I was chosen to be a corporal is beyond me.

"Go down this trench about twenty meters. You will come to a side trench on the left. Take it. Captain Erskine was there an hour ago."

They salute. I salute. They are very new to the front, indeed. Out here saluting is not so much in fashion as in Germany. Sudden death has a way of taking the formality out of life. Especially as we don't go in much for funerals. If a man gets a few shovelfuls of dirt tossed over him when he dies, he is lucky. We gave up on grave markers, even the most rudimentary, the first week. Too many men were dying. There was no time to mark their passings.

The two new privates toddle off down the trenches. "My, my, Karl, what an authoritative figure you cut. Father would be so proud."

"Shove it."

"Tsk, tsk, temper in an officer is unbecoming."

"I am not really an officer. Only a battlefield corporal."

"Well," Adolph says, "that will do until something better comes along." He pulls his pipe out of his pocket and sticks it between his teeth. At the moment we are out of tobacco, but he sucks on it anyway. I suppose there is some lingering flavor.

"How long?" he asks.

"How long what?"

"How long do you give those two? They are fresh off the farm." He shakes his head. "I give them a week."

I know what he means. New men either quickly learn the secrets of staying alive in the trenches or they perish. Veterans know how to stay alive. At least they know which chances not to take. Still, a falling shell breaks all the rules. Sometimes a man's time is just up. Often they die in silly ways. Only last week, Private Grosschek dove into the trench when the English unleashed a bombardment and broke his neck. The closest shell landed fifty meters away. Foolish. He was foolish. Such an unnecessary death.

Unnecessary deaths are not uncommon. One of our best machine gunners, Frolick, died because a small shrapnel cut became infected. Some weeks disease kills more men than bullets.

"Bastards," cries Adolph and throws a dirt clod at a pack of rats scampering down the trench. And bastards they are. At first, they came out only at night to eat crumbs we had dropped. Now they are bolder, or more desperate, and they come out at all hours, hunting in packs for food.

Rats are not finicky eaters. A dead corporal is as tasty to them as a crust of bread or a chunk of cheese. We used to shoot at them for sport. However, Private Heinson missed while shooting at a particularly large rat and the bullet struck a visiting sergeant in the foot, shattering several small bones.

I don't think the sergeant minded particularly. After all, that bullet was a one-way ticket out of the trenches. However, the captain was most unhappy. The sergeant was apparently an admirable NCO.

"It gets hotter every day," Adolph mumbles as he wipes sweat off his face.

My uniform is clinging to my back and legs. "Yes, it is really summer now."

"And to think I complained about how cold the trenches were last winter. What I wouldn't give for a blast of that good December air."

"I'd settle for a sultry August breeze." The air is dead calm.

"Yes, so long as it blows away from no-man's-land. Otherwise, the stench turns my stomach."

I turn and gaze across the open ground. Day before yesterday, the English made an assault. Their artillery didn't do enough with the barbed wire and the poor fellows got hung up by the dozens. It was comparable to being at a shooting gallery at some village fair. Swollen bodies dot the ground. You can hear the bottle flies buzzing.

I turn and look at my brother. "That was rough. The English, I mean, getting hung up in the barbed wire."

"I'd say so. I'd rather just go poof."

"Poof?"

"Yes, if my time comes here, I hope a big shell obliterates me. I hope I simply disappear." He makes a sour face. "None of this lingering and suffering for old Adolph. Not even for Kaiser Wilhelm."

He shivers like a wet dog. "And you, dear brother? If you have to die in this lousy place, how would you like to go?"

I look out into the far distances. The ground is quite flat and a man can see for miles. There used to be a small wood about a mile to the east and beyond that a hamlet. Our artillery has blasted them both to splinters and shards.

I do not want to die for I have seen the face of death and was not favorably impressed. Pain is not pleasant, even if is short lived.

"Well?"

"Like a hero, I suppose." I shift my eyes to his face. His cheeks are hollow. Rations have been short this week. "Jabbing my bayonet into the guts of a British officer would do."

"Maybe they will mail a medal home to mother." He laughs. Then his face changes and he falls silent. For a moment, his chin rests on his chest. Then he lifts his eyes to mine.

"I'm afraid your wish cannot be granted, Karl. For you see there are no heroes in war. Only poor fools who die for kaiser or king, as if they gave a good damn." He spits and shakes his head. "As if they gave a good damn."

For a moment he is silent. I am silent, too. Strange as it seems, I can hear birds singing. Foolish creatures. Don't they know there is a war on? Or are they relying on God? I seem to recall a passage in the Bible about sparrows.

Adolph pokes my arm. "I hear the field kitchen coming up. Let's go."

"Maybe they will have soup today."

He grunts. "I'm betting on more Swedes."

Twenty-nine

Trench Raid

I stand on the top step and peer over the edge of the trench. Before me, no-man's-land shimmers in the starlight. Tonight the moon is nothing more than a sliver and the wind is rising, making it an ideal night for a trench raid. Last month, the Thirty-sixth brought back a Hotchkiss without losing a man. I hope luck is with us tonight.

Below me are six hand-picked men. We are waiting on Lieutenant Banner, who is new to the platoon. Very few of the originals remain. Soon we will find out what sort of officer the lieutenant is.

Except for the wind, the night is quiet. The only artillery is well off to the south, at least three miles away and firing infrequently. No night in the trenches is ever totally quiet. Even in a thunderstorm someone will blast away. Last December, in the midst of a tremendous snowstorm, the French opened up with their 75's. One never knows with the French. I am not sure they think much.

Beyond no-man's-land the fires of the English are visible. For almost a month there have been no artillery exchanges along this sector and I suppose they are not worried. Still, there are other things to worry about besides artillery shells. I hear the men shifting around and turn and look down. Lieutenant Banner is coming. He moves easily, with a young man's stride.

"Corporal Schiller?"

"Yes, sir."

"Anything moving out there?"

"All quiet."

He pushes through the men until he stands directly below me. "All right, then, move out."

I twist round and swing over the lip of the trench. This is the moment we find out how intently the British have been watching. I have seen a trench raid jammed at the start by an alert sentry. My body tenses, half-expecting a bullet to smash into flesh and bone.

But there are no shots. The only sound is the coughing of one of the men waiting in the trench. I move out, keeping low to the ground, staying as best I can in the shadows. For the past week, the weather has been dry and the footing is good, except for dead bodies and shell craters.

Halfway across, I drop to the ground and wait for the others to catch up. From here on in we are better off moving on hands and knees, or sliding along on our stomachs. British sentries tend to be more alert than those of the French.

Bodies ease down out of the dark and sprawl on the ground beside me. The wind is still rising, blowing dust, providing cover for our approach. The night air seems heavy and I wonder if we are going to have a storm.

"See anything, Schiller?" The lieutenant's low-pitched voice sounds calm.

"No sir, it is very dark tonight."

"Better for us, eh?"

"True."

"Well, we'd better be moving on. Can't wait for daylight."

"All right, but from here we go on hands and knees. Without the moon it's hard to know exactly where the English trenches start and I'd just as soon not stumble into one."

"Yes, of course. Now get moving."

I start crawling, pausing every few seconds to listen. I wasn't talking merely because I like the sound of my own voice. Stumbling into a British trench would be like signing eight death warrants. To my ears, we sound loud as we crawl along. From before us comes the clang of metal against metal and I know we are getting close. I drop to my stomach as Lieutenant Banner eases down beside me. I can smell his sweat.

"Twenty meters," I whisper.

"So we crawl now, yes?"

"Yes," I whisper so quietly that the word is scarcely more than the expelling of a breath. I start crawling. He is crawling, too. Moving so close to me that I can hear his breathing.

Without warning, a voice floats across the night.

"Wind's up tonight?" The accent is unmistakably British. The voice smacks of London, a city I have often visited.

"Right," comes the answer. "Smells like rain to me."

"We could use a good shower. Dry as the desert the past two weeks."

"Heard from your old lady lately?"

I feel the lieutenant's hand on my arm.

"Last week. Had a letter."

"What's the news on the home front?"

"Baby's got a cold."

"What about Junior?"

"Got in another fight."

"Regular scrapper, ain't he?"

I feel the lieutenant's breath in my ear. "Now," he whispers.

Willpower drivers me up to my knees and I tug a grenade free and fling it at the voices.

The night explodes and we rise up and rush into the trench, shouting like Banshees.

Luck runs with us. We jump into the trench only a few meters from a bend in the trench and a mob of British rush around the corner, directly into our fire. We open up and they fall like dominos.

Those who escape our bullets plunge back around the bend and out of sight.

"We'd better move," I shout over the gunfire. "Grenades are going to start flying."

"Check the bodies quickly. See if they have maps. Find out their regiment. I'll toss an egg." He flings his arm forward and, seconds later, another blast shatters the night.

Private Gehrig and I rush forward and search the fallen bodies. All along the line, gunfire ripples. We have awakened both trenches. Just as I expected, the British start lobbing Mills bombs. The only thing that saves us is that they are throwing blind.

In the flash of the explosions, I catch a glimpse of a regimental patch. Canadian. Not what I wanted to see. Canadians are fierce fighters. I find an officer's pistol and jam it down the waist of my trousers. My hands are trembling and sweat runs down my arms. Yet I shiver. My blood feels like ice. Fear does that.

Our time is almost up. I search pockets and my fingers close on some papers. I snatch them up and shout at Private Gehrig. "Let's go."

We scramble up the sides of the trench as bullets pepper the ground like falling rain. One of our men cries out. Another stumbles against me. I shove him off and grab another grenade. I can hear my comrades running through the inky darkness. I turn and fling the grenade back at the trench. Five meters away a British bomb explodes and dirt clods smash against my face.

I am running, running and then going down, rolling and coming up running. Our mates in the trench are firing quickly, trying to give us cover. The others in our raiding party are nothing more than shadows. I go after them with my heart pounding. I think of the fallen and hope the papers are worth the lost lives. A bullet plucks at my sleeve, then I am diving into our trench.

Thirty

A Letter From Home

Karl, Our dear son,

Greetings from your home. We are all well, although Manfred is very quiet. There are days when he talks to no one. If you try to make conversation, he simply ignores you, or maybe grunts. Your mother and I, we try to never talk about the war or even allow it to be brought up, if we can help it. Of course you know how some people are. Mrs. Strophe down at the greengrocers is one. Etta Grub is another. You will remember her; she is one who caused all the trouble about Herr Austing. Also, Vicar Inglehoff is a notorious talker. You would think he would stick to religion, or at least to peace and comfort, but no, the war is one of his favorite topics. Your mother cringes whenever she sees him coming.

So, son, we talk to your brother, Manfred, only about the weather or the crops or what he thinks the mayor should do about the footbridge. As you know, it was old when I was a boy and since the war started no one has taken care of it. It is starting to lean to one side and just last week, when

Herr Schumacher was resting against one of the railings, it collapsed and he got a good dunking. Of course he is a fine fat fellow, although not so fine and fat as he was when you left.

The harvest was not good this year, especially the potatoes. Otto Picklesimer is forecasting a hungry winter. I don't much care for the old blowhard, but fear he may be right this time. The hogs and chickens are doing fair, but the cow has nearly dried up and I do not relish the thought of eating Swedes all winter. You recall how they used to grow when nothing else would.

Karl, my boy, I worry about your mother. Each week she looks a little thinner to me. On the other hand, the only place I am thinning out is on the top of my head. Ha, Ha.

Anyway, she gets thinner and last winter such a cough she had. I thought she would never get rid of it. I greatly fear another bad winter. Especially if there is not enough to eat. I hope you are getting enough to eat. Frau Graumiller had a letter from her son, Eric, last week. Remember him? He was a year or two ahead of you in school, a tall boy with unruly hair. When he wrote, he was in France, but closer to Belgium than you are (I cannot remember the name of the town). He is a corporal now, and says they eat a lot of soup. Do you have soup? As I recall, as a boy you were fond of potato soup and bean soup. Do they raise many potatoes and beans in the country where you are?

Ah, before I forget, yesterday I went to town to buy some salt and saw Helga. She was coming out of Levin's. She was with one of the Gass boys, the one with the clubfoot. Rumor has it they will marry next month. You will remember him; he was spelling champion at your school two years in a row. He did not make a strong, handsome man, but on the other hand, he is most unlikely to be called up. If the German army has to call him up, the war is lost. There, I have spoken.

Helga looked fine, only thinner in her face, but has developed a bit of a nervous twitch, which I suspect is due to the war. You may not have heard, but both her brothers were killed last month by the same French artillery shell. She said to say she wished you well.

In the papers there is much talk of the success of our troops on the Eastern Front. Good news, there, at least. About three weeks ago our men encircled a great Russian army. Many Russians died and we captured thousands. I am glad for the victory but wonder how the generals plan to feed so many prisoners when the German people go hungry.

It is wonderful that you are now a sergeant. Sergeant Schiller has a nice ring to it. I told Manfred about it, but he only nodded. Nod and shrug, that is all the boy does these days. Understandable, I suppose, but still worrisome.

Has there been any word of Adolph? To simply vanish in the mist one morning is most peculiar. You say there was no shelling at the time, but that he simply stepped into a great cloud of low-hanging mist and disappeared. Strange, strange, strange. Your mother is half-convinced the good God himself carried Adolph to Heaven. However, Adolph was never much on religion, so I wonder. Still, let the Lord's will be done.

I will close now to make the next post. Please know your mother and I pray for you every night. Surely you will be safe. Already we have given so much. But then, almost every family has given something. All three of the Von Heisel boys were killed last summer in some offensive. At least we still have you and Manfred—such as he is—and maybe Adolph. Who is to say?

Write when you can, son. Your mother and I miss you. She sends her love. I told her to send you a strudel, but she only shushed me.

Your loving Papa,

Henrich Schiller

P.S. Your mother's birthday is the twenty-second of next month. Write her if you can at all. Even a penny card would mean so much to her.

P.S.S. We hope you get leave soon. It has been well over a year since you were home, and you looked so tired then.

P.S.S.S. Your mother says to tell you to wear dry socks and you won't get pneumonia and, if you do catch a cold, to be sure and eat a big bowl of potato soup with lots of ground pepper. There, I have told you.

Thirty-one

Hand-to-Hand

A voice shouts in my ear, but I can hear nothing clearly. The British must have borrowed some 75's from the French and they are slamming us. For the last hour they have been hitting us harder than they have ever hit us before. Another shell screams overhead and seconds later the earth itself shudders. Bastards are finding the range. But worry is useless; you are either going to live or die. No hope of dodging one of those monsters.

The voice shouts again just as one of our trench mortars answers back. We are short on men in this sector, but we have plenty of artillery. From personal observation, I feel the side that makes the best use of their artillery wins the day. Our gunners are superb and, fortunately, a shipment of shells arrived only two days ago.

Again the voice shouts and I turn my head. It is Eckler. Before the war he was a piano teacher and, in his spare time, village choir master. Eckler is a thin, nervous sort, shivering every time the British start shelling. Still, he holds his position and stays alert on sentry duty.

"What?" I shout.

“I said, do you think this is it?’

“What do you mean?”

“Do you think all this shelling is the prelude to an attack, Sergeant?”

I shrug. Even after a month, it is still strange to hear myself called sergeant. To consider that I am a sergeant gives me pause. I think back to the first days of the war and good Sergeant Gruber. He was a veteran, a man with great military experience and bearing, plus he knew how to manage men. Alas, he took enough shrapnel to one knee to make a nice cookpot, so now all he is fit for is to train new recruits. At least he is back in Germany. It would not do for all the really good men to be killed. Already too many have given their lives. I think of Hans. He was one of the fine young men who lie beneath the grass in France. The thought of all their passings turns my stomach. I pull my mind back into the moment.

“Hard to say. One never knows with the damn British. They’re tricky bastards.”

“But this is the most shelling I’ve ever seen.” Eckler shivers against me like a wet dog.

“Yes, it’s pretty terrific. If I had to guess, I’d say they will come.”

“When? When do you think they will come?”

The air grows silent and I cautiously ease my head up and stare across no-man’s-land. “Not for a while. As yet, it is still too dark. They would lose their way.”

Eckler rubs his hands together. Once more the seasons are starting to change and there is a coolness to the morning. “Won’t this mist help us?”

He is right—the morning is thick with mist that shimmers white and ghostlike as far as a man can see. “Not as much as it will help them. They will be in the wire before we can even see them in such a pea soup.”

“Won’t the wire stop them?” The will to believe in the wire swirls through his voice.

“It should slow them down. But the only things that will stop them are hot lead and cold steel.”

The earth shudders and dirt rains down on us. That one was close. I sneak a glance at the eastern sky. Already it is growing light. I hope the mist lifts. If it doesn't they will be in amongst us before we can say Rumpelstiltskin.

I peer down the trench. I can see Fischer, the Shingledecker brothers, Hennie Studebaker, Corporal Jürgens, that lumpy private whose name always escapes me, and, just at the bend in the trench, four of the new men who have just come up. They have been thrown in the lion's den, but Captain Von Hermann had no choice. For over a month the British have been hammering us with blows falling like sledge hammers. Only yesterday a shell burst dead center of our trench, killing a half-dozen, including Lieutenant Blixt. He was a hard man in a fight and will be missed.

Command is asking a lot of these few men to hold this stretch of trench. But our losses have not been made good and between the shelling, trench foot, dysentery, and pneumonia we have lost a good many. So many that we have not made a trench raid in two weeks. Plus, we are overdue for a week out of the lines. Word is that the Seventy-first will come up before the week is out. One can only hope.

I turn and look the other way. A lieutenant I don't know runs that platoon. At least they are fresh, having come off leave only eight days ago and are near full strength. Snipers got two men the first night they were in the trenches. After that they smartened up.

The shelling rises to a new crescendo. Dirt flies in all directions and men curse. My bowels contract. Eckert shivers harder. I do wish he wouldn't. Shivering gets the wind up in me. I finger the cross that hangs around my neck and think of my Belgian. I wonder if she ever thinks of me. At times like this I doubt that it matters. I wrote her again last week, but death seems a foregone conclusion. Another shell screams overhead and smashes into our rear. I turn my head and try to spit the fear out of my mouth.

"Is it always this bad?" I hear more fear in Eckert's voice and it makes me mad. Fear is contagious. Being afraid is not a problem... every man is afraid. It's showing it that's bad form.

"Not always," I say, "but often it gets bad before an attack. Don't worry about that, though. Once it happens you'll be too busy to even think about being afraid."

Eckert looks up at me. I do not think he believes me. Too damn bad; the poor fool will find out soon enough. I wish even one of my brothers were here. There are so few of the originals.

Ah, here comes one now, scampering down the trench like the rat he is—Sergeant Meister. He too has been promoted. Months ago, I heard General Von Kluge speak of a war of attrition. Now I understand what he meant.

Meister eyes Eckert and snarls up his nose. To my way of thinking, no one in this trench should look down on another man. Before this day is out, we may all be dead.

"Well Schiller, this looks like the real deal. Colonel Langer has word that the British will make their big push today. "

"They've certainly flung enough steel our way."

"Yes, and their aim has been splendid. A big shell smashed dead center of the soup kettle. But that was no great loss."

"Not Swedes again?"

"You were expecting apple strudel?"

"I'm not that far gone, but a bowl of actual potato soup would be nice." A nerve twitches along my jawline and I rub at it. "Not sure how they expect men to fight on turnips."

Meister shrugs. "Yes, I'd give a lot for fresh bread and hot bacon." He grins, revealing his rotten teeth. "Guess I'll just have to keep going on cigarettes and what passes for coffee until the war is over."

The barrage intensifies, reaching a new peak. The screaming of the shells can drive men mad. My nerves quiver now.

A huge explosion smashes in our rear, there is a huge explosion. Horses scream and men shout. "I am afraid, Meister, that this war will be over for many of us today."

He gives me a hard look and I sense he is going to say something. His mouth opens, but he shuts it and shrugs. Say what you will about Meister, and I have cursed him a hundred times, he is no coward.

"I'm off now," he says, "Got to deliver a message to Lieutenant Mann."

"What's the message?"

"Hold at all costs."

"Wonderful," I say, "absolutely wonderful."

Meister laughs. Actually, he cackles. Then he ducks his head and pushes off the wall of the dugout. I watch him trotting down the trench and wonder if this will be the last time I see him. I have a bad feeling about this day.

The barrage abates, then resumes. But there is a difference to the sound. I cock my head and listen. Yes, the barrage is moving deeper to the rear. The famous British rolling barrage has started. I take a deep breath then call out to the men.

"Heads up now. The rolling barrage has started. They'll be out of their trenches any second. All eyes to the front. Fire when ready."

Beside me Eckert shivers like a wet puppy. I don't say anything, though. After all, my insides are quivering.

~ * ~

I peer out into the mist. The British have a morning out of a thousand to make their push. Never have I seen such a mist. It is thick and swirling and I see a dozen men moving through it, yet the next minute, I don't see any. It was only the light and the mist playing tricks on me. I wish I had a cigarette.

"I can't see anything, Sergeant. Maybe they aren't coming after all."

"Oh, they're coming, Eckert. I can hear them out there. Any second now and you'll see all the British soldiers you want."

Eckert makes a funny noise in his throat. I chance a quick glance down the trench.

"Eyes front, Fischer. They'll be on us before you can blink. Hennie, keep an eye on those new men and send that lumpy private down here. I want him by me when the shooting starts." That nerve along my jawline jumps again, and I rub at it like I am erasing a mistake on a school paper.

"Somebody whistle us up a breeze. We need to blow this mist on out of here."

One of the Studebaker boys gives it a try, but it comes out a squeak. He wets his lips and tries again, a good strong, marching tune this time.

"That's good. Keep it up."

But I am only talking to keep their spirits up. The old hands know that. Still, it seems to help the new men to hear their sergeant speaking in a calm voice. At least it sounds calm to me, even though I am shivering with fear on the inside.

"Come on, come on," I murmur to myself. "Come on, you British bastards. Let's get this over with."

Seconds later, as if the whistling is actually working, the mist begins to thin. Clear gaps form, spread. I can hear the sound of marching men, then a shouted order, and out of the mist steps a line of soldiers, bayonets at the ready.

"There they are!" I shout. "Fire!"

I swing my rifle up and sight down the barrel. The British are coming at a trot. In just a few steps they will be at the barbed wire. What's left of it, that is.

Off to my left gunfire crackles and I focus on a bowlegged soldier and squeeze the trigger. The butt of the rifle slams against my shoulder and I swing the gun to the right and sight on the next soldier in line. He walks with a slump as though he had a hump on his back. I squeeze the trigger again and old Humps flings up his arms and falls on his face.

Before I can fire again, an explosion rocks the trench to my right.

I elbow Eckert. "What was that?" I ask.

"Grenade," he says and his voice squeaks on the word.

Damn, I think to myself, Mills Bombs. Just what we need. I hate grenades. Artillery is bad enough, but after a time the shelling stops. However, it seems to me that the British have an inexhaustible supply of their lousy Mills Bombs and no compunction against flinging them in German trenches.

A bullet sings by my head and I duck. Eckert shouts and I lift my head. The British are running hard for our trench and I pull out my revolver. "Sanne," I whisper, and then they are on us.

A moonfaced British soldier stares down at me. For some reason I can't fathom, he seems rather surprised to see me. I point the revolver in the general direction of his helmet and squeeze the trigger. The lower half of his face disappear.

Eckert rises up and fires like a wildman. One enemy spins like a cabaret dancer and falls down into the trench. I am so proud of Eckert. If I had the time I would clap him on the back. But already more British flash forward to the lip of the trench. One raises an arm, grenade in hand. I fire the revolver and he doubles over.

Dozens of British jump down into the trench. A big beefy fellow knocks Eckert down and makes to go at him with the bayonet. I step forward and, at almost point blank, range fire a bullet into his chest. His hot blood baptizes my face.

All around me men scream and curse and grunt. English and German intermingle until there is only a wall of sound. I can feel it beating against my brain like a natural force.

Our trench is almost full. English and German solders grapple like wrestlers in some earthen auditorium. Too close for the rifle or bayonet, we go for the knife or the cudgel, even our hands.

A British corporal swings a hairy fist at my head and I step back and then I am falling. I have fallen over Eckert. The corporal grins and then he lunges at me with what looks for all the world like a butcher knife. What a way to die. If I had time, I would laugh. I throw up one arm in a desperate attempt to ward off the thrust. Instinctively, my eyes shut. No animal likes to witness its own death.

Only there is no death, no pain. I open my eyes. The corporal hangs limply in midair, impaled on Eckert's bayonet. What a man. Now he is a hero. If I get out of this, I am going to recommend him for a medal.

Grinning my thanks, I scramble to my feet. Another of the enemy is almost upon us. He swings the butt end of his rifle like a club. I step inside the arc of the swing and jam the barrel of the gun against his chest. I squeeze the trigger. Blood and gut spew out like lava from an erupting volcano.

A pack of the enemy comes lumbering down the trench. There are six or seven of them. There is no time to count. I pull the last grenade out of my belt and fling it at them. The force of the explosion sends me staggering back against the wall of the trench.

A bullet sings by my ear. Whether it is theirs or ours is impossible to say. My heart hammers in my chest and I gasp for air.

"Look out!" Eckert screams and I wheel around. Three of them are almost upon me. I fire at point blank range and the bullet blows one of the faces apart. I squeeze the trigger again and again, but there is no firing. I am out of bullets and out of luck.

One of the enemy is entangled with the body of his fallen comrade, but the other slashes at me with a wicked knife. I jerk my head to the side, but a second too late. One cheek burns and my blood runs hot against my naked flesh.

The man swings again and I step inside the blow and smash the revolver against his jaw. He roars with pain and I hope I have broken every bone in his face.

Suddenly his fingers are on my throat and I drop the revolver and jam my fingers against his throat. We're squeezing the life out of each other, stumbling wildly, two drunken dancers in a macabre waltz.

My throat burns and I see tiny black dots. My lungs gasp for air as the world whirls and the light comes and goes. He is very strong and I feel old and tired and weak, but I realize I must break the hold or this trench will serve as my tomb. I think there could be worse spots as the the darkness begins to seep in to my brain.

It is more animal instinct than any clever human thought, but I thrust a knee into his groin. I thrust with every ounce of strength I can muster. The world whirls and then he groans as the pressure lessens and I draw in great gulps of air. I chop at his larynx with the side of my right hand and he goes reeling down the trench. I bend and gasp for air.

Without warning, bullets pepper down like leaden rain. I glance up to see a squad of British firing down into the trench. Eckert moans, and I dive for the floor of the trench. No trench is ever straight, much to the displeasure of the engineers, and just here the wall juts inward, shielding me from the worst of the rifle fire. Perhaps I have bought myself another minute, but no more. They will be in amongst us again and I am out of bullets and hope.

Just then, at the nadir of my despair, a great shout goes up from our side of the trench and I turn my head and blink the dirt out of my eyes. A wondrous sight greets me. Reinforcements have arrived.

At a glance I can see that, as troops go, we have scraped the bottom of the barrel. I recognize Gettlefinger the cook, Hambrock the farrier, and Stolter, Kohl, and Kramer, all of whom are walking wounded. Even some of the stretcher bearers are there. Captain Vogel leads them and, running beside him, is his orderly, Hock. They are not a unit of any sort, but they are the most welcome sight in the world. They charge with great zest and in less than two minutes the trench is quit of the enemy, excepting the dead and a few fallen too badly wounded to resist.

I gasp for air as I try to gather my wits. Dead lie in every direction. They are young and old, English and German, privates and corporals and sergeants. Some, those blown apart by Mills bombs or our grenades, are only pieces of men. Not even their mothers would know them.

I am shaking like an aspen leaf before a hard November wind. My hands tremble and I have pissed myself. But I have lived.

I want to laugh and shout and sing, but all I can do is sob. Tears run down my face and mingle with the blood. I look for Eckert.

He is lying where he fell. His eyes are closed. Blood oozes from a hole in one leg. I kneel and touch his face. His eyes flicker open. “Sergeant,” he murmurs, but I press a finger against his lips.

“Be quiet and rest. You fought a good fight. Let’s get you bound up and back to the aid station.”

I look for the medical orderlies, but there are none to be found. So I rip off the shirt of one of our fallen and tear at it with my hands and teeth. I wrap strips around the wound. Eckert stirs when I touch his wound, but then he faints away. That is a small mercy.

My strength is coming back and I bandage Eckert as best I can, then gather him up in my arms. He is a slight fellow and life is flooding through my veins. I feel as if I could lift fat Major von Oppen two feet off the ground. Going up the ladder with Eckert over my shoulder is almost more than I can manage, but he is a German hero, so somehow I perform the task. Captain Vogel sees us, grins, and gives me a thumbs up. I grin back and keep on slogging toward the aid station. It seems incredibly important that poor old Eckert lives. In five minutes in that trench he has become like a brother to me, and I have already lost too many brothers.

Thirty-two

A Surprise

Steam rises from my coffee and I stare through it across an expanse of grass to a thin line of trees thick with squawking birds. I can see the birds when they fly as a flock, but they are too far away to identify. Probably starlings or grackles. Except for a fat roast goose on the table, I have never been overly fond of birds. Thinking about roast goose hot out of the oven does not endear me to my breakfast—a hard roll and two scraps of bacon. Still, I am not complaining; thousands in the trenches would gladly trade me their iron rations.

After the British assault, we stayed in the trenches for another week and then they brought us back for some rest, followed by training. There is talk of a late fall offensive. Offensive is now a word I find offensive.

I admit it—I am tired of the war. Still, though, it must be fought. If we do not fight that will not stop the French and British from attacking. I yawn, stretch, and sip on my coffee, going slowly so as not to scald my tongue.

At least our quarters are good this time. We are in a small village whose name comes thickly to my tongue, and a gang of us noncoms have taken over a house on the edge of town. It was formerly occupied by one M. Breton, a wool merchant who was smart enough not to put up any fuss when we arrived. Probably he has a place in the country where he has retreated to in order to better keep an eye on his flock. Idly, I wonder about the Aubiers and if they ever remember their German friend.

There is a quietude to this morning; even the birds have fallen silent. Sunlight filters through the leaves of the plane trees and falls warmly on my face. A truck rumbles by on the street that fronts the house and from far off I hear the voices of children calling out in play. It is difficult to think about going back to the trenches.

"Sergeant!" a voice cries. "Sergeant Schiller, are you back here?"

I turn to the sound. Two soldiers are coming around the side of the building, Dietz and Vogt, corporals who are staying here. Vogt has several envelopes in his hand and Dietz carries a newspaper.

"Yes, over here, under the trees."

"Ah you are a bum this morning." Vogt grins. "You were not out of bed at the crack of dawn like Dietz and me."

I rub at my eyes with my fists. "That's because you two are corporals, and I am a sergeant."

Vogt laughs loudly. "Ha, it's because you are lazy, too."

I shrug and sip my coffee. "Perhaps a bit."

"Well, seeing as how you are a decorated hero, Iron Cross and all, we will go ahead and give you your mail. Dietz wanted to hold it for ransom, but I said no, no, we must deliver the mail to the good sergeant."

"Ach, what do you want now, Vogt?"

"Why would I want anything?"

"I know you. You are always wanting something."

He screws up his face like he has a sore tooth. "Well, I haven't been home in over a year."

"Ha," Dietz chimes in, "get in line."

"Yes," I say, "Get in line, but first give me my mail."

"Well," Vogt says, trying to act like he has been insulted. "Here you go. And now, old Dietz and I are off to town."

I glance down at the envelope. The handwriting is not my father's, but it is familiar in a way. "Watch yourself."

"Spoilsport." Vogt laughs and elbows Dietz.

"Like I said, "watch yourself."

Vogt says something and Dietz chuckles, but I have already turned to the letter in my hand.

Dear Brother,

If you ever get to read this letter, I am sure you will be surprised to hear from me. Afraid I haven't been much of a correspondent since I got back from France. Actually, not much of anything. Being a one-legged man is not my idea of a life.

I write today to tell you that our good mother has passed. For the last few months, she looked very pale and seemed to eat less each day. Near the end, it was all Papa and I could do to get her to take a few spoonfuls of broth. Not that there is a lot to eat. Hard times are visiting Germany now. Reverend Gillsbacker says we are reaping the whirlwind that we sewed in 1914. I do not know about that, but I do know that if I never eat another Swede, I will not mind at all.

Doctor Himmelbeck came almost every day toward the end—Papa insisted—but there was nothing anyone could do. It seems her heart wore out. Probably caused by worry and poor diet. You know she was always a great worrier and this war, to my way of thinking, was the death of her.

We buried her in the rain in the family plot. Papa caught a cold that very day and, unless I miss my guess, it has gone into pneumonia. He coughs often and it sounds like each one will rip him apart at the seams.

A few of the men have come home and what a sorry sight we are. One-legged, both arms gone, nose blown off, eyes blinded. What a bunch of cripples! The whole town is nothing but cripples and children and old folks. Germany has come to a sad state.

I fear the war goes poorly. The papers hint at victories, but there are no proofs. Eric Werner came home last week on leave and told me things go badly on the Western Front. His regiment recently had to give up a ridge that cost them two hundred men last summer.

Oh, by the way, I saw Helga yesterday. She is married now. I didn't bother to listen to whom. I almost didn't recognize her. She has lost much weight, and her hair looks thin and dry and frazzled. She said to say hello, and that she wishes you well. There, I have delivered the message.

My half-leg hurts all the time and every week or so a tiny piece of shrapnel works its way to the surface. I have no real appetite and exist mostly on dry bread and whiskey, when I can get it. If whiskey is unavailable, wine will do.

Papa just had a terrible spell of coughing. Coughed up blood this time. Between us, Karl, I don't expect him to make it till Christmas. If I have my way, I won't be here either.

Sorry to be such a gloomy fellow, but such is my nature these days. I wouldn't have written, but you needed to know about Mama, and there was no one else. I hope this finds you well. If the bullet with your name on it has already found you, then I have only wasted a little paper and ink and time. I have more time on my hands than I want, so no loss there, eh, brother?

Until we meet again, wherever that may be.

Your brother (or what is left of him),
Manfred

I read the letter twice, then fold it and put it in my pocket. I stand up. I will go for a stroll downtown. Perhaps I will find Vogt and Dietz and we will have a coffee. I will think about the letter in the dark hours of the night. Tears are not noticed then.

Thirty-three

Violets in the Spring

This spring, I am afraid
that good Mother Earth
will put forth not crocus and primroses,
but the alabaster
skeltons of dead Germans,
not lady's slippers and violets, but
the shining skulls of the Austrian dead

The eastern sky is a blue so pale it hardly seems a color. The moon still lingers, fading gently as the new day stretches across the earth.

The poor earth is a sad sight. Great holes have been gouged in soil so that a man cannot walk a straight line for twenty meters. For as far as a man can see, not a single tree stands unbroken.

And everywhere are the bodies. Many lie where they fell when the English beat us to the punch last fall and made their big push here and along the Somme. Dirt thrown up by exploding shells has covered a few, but others lie face up to the sun or face jammed into the French soil. First, they bloated. Then, they rotted. Now, they are skin rudely stretched over broken bones. Even buried bodies do not stay underground. Between the daily artillery barrages and the freezing and thawing of the ground, the dead work their way up to the surface; an arm poking through here, a leg there, sometimes only a head without a body. In no-man's-land, every day is the day of the dead.

But this morning I have resolved not to think of the dead, for last night the wind shifted and the warming breezes carry the promise of spring. For weeks, we have been teased by hints that spring was on its way, but now, deep in some instinctive chamber, I sense it has truly arrived.

My dysentery has abated and there has been no shelling for several hours. Taking advantage of the quiet, the field kitchen has come up and, for the first time in weeks, we have hot coffee, bacon, and fresh bread. Such wonders make me feel like a new man. A morning stroll seems in order.

I wander off down the trench, pausing here and there to clap a man on the shoulder or make some pleasant remark. From some secluded spot a bird begins to sing and he sounds exactly like the birds that used to nest in the lilac bush outside our back door.

Remembering that bush is bittersweet. My father passed just before Christmas and Manfred has simply vanished. No one knows when or how he left or where he went, but I have a good idea.

My old enemy, formerly corporal now Sergeant Meister is strolling down the trench toward me. Except for Heinson, Glotz, and Mohrmann, the son of the banker, he and I are the only originals. That is what we call ourselves. Hard to fathom, but all the rest of our original companions are dead or invalided out, like poor Manfred, or simply missing, like Adolph. We have started a pot, and each week we put in a mark. The last one in the platoon wins the whole caboodle. Meister always claims to feel lucky. I am not so bold.

"Morning, Schiller."

"Good morning, Meister."

He stops, sniffs the air, then lifts his eyes to a sky growing ever lighter. "Well, my friend, it seems you and I have lived to see another spring."

I nod. "You sound surprised."

Meister laughs. "One never knows. I recall old Gruber saying that the only thing for certain is that something will happen different today than what happened yesterday, and it will probably be bad."

We both laugh. I still am not fond of the man. He thinks too highly of himself. But war has a way of throwing the least likely of people together. What is it the British say? Ah, yes, strange bedfellows.

"Have you heard from Gruber lately?" I ask. I always liked Sergeant Gruber. He treated a man like a man and always pitched in and did his share of the work, no matter how dirty. That is far more than most of the officers today will do.

"Yes, indeed. I was going to tell you last week that I had received a letter, but that very night those infernal British launched that big trench raid and drove it straight out of my mind. You recall that one? It was when Lieutenant Feldstein was killed."

"Yes, one does not forget such events. So Gruber does well?"

"As well as can be expected, he says. His arm aches something fierce whenever the weather changes and he still limps badly, but his appetite has returned."

"Ah, a good sign."

"Yes, and he wrote that he would be a father this summer."

I feel my face crease into a smile. "The old devil."

We both fall silent for a moment, remembering our comrade who has survived the war. Survived at great cost, but he has survived. The bird starts up again. Cigarette smoke floats in the cool morning air and, even though I smoke infrequently, I want a cigarette very much. Further down the trenchline a man laughs, a good hard, belly laugh. I have not heard such a laugh in weeks. As if to drown out the laughter, the bird sings louder. Meister cocks his head and listens.

"A thrush," he says. I must give him a funny look because he shrugs and looks away almost shyly. "Before the war I was a bird watcher," he says. "Each spring I would take a long hike in the Black Forest to see how many species I could identify."

I don't know what to say. In some obscure way, I am embarrassed for both of us. I look away. From far off, miles behind the lines, comes the whistle of a train. Memories of that first train ride of the war flood my mind, followed by memories of the hospital train.

"Oh yes," Meister says, shaking me out of my reverie. "A letter came for you yesterday. Corporal Hoppe forgot to give it to me until this morning." Meister shrugs. I shrug. What else is there to do in such a situation?

Meister reaches inside his tunic and pulls out an envelope and hands it to me. "Well, I'd best be off. Have to answer a call of nature, you understand."

"Yes," I say, trying not to think about his words. What an unpleasant image? I glance at the envelope. I had hoped it was from Manfred, but I do not recognize the hand. The writing looks like a woman's. "See you."

Meister turns, raises a hand, then strolls away down the trench, headed for the latrine.

I watch him until he disappears around a bend. Then I turn my eyes to the envelope. It has traveled hard and is stained and wrinkled, and one corner is torn. Letters are to be savored, but curiosity gets the better of me, and I tap the letter down and rip one end open.

The greeting says, *Private Karl Schiller,*

My eyes fall to the bottom of the page. It is signed simply Sanne Desmet.

My hands tremble, and I feel my heart start to beat faster. I had all but given up hope. This is not a letter to read in the trench. No, it must be read in some special place. I fold the letter, slide it back into the envelope, then stuff the envelope in the inside pocket of my jacket. It is a nice jacket with only one bullet hole and a small bloodstain. I liberated it off a dead British lieutenant.

~ * ~

There is warmth in the sunlight today. It is by far the warmest day of the year. Under my uniform I have begun to sweat. Bees hum close by and I can hear frogs. It is so pleasant to be away from the trenches, even for an hour, that I could close my eyes and imagine I was in Germany before the war. I remember when Helga and I used to take walks in the spring. Suddenly our last visit before the war pops into my mind and I hear the old footbridge creaking beneath our feet.

I must be a kilometer behind the lines. It was a nice gesture by Captain Holtz to allow me a half day out of the line. The road slants up a hill and when I reach the crest I can see the shattered remains of a grove of trees. Under the trees there is green grass and, even though the trees have shattered limbs, it looks cool and inviting. I step off the road and, as I do, I notice my boots are coated with dust.

I cross open ground—it must have been a meadow before the fighting—and as I draw closer to the grove, I hear water running. I step more quickly toward the shade.

Among the trees the air is still and there is a silence like you hear in the great cathedrals. But then I realize it is not truly silent here—I hear the hum of unseen insects close by and from across the open ground the lowing of cattle.

A gnarly old oak still stands in the heart of the grove. A shell has ripped out the crown, but enough of the canopy remains to throw a dark patch of cool shade. I sit with my back against its aged trunk. Surely this tree was young when Napoleon ruled France.

I am torn about the letter in my breast pocket. Perhaps she was glad to hear from me. Or it may be that she has regretted our interlude, or felt a delayed anger at my actions, and spelled out her unhappiness on the piece of paper. I want to read it but am afraid to open it. There is really no good reason why the letter should matter so much to me. After all, it was only one night, a mere parenthesis in eternity, and I was rather inebriated.

Still, her response does matter, perhaps because I have lost so much. My mother and father and one of my brothers are dead. The other two might as well be dead to me; I have no idea where they are, or even if they live. I close my eyes and take a deep breath, drawing spring into my nostrils, tasting its sweet flavor in my mouth. I open my eyes and pull out the envelope. As I tug the letter free, I notice my hands tremble.

I open the letter. Dappled sunlight falls on the paper.

Private Karl Schiller,

You must imagine my surprise when I received your letter. When you left that morning, I told myself I would never see you again. I looked upon you as nothing more than a violent whirlwind passing through my life, upsetting my balance then moving on.

For a long time—at least a month—I was uncertain as to whether to respond. Even as I write these words I am of mixed mind. Why should I write you, I ask myself, after all we had only a few hours together? Furthermore, you got me drunk and took some advantage of me, although I must admit that I was somewhat cooperative.

In addition, I hate the Germans. You must not be surprised by that. Not only did a German seduce me, but a German killed my brother. In these horrible, terrible, awful times, I have been left alone. My parents are old and feeble and need far more from me than I can give. Every minute I am not helping them, I am trying to keep the farm going. It has never looked so awful, and I am ashamed. But what is a woman alone to do? Besides, none of the farms around me look as they did before Germany invaded.

The days are long and hard, with brutally hot summers and icy snowbound winters. But what has not killed me has made me stronger. I am a different Sanne Desmet than you remember, if you remember me at all. Do you remember me? If so, is it with fondness? That is the question I have asked myself every day since you left.

Part of me did not want to write you, but still, I told myself, you did write and when a person gets lonely enough, they will grasp at the flimsiest of straws. So I should be polite and remember my manners and thank you for writing, but I won't.

The war is all anyone talks about, yet it is hard for me to make sense of which side is winning. On the rare occasions when I see a newspaper, it seems to me that all they write about is men dying. So many men. My brother. The village schoolmaster. A boy named Leopold who was sweet and kind and generous. Our hired man, who never knew his parents and never had the chance to marry.

I am sure you have seen more than enough death, maybe enough to slake even a German's thirst for blood. Perhaps many of the men who sacked our peaceful village that night are now dead. Perhaps you are dead. If you are, perhaps God will grant you forgiveness.

In your letter you express some regret, mixed with certain feelings for me. I wonder if your words are true, of if you are playing games with a poor Belgian woman? I confess to certain feelings for you, but I must warn you, they are a sad jumble at best.

It would probably be best to forget you, but, for a number of reasons, I cannot. Will I ever see you again, I wonder, and want to cry. But what would that accomplish, except to cast a deeper sadness on my soul. So, although I cannot totally forgive you, I also cannot forget you. Thus, should you ever journey this way again, I would like to see you.

Perhaps, I tell myself, you will write me again, or perhaps you will forget me, or even perhaps you are dead. Perhaps covers much ground, but I take the chance and write. Time will tell the balance of our story, if there be any.

Your Belgian,

Sanne Desmet.

Three times I read the letter and still I am not sure quite how to take it. In the end, I decide to view it in a positive light. After all, there is that line where she indicates she would like to see me if I am ever in her part of the world again. I try not to think about the mixture of feelings.

I take a final look at the letter, fold it, and put it back in my pocket, then lean back against the trunk of the ancient oak and look out across the little glade. Already the grass is green here, tall and thick, lush even. Tiny white flowers, no bigger than the buttons on a man's shirt, grow in great profusion. Running through the center of the glade is the brook, a narrow band of water only a few inches deep running along at a surprising clip. The land slopes here. Not a lot—only a few inches—but enough to create little ripples where it flows over white rocks.

The sound of the moving water arouses a thirst in me and I get to my feet and walk to the edge of the water where I sink down on my knees. The ground is mossy and soft and I think I would like to lie here and sleep. Instead, I drop my head to the clear water and drink. The water is cool and refreshing and I drink for a long time before I lift my head. As I do, I see a flash of blue on the far side of the brook. I look again. Violets, wild violets. Violets, ah violets. I think of the letter in my pocket and the violets as good omens.

Maybe I will pick a mess of violets for Sanne one day. What woman can resist flowers? What foolishness a man thinks. She is more likely to laugh in my face, or send me on my way with a few well-chosen words than be happy to see me. And I will not blame her. No, the blame is all one sided in this case.

I take a final glance at the violets. There is no need to pick them. Violets are for lovers, not for the trenches. I push up. Time to be heading back. I do not want to abuse Captain Holtz's generosity.

Thirty-four

Once More

Over the top is the cry
and we spring to our feet and
climb the parapets
and, without another look,
we gasp a great lungful of air,
push our bodies out of the
trench and into no-man's-land,
to face the barbed wire, bombs,
and bullets,
taste the fear in our
mouths and feel the piss
running down our legs
while we pirouette in the arms of Old Man
Death

It is four o'clock in the morning. All the officers and sergeants gather around Captain Holtz to receive our final orders. Tonight the moon is bright, shining down us with an unusual intensity. Surely that is a sign of something. Of what, I cannot say. There is a chill to the air this morning. Summer has been long and hot and it is difficult to realize the seasons are changing.

"All right now, let's go over this once more. There must be no slipups. Our wing is the fulcrum on which the rest of the attack hinges. Come in, come in, everyone come in closer."

We shuffle around, bumping into one another, pushing to get closer to Captain Holtz. Bodies collide and somebody curses softly.

"Silence," says Captain Holtz in the stern voice he uses when he wants to be serious. We all straighten up and the murmurs cease. He waits until there is only silence.

"All right, pay attention. In the morning there must be no mistakes." He coughs softly, turning his head away, then back to us. All summer he has been coughing and he looks pale, but he never flags. Always he is always on his best behavior. We all admire Captain Holtz and do not want to let him down.

"At five o'clock we will begin the movements. Lieutenant Seivers, your platoon will pull out first. Hoffmann, yours will follow. Then yours, Schiller. You three will swing your men down the Pernese Road all the way to the crossroads. Then you will take the left-hand turn and advance as quickly as you can down it until you come to Charnone. There may be French soldiers stationed in the town. Our scouts have indicated this is a possibility."

He coughs again, a deep racking cough this time, and, for a moment, he bows his head as if in prayer. Then he takes a deep breath, blows it out, and lifts his head. Moonlight covers his face so that he looks a ghost.

"Now, this is critical. You three must keep your men moving forward. Brush aside any resistance but keep moving. General Keller is certain that if we can make the Morsine Bridge by daylight we will catch the French at their breakfast and a breakthrough is all but guaranteed. They will not be expecting you. At five-thirty our artillery will open up with a massive barrage, but it will be three miles to the north. They will suspect nothing.

"Push across the bridge and keep moving. Speed is of the essence. One of our planes observed a major troop movement yesterday. The French are swinging their left flank around in order to strike a blow at us, probably near Vechim. It is thought that the British will slide over to cover the opening, but our artillery has damaged the rail lines and they will have to march. They appear to be making preparations to begin this morning, but even if they leave at daylight, they cannot possibly be in position before noon.

Captain Holtz curls one hand into a fist and pounds it into the palm of the other. "This is what we have been searching for months. Being two armies, the enemy is not as unified as we are and with so many moving parts it had to be only a matter of time before there was a gap in the line. If we can get to that gap before the British, we can pin them back. Then General Von Klaze can roll up and smash them.

"Now, you three must keep driving your men. There are to be no rest stops, no looting, and no lagging. If a man lags, shoot him. Speed is critical. We have a window, an hour, maybe two. No more. You three must get your men into position and hold the British off long enough for Colonel Messer to get the Fifty-third up. They have been on leave and have received reinforcements, so they will be just what we need. Only they are not here. Already they are on the march, but without hope of supporting you before early afternoon. For an hour, two, three you will have to hold the British off. Also, if the French get wind of our attack, they may wheel back and attack you from the rear.

"So be alert at all times. I am supremely confident in your abilities and those of your men. You are all battle-hardened soldiers and know what is required. So once more I call on you, as good German soldiers and members of the proud Twenty-sixth, to step forward into the breach."

Someone cheers and then others join. I cheer, too, but for what I do not know. We are being thrown into a narrow gap between two great wheels, one British, the other French. It appears to me as if we stand a splendid chance of being crushed.

Captain Holtz smiles. In the flickering torchlight, I can see the tiredness etched in his face. His shoulders sag and his head leans to one side as though it is too heavy for his neck to hold. After a few seconds he waves a hand.

"All right, gentlemen, you know what you are to do. I am counting on you to achieve success. Germany is counting on you. If we can break through here, separate the two armies, smash the British, then wheel and smash the French, we can turn the tide of this war."

We are all listening carefully. Emotion runs through the captain's voice like an underground stream.

"As you know, our armies have suffered reversals over the past few months. Verdun still holds out. We were turned away from the gates of Paris. We have bogged down all along the Marne. At home the harvests have been poor and our fathers and mothers, even our children go hungry. In the spring they will call up the next class three months early. In addition, many men older than some of you have been called up."

The captain pauses, draws a deep breath. "It is safe to say, gentlemen, that what you and your men are able to do over the next few hours may change the direction of the war. Now go and get your men ready. Synchronize watches. I have four twenty-two. May this be our blessed hour. My thoughts go with you. I wish I were leading the attack in person, but I have been ordered to stay at the command center. In many ways I envy you. Now go."

For a few seconds, we all stand and stare at each other. Like so many sheep, I think. Then men begin to walk away, disappearing into the darkness. As I follow, I wonder how many of us will live to see sundown.

Thirty-five

Breakthrough

We move through country I have never seen, marching quickly through the dark. Already we are on the Pernese Road. My men march with vigor, given the early hour. Before us go larger platoons commanded by Lieutenant Seivers and Lieutenant Hoffmann. They are both good officers, although Lieutenant Hoffmann is not a lucky man. Twice he has been severely wounded and only came back from medical leave last week.

Trees line the road, rising up like silent, giant sentinels. Birds flutter in the trees, too sleepy yet to fly. I can smell new mown hay and freshly turned earth. A man could do worse than die with those scents in his nostrils.

This is a good road, as yet touched only lightly by war, and, after all those weeks in the trenches, it feels good to stretch out and march quickly down the hard-packed earth. A runner comes hurrying back from the front, goes by, then curls back and settles alongside of me.

"Private Hosler, sir. Lieutenant Hoffmann sent me back to tell you that you are almost at the crossroads. Charnone is less than a mile away. He said to remind you that you are too push on through

Charnone if at all possible. Fire if fired upon, but otherwise, keep moving."

"Thank you, Private. Go back and tell Lieutenant Hoffmann I understand. Tell him I will see him at the Morsine Bridge."

"Yes, sir." We exchange salutes and the private disappears into the darkness. For a moment, I can hear his footsteps, then only a heavy silence.

Corporal Keller marches beside me, mumbling words I cannot discern.

"What's that, Corporal?"

"What's wrong with Lieutenant Hoffmann? He should know he can count on us. Have we ever let him down?"

"No, but this attack is critical, so Hoffmann is taking no chances. I don't blame him."

"Do you think we have a good chance, Sergeant?"

I glance off toward the east. Daylight is coming. Already a hint of pale blue glimmers in the eastern sky. Birds chirp. My stomach grumbles.

"Hard to say, Corporal. Nothing ever goes quite as the generals plan in any battle, but if we can catch the French asleep, or even at their breakfast, then, yes, the odds shift to us."

"Looks like good weather," Keller says.

I glance again at the sky. For a change, we have a dry spell. Dust I don't care for, but it is better than being mired in mud.

"Agreed, Corporal. Now go and tell the men to pick up the pace. I want Hoffmann to feel our hot breath on the back of his neck when we get to the Morsine Bridge."

~ * ~

Charnone is clearly visible. Pale daylight covers the ground, although shadows are still deep on the west side of the buildings. The morning is still new and the streets appear empty. Already the men under Lieutenant Seivers' command are striding into the village. With my field glasses I can see the windows of the houses and the chestnut trees that line the main road. I swing the glasses around and search for Hoffmann. He is about a hundred yards ahead, standing just off the road, peering toward Charnone, shading his eyes with his hands. He is a good officer, a very brave man. We are always criticizing each other, but only in jest. My men march past me and I lower the glasses and march alongside them.

Larks sing out from the tall grasses that grow beside a ditch. On the far side of the ditch is a meadow where horses are grazing. The day promises to be warm. Already a thin sheen of sweat is forming on my brow. Private Hench whistles as he marches. He also has a wonderful singing voice, baritone. I cannot carry a tune in a tin bucket.

Suddenly the morning is filled with popping sounds. For a moment I am unsure what they are. Then it comes to me—gunfire, distorted by the buildings. Seivers' men have met resistance. Now we shall see how light the French resistance is.

"Double time!" I shout, and the men pick up the pace. Before us, Hoffmann has swung his men out to the left of the road, and I order mine to the right. As usual, old Hoffmann has a good plan. If Seivers meets resistance in the middle, he will swing left, and I will swing right. It is doubtful the French have enough men to thwart all three thrusts.

We are off the road, moving rapidly across open ground. A line of trees curls off to our right, but before us is only meadow. Birds whirl up and a rabbit bounds out of a bramble patch and hightails it off toward our far right flank. The gunfire is louder, sharper, and I can hear our own guns answering those of the French.

"Remember," I shout, "push on, don't get bogged down. Pass it on, pass it on."

Above the sporadic rifle fire, I can hear my order going down the line. My men advance in perfect order, on the double. Hoffmann would be jealous, the kaiser proud.

Washing is hanging on clotheslines and a wagon with two draft horses hitched to it stands before a greengrocers. Church bells ring out as the level of gunfire rises, then rises another level. As I expected, our scouts have missed the mark, again.

We are running hard. Off to my right, a man stumbles and falls. He does not get up. I cannot see who it is. Private Mercker cries out, drops his rifle, spins around and falls face first to the ground. The French are picking us off like rabbits, but they are not visible. Where are they?

My eyes search the streets. A bullet sings by my ear. All along the line men are diving for the earth, seeking protection or camouflage. I drop to the ground and peer up at the buildings. Maybe the French are on the rooftops. No, they are not there. Something flashes a little lower and I pull out the field glasses and focus the lens.

Ah, they are shooting from the windows. What I wouldn't give for a field piece or two. I would blast Charnone off the face of the earth. We cannot allow ourselves to be pinned down like this. The attack depends on us keeping moving.

I look left and see that Seivers' men are pinned down. There must be a lousy Frenchman at every window. I cannot see Hoffmann or his men.

"Fire at the windows!" I shout. "Fire and advance."

All around me rifle fire rings out. Most bullets thud against the mortared walls but here and there glass breaks. "Fire."

Another round rings out as I am scrambling to my feet. "Charge!" I scream, and my men rise like unwieldy beasts and follow me.

Thirty yards to go and still the bullets whine by my ears. One burns the fleshy part of my left arm, but I keep running. The first building is only a dozen yards away and I pound on, trusting to luck.

I make it, and for the moment I am safe. Safe, but alone. Then Corporal Keller and a dozen men make the shelter of the building, all breathing like hard run horses. I suck in air. More men arrive and again we are quite a good sized squad. Not as numerous as we were at daybreak, but large enough to make a difference.

When I get my wind back, I face the men. "Remember, our orders are to keep moving at all costs. The French are in the houses and buildings. They are shooting down at us, but if we stay close against the buildings, they cannot see us. Follow me."

I whirl and start out, tugging my revolver from its holster. What I said was true, but only to a degree. Frenchmen in the building we are close to cannot see us, but others across the street, or a building or two down the street, can. Still, I can't say that. We must break through. To be held up for an hour while we clear Charnone means disaster. There is nothing to do but trust to luck and keep moving. Either a bullet has your name on it, or it doesn't.

We make one block and I try for two. A bullet smashes into the wall beside my head and masonry rains down on me. I glance across the street and see a face at a window. I snap off a quick shot without really aiming and am pleasantly surprised to hear the tinkle of glass.

Behind me a man shouts, "I'm hit!" but I do not even turn around. There can be no pauses in Charnone. I am sure Hoffmann is doing the same. Already the gunfire is lessening. The bulk of the French must have been in the center of town and out here on the wings we are breaking through. My breath rasps in my throat and my lungs burn, but I pound on. Keller runs beside me, with a dozen men on our heels. We are free and running like men possessed, heading for the far side of Charnone. The wounded will have to take care of themselves and the dead won't mind our pushing on.

~ * ~

Perhaps a hundred meters ahead is the Morsine Bridge. We kneel or lie in the tall grass along the crest of a small hill and stare down at the river, the bridge, and the French infantry. Without the glasses the French look like toy soldiers. I lift the field glasses.

No more than a half-dozen men are on the bridge. On the far side of the river the French have established a small camp. Two columns of smoke rise between some tents, pointing at the sky like gray fingers.

Although we are behind schedule, quiet still rules the morning. Three or four men meander among the tents. The rest of the French seem to still be dreaming. Well we shall give them a rude awakening.

I swing the glasses back to the bridge. Yes, the soldiers there are armed. Worse, the ground directly in front of the bridge is open country, with the grass mown close. Further down the bank on both sides there are trees, but all close to the bridge have been chopped down. Without a diversion it will be a slaughter if we rush the bridge. If I had a full platoon we could simply overwhelm the defenders, but platoons are not what they were in 1914. The others should be up soon—Hoffmann, especially, is a driver—but time is of the essence.

"Keller?" I call out in a low voice.

"Yes, sir." In an instant, the good man is right by my side.

"We are going to need a diversion, or they will cut us to ribbons. See that darker stand of trees where the river starts to bend?" I point. "There, off to the right, maybe forty or fifty meters downstream."

"Those taller ones?"

"That's right. Now pick out half dozen good men, then swing around and come in from the south. Make lots of noise, gunfire, shouting, that sort of thing. But your attack will only be a feint. The whole idea is to make the French think an attack is coming there. Keep them occupied and the rest of us will take the bridge and get a machine gun set up. That ought to hold them off all right. Understand."

"Yes, sir."

"Good, now Hoffmann and Seivers should be along any moment, but we can't wait. Let's take that bridge, drive off this little band of Frenchies, then start working our way between the two armies. Messer should have the Fifty-third up in a few hours. Just follow my lead. If I go down, you know what to do."

"No need to worry about that, Sergeant. You are indestructible."

"Horseshit, Corporal Keller, but good luck anyway." We shake hands and Keller moves down the line of men, tapping one on the shoulder, then another. In less than a minute he is ready to move off. At the last moment, he turns and snaps off a salute. I salute back and he spins on a heel and takes off at a trot. Six men in field gray follow him. They look like pictures of wild Indians in America I have seen in books. In seconds they curl out of sight under the brow of the hill.

It will take them at least a quarter of an hour to get in position, so I lift the glasses again and survey the French. The number of men on the bridge has grown and now, six or eight men move about between the tents.

High above us, a hawk rides the thermals. The sun is up, gaining in intensity. Time seems to move in tiny increments. My mind begins to drift. Partly because I am no good at waiting, and partly because before any battle a man thinks of everything else he can think of so he won't have to think about dying.

I wonder where Hoffmann and his men are and if Colonel Messer's division is making good progress. I wonder what the French are planning for breakfast. I wonder how many of my men will die today.

Often before a battle I think about being killed, but for some reason I cannot name, I do not think I will die this morning. Perhaps that is a good omen, or maybe I am simply tempting fate—always a foolish thing. Still, it does not seem to me that I will die this morning. Time, of course, will tell.

I look down the line of men. Some look nervous, while others smoke or chew on a dirty crust of bread they have pulled from their pockets. One man scribbles words on a scrap of paper. Perhaps he is writing a final note to his mother, or lover, in case this is the day he finds that one bullet with his name on it.

I glance at my watch. Only a few minutes more and Keller should launch his diversion. I should give orders to the men, but out of nowhere I think of Sanne. Her face floats before me like a wandering moon. She is not exactly beautiful, but there is something about her I cannot forget. I wonder if she still lies in bed, or if she has already begun the day's chores. Maybe, even at this very moment, she has gone to that old barn to milk the cows.

There are people who believe that if you think of a person, that mere silent shifting of your brain will make them think of you. My father knew a man in Berlin who swore that this phenomenon was true. He claimed to have irrefutable evidence. However, as far as I know, he has never shown anyone his evidence. Still, it is pleasant to think that such a thing might be true. And one must admit that the world is full of many strange things.

I swing the field glasses up, and off to the right I can make out the movements in the tall grasses and see strange shadows darkening the ground. It is time, so I shake the cobwebs out of my head, ease down the slope a few yards, then call the men to me.

"All right, this is it. Corporal Keller and his men are going to create a diversion for us. Our job is to take the bridge, then hold it. The rest of our men will be along soon and then we will push on. Now, the only way to take the bridge is by direct assault, which means we will be attacking across the open ground in front of the bridge. The last forty yards will be nothing but one full out thrust forward. The French do not have many men on the bridge and we should be able to overwhelm them easily. However, we must keep moving forward. If we stop to seek shelter or come to the aid of a fallen comrade, we give away our advantage. So keep pushing forward, no matter what. There will be time to care for the wounded after we take the bridge. Now this attack should be over in less than five minutes. It is simply one big push. I will be leading the attack and, remember what I say. If I go down, do not stop for me. Take the bridge and hold it."

I pause and look around at the men. All look grim, but determined. They are brave lads. Many have received only minimal training, but they are willing, and I sense they will obey orders. It would be hard to ask for anything more.

"Any questions?"

A few feet shuffle, and a man coughs, but nobody speaks. "Let's go," I say. "Remember, keep moving, always keep moving."

~ * ~

Gunfire off to our right, and I pick up the pace. While the diversion should work, it will not hold the French long. They generally lack brilliance in their thinking, but they are not grossly stupid.

The ground in front of the bridge is not as flat and smooth as it appeared from the crest. Slight dips and risings up create better cover than I expected. So far, the French have not seen us. From the far side of the river, men begin to shout and the gunfire rises in intensity. We are in a swale now, but ahead I can see the land sloping upward before leveling out. Once we reach the level ground it will be time for the rush to the bridge. I only hope the diversion works.

I twist around to glance back at my men. They are coming on, moving steadily. Certainly, a few appear apprehensive, and I know all must be feeling fear—a man never loses his fear prior to a battle, no matter how many he has fought, but they these brave Germans hide it well.

I wonder those thoughts that are the same before every battle. Will I be killed or wounded today? Will I break and run? Will the attack succeed?

Then I think of my brothers and my comrades who have died. As always, for a moment, I see the faces of my mother and father. Then I think of Sanne. Strange, but she is almost all I have left outside of the army. The Aubiers, if they still live, will probably never speak to me again, Helga has found another, Hans and Mother and Father are dead, and Adolph has disappeared, and who knows if Manfred still lives. Except for my comrades in uniform, I would be a lonely man. So, I think of Sanne, fiercely proud angry, defiant, yet lovely in her unique way. Then I smile and start running as hard as I can up the slope.

I pop out into the clear like a ferret popping out of his hole. The bridge lies directly ahead, no more than thirty meters. A dozen Frenchies line the bridge, but their attention is drawn to the gunfire off to the right. Some are even firing at Corporal Keller and his men, though they are far enough away to make any hit a lucky one, and probably not fatal. I run hard for the bridge. It will be better to be in amongst them before they know we are there than to take a few potshots on the run. I don't like those odds.

Twenty meters and I hear my men pounding behind me. One long-legged private has drawn even on my right and a pair of slender, younger men are outpacing me to my left. For a soldier, I am getting to be an old man.

A Frenchie turns on the bridge, and I watch his face change. Then he is shouting, and all his comrades whirl about and begin firing. They fire in a hurry, without taking proper aim and the bullets go wide or high.

Only ten meters now and a bearded Frenchie rushes forward and smashes into the private with the long legs. Another lunges at me with fixed bayonet, but his thrust is awkward and I step aside and smash my arm against the back of his head as I run by.

Suddenly I am in among them and we smash at one another with fists and cudgels and the butts of rifles. I lock arms with a swarthy sergeant and we spin around the bridge like tops, smashing into other men crashing against the side of the bridge. He gets a hand on my throat and black dots dance in front of my eyes. His breath is hot against my face. It smells of garlic. What a crazy thing to notice.

It is hard to breathe and, with the strength of the desperate, I jerk my right arm free and drive my fingers into his eyes.

He screams and, as the pressure on my throat eases, I smash my fist against his jaw and send him reeling. Another Frenchie rushes up, with bayonet fixed, jabbing at my face. I feel the sharp point slice against my ear, but he has made a fatal mistake. He should have gone for my abdomen. I have my knife drawn and drive it into his throat. He drops like he has been shot.

More French are rushing toward the bridge, but my men have come up and we control the bridge. As if by magic, they kneel in a raggedy line and aim their rifles.

"Fire!" I scream and the raggedy volley decimates the front row of the French. Still they come, jumping over their fallen comrades and I am forced to admire their dash.

Every man on the bridge is firing as fast as he can, but there are many French soldiers and they are almost upon us. I jerk my pistol out and fire at the nearest Frenchie. His face blows apart. He is so close his hot blood and brains splatter my face. I fire again and a corporal goes down, clutching his stomach. I fire again and again—the French are packed so tightly I cannot miss.

I am out of bullets, so I tug a grenade free and fling it at them. A dozen fly in all directions. They begin to fall back, firing as they go. Then, as if by some signal I do not see, they all turn and run. If I had more men I would order them forward, but we must hold the bridge till Hoffmann and Seivers catch up. I turn to tend to the wounded. My entire body is shaking.

Thirty-six

Night of Thunder

"What I want to know is where in hell is Colonel Messer and his division?"

Keller's voice is bitter. Hard to blame him, considering.

"He must have gotten hung up," I say. "You know how clogged the roads can get."

Keller laughs, but it is not a happy sound. "Sure enough. It was god-awful in Belgium, wasn't it? All those refugees. We could hardly move."

"Yes. You were with the Eighty-sixth then, isn't that right?"

"Actually, the Eighty-eighth. That was quite a division back in '14. We were something else, thought we were good enough to win the entire war just by ourselves."

We both chuckle at that, but then the British artillery starts up again and you can't hear yourself think, let alone carry on a conversation. Streaks of fire paint the night and the very earth shudders with the impact of the shells. They've been at it on and off since an hour before dark and they haven't gotten the range yet. Either their spotters or their gunners aren't very good.

"Messer should have been here now," Keller shouts as the barrage eases. "He was only supposed to be half a day behind us."

"Yes, and Charnone was supposed to be pretty much unoccupied, too. Tell that to Hoffmann and Seivers."

"Heard Hoffmann got it again."

"Yes, he's the unluckiest chap I know. Brave as a lion but can't seem to help getting wounded every time he goes into battle."

"Thigh this time, wasn't it?"

"That's right. Dumdum shattered his thighbone. His war is done at last."

Keller snorts. "Lucky bum. He's well out of it, isn't he? Well, good for him. At least a few of us will survive this lousy war."

A shell smashes just beyond the defile we're in. Dirt rains down on us.

"Bastards are getting closer," I say as I turn and look at Keller. We are only inches apart, but his face is no more than a pale blur against the dark. "Thought you were the patriotic sort."

"Oh, we all start out that way, don't we?" He chuckles at his own words. "Starts to fade pretty quickly when you catch a bullet or see your friends lying all around with their guts in their hands." He coughs. "Wish I had a cigarette."

"Yes, a pipe would be nice."

He jabs me in the ribs. "Ha, I tell you what would be nice, Sergeant, is for Messer to get up here with his division and relieve us."

"Don't kid yourself," I say. "There won't be any relief this go round. Lieutenant Seivers says we attack in the morning, Colonel Messer or no Colonel Messer."

Down the line a man moans in the dark. As best we could, we have gotten the wounded in. All three squads have suffered losses. I don't see what Seivers hopes to accomplish with so few, but he has his orders. And a good German soldier, especially an officer, always follows orders. I am tired of following orders, but so, I suppose, is everyone else.

Another shell screams overhead. Seconds later it plows into the ground with a blast that makes my ears throb.

"By morning, they'll have us coordinated."

"Perhaps," I say, although I think Keller is right. "But maybe we won't be here. Seivers says if Messer comes up tonight, we'll start to swing the left flank around. Give the British one helluva of a smash at first light."

"If the French don't get here first."

"Don't borrow trouble, Corporal."

Keller falls silent and I wonder what is going through his mind. He is a good soldier and I figure he has already calculated the odds. They look long to me, any way I figure them.

Shells rain down on us as the enemy is at last getting the range. Never have I felt so helpless. The defile is not deep and there was no time to dig, so we are dreadfully exposed. If they fine tune the range we won't have to worry about what the morning will bring.

"Sergeant?"

"What?"

Keller stirs. His body presses against mine for a second then moves away. He is probably trying to work his way deeper into the earth. That is only natural.

"After the war, if we make it I mean, what do you plan to do?"

"Hum, that is a good question." And it is. For some reason of late, I haven't given much consideration to what might happen after the hostilities. Too busy trying to stay alive, I suppose.

"I don't know. Haven't given it much thought."

"Will you go back home?"

"Perhaps, but not right away. All my family is gone, you see."

"That's rough."

"Not as rough as some poor bastards have it."

"True. No legs is lousy, and so is no arms."

"Or no nose."

"Or being blind."

"Yeah, I'm lucky when you consider everything." And I am. At least I'm still alive and have all my body parts.

"No, I won't go home." I laugh a little, softly, almost to myself.

"What's funny?" Corporal Keller asks.

"Nothing really. I was just thinking that after the war I might like to go back to Belgium."

"Why in the world would you want to do a crazy thing like that, Sergeant?"

I don't answer immediately because I am unsure how to say what I am thinking. Eventually, I clear my throat. What I wouldn't give for a shot of whiskey, even a cup of coffee.

"Well, you see I met a woman there. One I liked rather a lot."

"Did she like you?"

I think for a moment. My legs ache and I stretch them out, trusting the British won't quite get the coordinates right.

"Maybe not so much at the time, but time changes things, you know?"

"Yes," Keller says. "Time and suffering and death. That holy trinity changes a lot." Again he shifts position. "Was she pretty?"

I reflect. "Not beautiful, no. Nor flashy like a cabaret dancer, but nice looking. She had the kind of face a man would like to grow accustomed to seeing."

"She sounds nice."

"She might be," I say, "under the right circumstances. What about you? What will you do when the war is over?"

Keller is silent for so long that I am afraid I have offended him in some unintended way. Then he laughs a little, low and throaty—a genuinely amused sound.

"I know it sounds silly, Sergeant, but I've never really thought about that. Not really. Suppose I will just go back home. My father is a butcher and I helped him. And that was all right before, but now—"

"You want something different?"

"Sarge, I don't know. Being a butcher wouldn't be bad and I really don't know of anything else I want to do. Still, I feel like there might be something out there, now that I've seen a bit of the world."

"At least of France and Belgium."

"*Ja*, you are correct, of France and Belgium."

Another barrage threatens to shatter the night into fragments. Shells scream overhead and land all around us with maddening frequency. If we stay here it is only a matter of time until one comes along with our names on it. I wish Messer would hurry. If I have to die, I'd rather die on the move. The barrage goes on and on and on and on, as though it will never end. Finally, the British gunners grow tired or they run low on shells. You can almost hear the silence falling.

"Apparently, we are actually quite close to the Belgian border."

"Where did you hear that?"

Keller coughs. "Overheard a couple of the officers talking. They said it was less than twenty miles to the east."

I settle back against the curl of the defile. "I thought Belgium was a long train ride away."

"Yes. Thank goodness we didn't have to march."

"If the generals had to march, this war would soon be over."

Keller thinks my remark is quite funny. He laughs a little.

"A German general march...you must be out of your mind."

Something in his remark strikes me as holding truth. I reflect for a moment.

"Perhaps you are right," I say. "I must be a little mad. We all must be a little mad. War makes men crazy, you know."

"Yes," Keller says, "I know."

Thunder rolls again over the British lines, only the sound is not of nature. Shells scream overhead like wounded horses. Trees splinter and men cry out. Thunder rolls.

Thirty-seven

Paris Over The Next Hill

I have begun to wonder
if Paris is only a figment
of my imagination,
a mirage of the mind,
a never-to-be-kept promise
always glittering ephemerally
just over the next hill

Branches slash our faces and vines thicker than a man's arm tangle our feet. Bullets whine around our heads while sweat runs down our faces.

None of this matters, not now, not when we are gaining ground. Messer and his division came up just before daybreak and, after a hastily convened briefing, we began the attack. There had been just enough light to see.

I held no great expectations, not after the bombardments of the night before. But our luck must have been in. By blind chance we stumbled on a gap in the lines, a gap between the armies, so we curled to the north and raced headlong into the French. They were trying to cook breakfast. We charged out of a little woods screaming like wild Indians and smashed into them on the dead run. They broke like rotten sticks. Behind them was open ground. At least it has been so far.

All morning we have been pushing on. More territory has been gained in the past three hours than we gained all last fall and winter, and still we are moving. The open country has given way to a thinly wooded upslope of land that seems bereft of enemy soldiers.

Keller slogs beside me. Off to his left I can see our men, a thin gray line moving between the trees. These trees are small and scattered, second growth, not at all like the ancient forests of Germany. I can feel the miles in my legs and my lungs burn. The others must feel the same. Never have we moved so far so fast, yet still we must push on. Opportunities like this are too precious to waste.

Scattered gunfire...but where? I can hear shots, but in the timber it is hard to place them. A bullet smashes the trunk of a birch a foot from my head and I dive for the ground. Keller is on the ground, too, and, I wonder if he has caught a bullet with his name on it. But he turns and looks back at me, then waves me forward. I crawl toward him and we move out as one.

We crest a rise and I peer over the edge, but all I can see are more trees, then a meadow, and, finally, the roof of a barn off to the west. "Where are they?" I ask.

He points to our left. "Over there."

I follow his pointing finger. Ah, yes, there they are, tucked in behind a stone wall that runs on the far side of a dirt road. I nod. "And we were doing so well," I say.

Keller grunts then ducks his head as a machine gun opens up beyond the wall. When the firing dies, he turns his head.

"Yes, and I was just thinking, if we can push on for only a few more miles it will be Paris over the next hill."

"It was too good to last," I say.

"Yes, but we had a hell of a run at it, didn't we, Sergeant?"

"We most certainly did, Corporal."

Footsteps sound behind us and we turn to see who is coming up on our rear.

It is more of Messer's men, maybe a hundred of them. They drop beside us as the machine gun crackles. The bullets make a zinging sound, a sound that makes a man's blood run cold. A lieutenant flops down beside me.

"British or French, Sergeant?"

"British. They've dug in behind that stone wall."

"What stone wall?"

I point.

"Oh yes, I see now. How many do you think there are?"

"Hard to say. We've only been here a minute or two."

The lieutenant lifts his head and looks around. I do the same. The little woods is filling up with German infantry. There are more soldiers than trees. I turn and look down toward the stone fence. The enemy has brought some light artillery up and it will soon make the woods a hot place.

"We have to break through, Sergeant. Victory is almost within our grasp. Colonel Messer himself said so, and General Lietz is arriving today to take command. The war could be taking a turn today, a turn in our favor."

I hope the lieutenant is right, but as I peer down at the stone fence it looks to me like the British are making a stand. Reinforcements are coming up. They are visible in the rear of the British lines. From here, they appear as so many ants. The British artillery opens up. The first shell smashes into the top of an oak and leaves and branches fall on us like strange hail.

The lieutenant jabs me with an elbow. "All right, sergeant, the reinforcements are up."

I glance around. The little woods is jammed with German soldiers. More lie in the tall grasses on either side. There must be five hundred of us, maybe more. Beyond the woods, I catch faint glimpses of more gray uniforms.

"Good, good, but what about that stone wall? It makes a perfect barricade."

The lieutenant smiles and points down off to the left.

I look, but don't see anything but the infantry I saw before. "What?"

"Look back a little, just beyond that rise of ground."

I turn my head and there, coming out of a natural depression in the earth, are three, no four of our field pieces.

"They will smash that wall to pieces," the lieutenant says with satisfaction.

I nod. The lump in my throat is forming. The one that comes just before every attack. "How did they get those pieces up here so quickly?"

"General Von Klaze issued stern orders, and Colonel Rupp is just the man to carry them out."

"Yes, the colonel has that reputation."

"Yes," the lieutenant says, "as reputations go, that's not a bad one." He is silent while his eyes scan the ground before us, but I do not think he is seeing anything. I know that look. He is trying to see beyond what is visible. He is trying to see tomorrow, but, as we all know, that is promised to no one. His throat works as he turns and stares at me. His eyes are green.

"We go on the whistle. Pass the word." He turns his eyes back to what lies before us. I turn and give the orders to Keller.

~ * ~

Although I know it is coming, my body jerks. Even when attack is certain, your mind can never quite accept the prospect of death. I scramble to my feet and run with the others down the slope. We are no more than twenty meters from the woods when our artillery opens up. For once, it makes me happy to hear the shells screaming over my head.

The first shells fall short and the second volley flies too far, but our gunners are getting the range. German gunners are the best in the world. The enemy stands firm, however. They mass a row of making guns on their right flank and begin firing. Our men fall like a long row of dominos.

A shell smashes into the wall and stones fly everywhere. Some of the enemy turn and start running. A man to my left throws up his arm and falls forward. Not all the enemy have left. Keller is beside me on my right and the lieutenant runs beside me on my left. For once, I feel invincible. We cannot be stopped. Another shell crashes into the stone wall and a gap wide enough to drive a train through appears. We run for the gap. A bullet rips through my sleeve but I only laugh. I must be crazy, for Paris seems to be just over the next hill.

Thirty-eight

Deeper

Never have we been so far behind enemy lines. For two days and nights we have been off the leash. The British do not know exactly where we are. Neither do the French. Even our own generals can only guess. Every step has driven us deeper behind the enemy lines.

Our eyes are gritty and our throats parched. Our stomachs growl and blisters the size of American silver dollars tattoo our feet. Yet, never have we been happier. In the short time since we raced through the gaps in the stone wall, we have looted a supply dump, blown up an ammunition wagon, and scared the devil out of two villages too small to have names. I cannot say whether they are French or Belgian; screams sound the same in any language.

The third day has dawned cloudy, with the wind out of the west and the promise of rain suspended in the air. We are maneuvering through a nasty patch of ground where trees grow thick and low and numerous vines hang down from the limbs and run along the ground, ready to snare a careless man. The canopy is so thick and close that only a feeble light penetrates. A nasty odor pervades the woods; it smells a little like rotting vegetation and a little like death.

The trail has narrowed and we walk single file, seeing only the back of the man in front of us. Long ago I lost any sense of where we were. Inside the woods it is so dark that it is no longer possible to tell what direction we are traveling.

Sounds are muffled within the trees, too. Now and then the sounds of big guns come to us, but it is impossible to tell whose they are, or where they were firing. Once we hear a train whistle. It sounds quite far off. I am sure I hear cattle, but Keller says that is only my imagination. Insects whine about our ears and small creatures rustle the leaves of the underbrush.

"I do not like this place," Keller mumbles from behind me.

"Why's that? It seems a lovely place."

"Ah, the jokester today, are we? This is a nasty damn wood if I ever saw one. It stinks of death."

"Ah, Keller, that must be your breath blowing back in your face."

Keller says something, but there is a ruckus near the front of the line and I cannot make out his words.

"What is going on?" I ask the man in front of me. He has without a doubt the worst mustache in the entire German army.

"Hold on," he says, "word is coming back."

We have stopped moving and I can hear the breathing of the men and what sounds like motorized vehicles. But that must be my imagination. Men whisper and I see a few stepping off the trail into the underbrush. Something is up. The man with the infamous mustache turns his head. "Captain Goetz wants you. He thinks the enemy are just beyond the woods. He says to bring your field glasses."

I hustle to the front, tugging the field glasses from around my neck. It makes my head hurt to remember the number of times I've gone to the front like this, to use the glasses myself or pass them on to some senior officer. After a while it occurs to a man that maybe he is using up all his luck. Many soldiers think that war is simply another roulette wheel—it just keeps on spinning and the more times the wheel spins, the more likely it is that your number comes up. But I am a soldier, a good German soldier, so I follow orders.

Captain Goetz and his officers are crouched down at the edge of the woods. Twenty meters beyond the woods the ground falls away sharply until it plateaus for another fifty meters. Then it falls off again to another terrace. Hundreds of tiny men are moving about the second terrace. At the farthest point of my vision is a village where the houses look like doll houses.

"Captain?"

"Yes, what...oh, it's the man with the field glasses. What is your name, Sergeant?"

"Schiller, sir."

"That's right, Schiller. All right, let's see those glasses."

I hand them to the captain and he swings them up to his eyes. While he peers through the glasses, I study his face. There is something wrong with it. I noticed that when he turned to look at me. One side looks normal, but the other is distorted–the cheek caved in and the eye socket malformed. War is hard on soldiers of every rank.

Captain Goetz studies the figures below for a long time. My mind begins to wander and I glance at the other officers. I do not know any of them. Most of them look young, younger than I am at any rate. Many of the older officers have been killed or wounded so badly they had to be sent home, or back to Germany to train the new groups. I am curious as to what the captain is seeing.

"Thank you, Sergeant." Captain Goetz hands me back the field glasses. "You may go back to your unit. Pass the word that we will wait here for a while." He sees the questions in my eyes. "Those are English soldiers down there, a division at least, with more coming up. Keep that to yourself, Sergeant. By your face, I can tell you are a veteran, and I am relying on you. Tell the men only that we are going to rest here briefly. When the moment is right, I will give the order to advance. Understand?"

"Yes, sir." I slip the strap of the field glasses around my neck and start moving back down the line of soldiers. I can feel their eyes on me. I can sense them trying to read my mind.

Thirty-nine

A Day Of Reckoning

The long day has finally ended and much of the night is gone, yet we are still in the woods. Clouds cover the moon. Keller and I have worked our way to a place where there is a break in the canopy and we can see the sky. Occasionally, a star pops out, only to disappear seconds later. Rain still seems in the offing, although not a single drop has fallen.

"What time do you think it is?" Keller's voice is groggy with sleep. We have both dozed at times during the night, but tree roots poking up through the ground and the knowledge that the enemy is just over the crest keeps one's mind churning.

"I don't know. Late, I think."

"Nearly morning?"

I peer at the sky, but all I can see are clouds and darkness. Still, the night has that end of the darkness feel. Before the war I would not have known such a sensation, so I can truthfully say the war has taught me much. "Feels like it," I say.

"Good. This is one morning I'll be glad to see. Don't mind admitting this woods gives me the creeps. Death is here. I smell its stench."

"Probably just rotting vegetation."

"*Nein*, corpses."

I rub the back of my neck. Although we have rested most of the day and night, I am exhausted. Marching suits me better than sitting. "You may regret your wish. This darkness is good cover."

"Trust me, Schiller, this is not a healthy place."

Before I can respond, whispers travel down the line—time to move out. Go single file and as quietly as you can. Keller turns and passes the order to the next man waiting in the darkness.

Although leg muscles protest, I am glad to get to my feet. Keller is right—a stench clings to these woods and I would not bet against there being corpses not far below the grass. Many sections have been fought over two, three, even four times and it strikes me that this woods is a likely place for a wounded man to crawl into to die. The shade would seem inviting to a bleeding man on a boiling summer day.

We are moving, trying to go silently, but roots catch the toes of our boots and vines grab our ankles and sleepy men stumble against one another.

Before I am quite ready, we step out of the trees into a patch of pale moonlight. I hear my name being whispered hoarsely. Startled, I whirl around and find myself face to face with Captain Goetz.

"Schiller, is that you?"

"Yes, sir."

"Thought it was. You strike me as a good man, and I want you to stay close to me. I may need those field glasses again and I can always use some good veterans. Most of the officers are so young and inexperienced, and many of the old ones are losing their nerve. Experienced men with sound nerves are hard to find."

"What about my unit?"

"Lieutenant Grushar will take over." He nods at a youngish man standing just off to his right.

"Can Corporal Keller accompany me? He, too, is a veteran and his nerves are like steel."

"Well, all right. Now quickly introduce the lieutenant to your squad then hurry back. We need to make time. It appears there is a small gap between two large English divisions and we must take advantage of the opportunity."

"Yes, sir." I nod at the lieutenant and we turn and step off toward my men.

~ * ~

We are crossing a turnip field outside a small village whose name I do not know. It is late in the afternoon. We left the woods only a few hours ago, but it seems like a week. I thought we had marched before, but never have I marched so hard or so long. All afternoon we marched at a pace I never imagined men could maintain. Captain Goetz has been driving us and we grumble, yet we know he is right. We have gone too far and become detached from our brethren. We must reconnect with them before the English or the French stumble upon us. After all the damage we have done, they surely are looking for us. If they catch us out here alone, it will undoubtedly be our day of reckoning.

Despite the captain's urgings, our steps have begun to falter. Before the day began we were very tired; now we stumble over clods of dirt and stagger when we step in a furrow. All we have eaten today are the few crusts of bread we carried in our packs and raw turnips. Still, for once, even the Swedes tasted good.

Keller and I plod along beside the captain. I glance at his face. Lines of exhaustion are etched in his flesh. Still, he makes no complaint. He turns to his aide who carries our maps. "What is the name of this village?"

The aide shakes his head. "I do not know, sir. I have studied the maps carefully and this place is not listed. It must be very small and unimportant."

"Are you sure you are looking in the proper quadrant? Every town has a name."

The aide shrugs. He looks very tired, which I can understand. "It is hard to say, sir. We have marched so far and often in the dark..."

"Yes," says the captain. "That is true. Still, we need to get our bearings." He bends his neck and plods on. We plod after him. At the end of the field stand remnants of a stone wall. He halts before the wall and turns to me.

"Sergeant Schiller."

"Yes, sir."

"We need to know where we are."

"Yes, sir."

"So I need you and your corporal to slip into town and find out what the name of this place is and if there any French or British soldiers nearby. While you're at it, try and find out if we are in Belgium or France."

He nods at his aide. "Lieutenant Mozelle here notes correctly that we have done a great deal of marching over the past three days, or is it four?" He shrugs. "In any case, we seem to have marched off our maps and need to pinpoint our location in order to make certain we are headed back toward our lines. Understand?"

"Yes, sir," I say. We surely don't want to wander into the enemy's lines. That would be a sad end to our tour.

"Now, you must not give us away. If you can, liberate some civilian clothes from an unattended clothesline. If things go badly, just say that you have been lost from your regiment for a week and have been wandering so that you no longer have any idea where they are. Above all, don't get captured as a spy. Spies are not tolerated in any country." He pauses as he rubs at his eyes. "Do I make myself clear?"

"Yes, sir."

"Then go, and may luck go with you. Oh, Sergeant?"

I turn and look him in the eye.

"Before you go, why don't you leave your field glasses with my aide? They will only be in your way."

I nod, pull the strap over my head, and hand the glasses to the aide. He looks at them for a moment, then slings them around his neck. I turn, nod at Keller, and we start forward, crossing the wall in one of the fallen places, then hurrying across the road. On the far side is a small orchard, apples by the look of the trees, and there the shadows are already deep.

~ * ~

Dusk has fallen by the time we work our way into the village. We have taken the captain's advice and disguised ourselves as best we can. Keller found an old pair of pants in a potting shed and put them on over his, then turned the blouse of his uniform inside out. It looks strange, but with darkness coming on that should not matter. I had no luck with pants, but did lift a worn, blue jacket and a driver's cap off a wagon standing outside a barn. I, too, will count on the friendly darkness.

From the far end of town, a church bell tolls and I wonder what that signifies. I sense Keller looking at me, but I just shrug for we cannot speak. Our accents would give us away, even if we knew which language we needed to be speaking.

We are entering the village from the northeast, cutting through back yards, churchyards, and graveyards. An alleyway runs between two buildings. If my sense of direction is good, it will take us to the main road. I point to it, Keller nods, and we start down the alley. Like all the roads have been today, it is unpaved and I can barely see puffs of dust rising where our feet strike the earth. My nerves are on edge, but at least they have pushed back some of the exhaustion. The church bells stops tolling as we step out from between the two buildings onto the main road.

The village has no streetlights, for which I am glad. It will difficult enough to pass in the dark, or near dark. Still, a faint blue hint of daylight lingers and light spills from some of the buildings, so Keller and I stay in the shadows when possible.

Acting like we are simply out for an evening promenade, Keller and I stroll down the street. Actually, it is the main road and several other people are doing the same. Each time we pass one I wonder what they think of us. Even if our clothes pass inspection, we are strangers in a small village, and strangers in such places stand out.

Midway down the second block, a man comes rushing out of a doorway and caroms off Keller. "*Pardon,*" he says in French, and

Keller grunts and nods. The man hurries off into the gathering dusk. A nice meal with his family awaits, I imagine, or an assignation.

Two ladies walk toward us, moving rapidly for ladies, and I guess they are late for some event. Keller smiles—he has a nice smile—and I doff my driver's cap. The ladies nod, but do not speak.

Up ahead are brighter lights and voices raised in conversation and singing and laughter. We walk toward the lights that come from a café on the corner. My hope is to find an old newspaper that will give us some sense of where we are. It would be no job to pick up a discarded newspaper and stuff it in a pocket. I nudge Keller with my elbow and nod at the café.

We are close enough to distinguish voices. They are speaking French, but not with a Parisian accent. Still, I can understand most of the words. However, although I am virtually fluent in French, I could not begin to mimic their inflections.

The café has a menu posted on a board just outside and Keller and I pretend to study it. We try to look like men deciding whether to enter or not. From time to time, I cast a glance at the tables hoping to see an abandoned newspaper. Even one several days old would be useful. Not for the war news though, the papers never get that correct.

A multitude of aromas mingle in the air. I can smell the bouquets of various wines, freshly baked bread, and sausages and onions frying, and sweat and perfume, and the scents of the horses standing just down the street in front of a delivery wagon. It is the scent of the freshly baked bread that is most painful—it nearly drives me mad and saliva fills my mouth. For an instant, I wonder how it would be to dine at such an establishment with Sanne. Foolish men dream foolish dreams.

We cannot stand there long. Already one of the waiters is giving us the eye. Luck is not flowing with us tonight. I have not seen a single sheet of newspaper. What a disgrace to the clientele. The waiter starts toward us, but a thickset man at a nearby table calls out and the waiter turns. I nudge Keller and jerk my head toward the darkness. Time to move on. Enough light falls from open windows to allow us to see handbills nailed to buildings or posts. Perhaps luck is only meters down the street.

We turn and step back into the street. A few steps later, I turn and see the waiter is staring after us. I tell myself he is only looking for customers, but I do not believe it.

We walk past stores closed against the night, empty lots, and by dark alleys. A cat lying in a window box stares intently at us. Down a side street a dog barks and, from behind one closed door, come the sounds of a piano. Whoever is playing has a light touch. I love music but have no talent for it.

The street bends to the right and, again, we hear singing. Only this time the voices are rougher and the lyrics are, to be kind, coarse. Lights splatter through partially shuttered windows and the smell of wine and whiskey and piss is strong. A bar. What I would give to spend a pleasant hour or two inside those walls. But, alas...

Just as we pass, the door swings open and three men step out, laughing and pounding one another on the back. I nudge Keller with my shoulder and we ease deeper into the darkness.

It is not easy to follow the conversation—they have all been drinking—but I gather that two of the men are asking the other if he wants them to see him home. He gestures wildly with his arms and shakes his head with vigor. "No, no," he says, "I am perfectly capable of seeing myself home. It is only a matter of a brief walk. The air will clear my head."

One of the other men says something I don't catch and then they are all laughing again. Keller and I get our backs up against a wooden building that smells faintly of moldy grain. Hope rises in me.

The men talk some more, something about a fellow named Josephs, but finally they say their good nights and pat each other on the back. Two of men turn and start down the street, going in the direction from which Keller and I have just come.

The other man coughs, then laughs a little to himself. Finally, just as I have hoped, he begins to meander off alone into the night that has now fully fallen. There is no moon and our faces will be no more than blurs to him. He has a decidedly leftward lean as he walks.

He is singing softly to himself, not unpleasantly. The song is one I have heard. It is about a poor girl who pines for a rich man. I let our fellow get twenty meters ahead, then nudge Keller. We step away from the building and stride down the road, following in the drunk's footsteps.

For a few meters he walks a straight line, or at least a gently curving one. Then he stumbles, catches his balance, and walks on. Even in the poor light he is easy to follow. If there was no light we could follow him by the noise of his footsteps. He is not careful and puts his boots down heavily, as though striking the dirt harder keeps him upright.

He weaves from side to side, but Keller and I follow by keeping close to the buildings on the left-hand side of the road. Now and then he passes a house from which light spills and, once he seems about to turn and knock on a door, but he lurches forward only to stumble again. This time, he stumbles against a wagon parked at the edge of the road. He sinks to his knees, but, with much grunting and cursing, pulls himself erect.

As if the effort has miraculously revived him, the man walks absolutely normally for twenty meters, thirty, forty, fifty. Then, just as I am beginning to doubt, he collapses in the middle of the street. Keller and I hurry forward.

"Oh," he groans, "Oh."

"What is wrong, friend?" I ask. My accent should not bother this drunken boob. "Are you ill?"

"No, I have slipped and fallen. My legs are injured." He thrashes them about in the dust. The fool reeks of wine. Even his clothes smell of it, as though he has spilled it on himself, or sweated wine from his body.

"Here," he says in a loud, rough voice, "don't just stand there. Help me up."

"But of course," I say and Keller and I each get an arm under a shoulder and tug the rascal to his feet. He sways like a young willow in a gentle breeze and we each get a good grip on an arm.

"Can we walk you home, friend?"

"Yes, my legs are worse than I thought. I must have injured myself terribly." He belches.

"We had better get you straight home," I say. "Do we keep walking down this street?"

His heads flops to one side and he eyes me from only inches away. "Do I know you?" he asks and belches again, more gently this time."

"No," I say, "I don't believe so. We are strangers. We heard there was farm work in Linze and are trying to get there. I'm afraid we have taken a wrong road."

The man lifts his eyes to the sky. Here and there a star sparkles, but the moon is dark and I wonder what inspiration a drunken man hopes to draw from such a sky.

"Linze? Linze? Yes, I have heard of that place, only...Ah, yes, you have come too far to the west. You are nearly to Belgium. You must have taken the wrong turn at the crossroads outside of Mersette. You are in Rein. We are only a small village and there is no work here."

"Has the war come to this place?"

"Oh, a little." He shakes his head. "We had better start walking for I am not feeling well."

"So the war has been here?"

"In a way, *oui*." We start walking, or rather Keller and I walk and more or less tug the poor fellow along. His legs keep going limp and, if we did not hold him upright, he would again soon be sprawling in the street.

"The war," I prompt. I have no fear of making this imbecile suspicious for he is rotten drunk.

"Oh yes, well many of the young men of the village have gone off to the army. Only not all. No, indeed. The mayor's son has not gone. They say he has a disease of the blood. But, me, I think it is only that he is afraid to go. Those Germans are brutes, you know?"

"So I hear," I say. Keller snickers, but the drunk keeps talking.

"No Germans around here, thank goodness. See, friend, we are well protected. The English lines are only five kilometers to the east and our brave French soldiers hold the line just across the border,"

"The Belgian border?"

"*Mais oui*, it is no more than a dozen kilometers west."

"Many soldiers in town?"

He stumbles and it takes a moment to right him. "A few," he says, "now and then. But none lately. Rumor has it that some renegade band of Germans is marauding all across France. All the troops are out looking for them."

He makes a small sound, sniffs, then coughs. I am afraid his cough is going to turn into another attack, but it eases, and he peers up at me. We are standing at the edge of a pool of light falling from some upstairs room. We have walked some distance and his eyes look clearer to me than they did before. Perhaps the exercise and the fresh air is sobering him up. I must exercise caution.

"You are very curious about the soldiers, *mon ami*."

I force myself to laugh. "With good reason. I have no desire to join them."

"You are not a patriot?"

"Of course I am a patriot. However, I have already suffered much. Three of my brothers have died for France. I am the only one left who can support my mother and father. They are old and not well."

"I am not well, either."

"Yes, your legs are injured."

It is the drunk's turn to laugh. He sounds like a comedian I heard once in a cabaret before the war. "Actually, I am rather drunk tonight."

"Ah,"

"Yes, I too have suffered. I would join the army, but I have the rheumatism. It is very painful, especially on rainy days."

"Then it is certainly understandable why you are not a soldier, as they must live life rough. And a drink to ease the pain, well, that is only to be expected."

He nods as though I have spoken extraordinarily wise words, instead of the blabber I have been spouting. He nods, then peers at a house across the street. It is small and seems to lean to one side.

"I think that is my house," he says.

"Then we should bid you *adieu.*" I do not want to face a French housewife. They have the reputation of being clever.

"Yes, my wife will let me in." He clasps me in his arms and kisses both cheeks. His breath is lousy. "Thank you for coming to my aid."

"It was nothing."

"Ah, but it was. I tell you...'

"Alas," I interrupt, "we must go as we have friends waiting."

"May the good God go with you, good Samaritan."

"*Adieu.*"

"Hey, wait, I didn't catch your name."

"Barabbas," I say as Keller and I turn and step lively across the night.

Forty

Left or Right

"So, it must be that we are here," Captain Goetz intones. He sounds puzzled, as though the calculations didn't quite work for him.

"Where?" asks a lieutenant whose name I do not know.

The captain jabs the map with a forefinger. "Here, right here at this tiny blue dot." He shakes his head. "I saw it yesterday, but there was no name with it, so I thought it was just a drop of ink some clumsy printer spilled." He jabs the map again, then jerks it off the top of the stone wall and rolls it up with vicious twistings. His face is closed tight and lights flash in his eyes. His anger is alive and the rest of us are afraid. We look at one another, then back at him, then down at the ground.

He lets out a long swoosh of air and I risk a glance. His face is calmer and his eyes are hooded. "All right," he says, "now we know where we are, so we have a good chance at making it back to our lines. I think I know where we made the first wrong turn. It would take too long to reverse our path, so we will have to cut across country and try to hook up with our regiment. The roads look good, at least on the map, and we know where our enemies are. If we can believe a drunk, that is."

He gives me a hard look, but I let it slide on by. What else can I do? I am no trained spy. Keller and I did our best.

The captain glances at the sky. "It has been daylight a good hour," he says. "We must not waste this day. Every minute we stand here, we are sitting ducks for the first British or French officer to motor by."

He gives us the eye—that is what we call it. We used to call it the evil eye, but we have been hardened.

"Shake your men out and let's get on the road. Moving by daylight we run risks. However, just standing here by the side of the road is tantamount to surrender, and Captain Gerhard G. Goetz does not surrender without a fight. Now, gentlemen, I suggest we get a move on." He spins on his heel and steps through a break in the wall, moving so quickly that, for a moment, we are all too surprised to react. Then we run for our men.

~ * ~

The mist is thick this morning, nearly as thick as the porridge in my head. Four hours of fitful sleep last night has done nothing for my brain. Yesterday we marched all day and I cannot begin to say how many kilometers we covered. Even after all the light had faded we marched for an hour. We marched until the captain's torch failed. Then we were up before good daylight. Now, even though it is the middle of the morning, we can see no more than twenty or thirty meters in any direction. Depending on your point of view, this could be good or bad.

"It is like marching through soup," Keller says.

"Yes," I say, "hard to know where we are going."

"Best I can tell, generally north and west, but that's a guess."

"As good as any, I suppose." Keller has a naturally good sense of direction—better than mine at any rate.

"Any idea how much further till we start seeing some of our own?"

Our boots thud against the packed earth. A man coughs. Hidden in the mist, a bird begins to sing. If it weren't for the prospect of being shot, this would be a pleasant stroll. The air is cooler this morning, filled with the scent of new mown hay.

"Not really," I say. "The captain said it might be two days, or three. Even then, he was only going by the map and where our regiment was when we broke through. By now they could be miles away."

Keller nods and falls silent. There really isn't much more to say. Either we make it or we don't. It is rather like the bullets that go zinging by your head—either have your name on them, or they don't. I smile at myself. I have become a fatalist. War will do that to a man.

I am glad Keller is silent. For some reason, I have no desire to talk this morning. Perhaps that is due to a shortage of sleep, or maybe it is that sick feeling in the pit of my stomach. I am becoming an old woman, or a gypsy.

The wind stirs, and across the road the fog parts like a silver curtain being pulled apart. I can see a hedgerow, then a field beyond. An old horse stands in the field, surrounded by a few sheep. A dog barks from some unseen farmhouse, while behind me a man stumbles and curses.

Suddenly, for no reason I can name, I think of Sanne and wonder what it would be like to be walking with her. I wonder if she ever thinks of me, in a positive sort of way, I mean. Certainly she must have experienced many dark thoughts about me.

The road briefly goes up a rise and then down a slope. Fog has surrounded us again, thicker than ever, so it is difficult to see clearly the man in front of you; trees rise out of the swirling mist along the side of the road, reminiscent of figures drawn by an amateur.

Sounds are also distorted by the mist. The dog barks again, but I could no more tell from which direction than a locust could. A bird calls out and the notes sound strange. I have not heard such a bird before. I hear a metallic click and then the sound of a man sneezing. These sounds seem to come from the trees growing along the left-hand side of the road, but that makes no sense. It must be the mist distorting them.

"Did you hear that?"

I turn to Keller. "What's that?"

"What?"

"That noise I just heard. Sounded like it came from those trees."

"I didn't hear anything special. What did it sound like?"

"I'm not sure. But sort of like a click."

Keller rubs at his face.

I glance back at the trees. "Maybe like a rifle bolt being jammed home."

He has a puzzled look on his face. I tilt my head and listen hard, but all I can hear are footfalls mingling with the sounds of men breathing heavily on the march. Then I hear that strange bird again. I glance at Keller. Then another sound seems to come from the trees. Unless I miss my guess, it is the sound of a muffled sneeze. I roll my eyes, and this time Keller nods. I reach down and ease my sidearm out of its holster. Keller wraps his fingers around a stick grenade. Maybe we are only imagining sounds. When a man grows overtired, his mind does strange things.

I step quietly now. Goosebumps cover my upper arms and a single trickle of sweat runs down my spine. Behind me, maybe two rows back, someone starts to whistle tunelessly. Bees drones in a patch of clover next to the road. The air has gone dead calm.

"Drop your weapons!"

The voice is English. From the trees, British soldiers rise like sudden stalks of corn. My throat seems to close. Weakness flows through me like water and I feel my fingers loosening on the revolver.

"Go to Hell!"

It is Captain Goetz who shouts those words then, just as if he has called down the fates, all hell does break loose. At least it sounds as I imagine hell for I see nothing as I dive for the ground. Bullets whiz, and a man groans, "I'm hit!"

Keller is on my right and a private named Graff is on my left. Graff is shaking as he tries to fire his rifle. Keller's right arm swings forward and my eyes follow the arc of his grenade. It explodes against a tree and splinters rain down on us.

I twist around and point the revolver in the direction of the British. At first, I can see only dirt and trees. Then I catch movement between two trees and squeeze the trigger.

I hear Graff's rifle bark, but only once, and I risk a quick glance. No more than that is needed as the top of his head is gone. I think he was a salesclerk from Bremen.

The British are rapidly ramping up their fire and all up and down the road men cry out in pain. A bullet smashes into the road inches from my face. Another tears through the fabric of my uniform. Suddenly there is a lull in the firing and I hear the captain's voice. He is still cursing. Just for the hell of it, I pull the trigger one, two, three times.

I kick Keller in the leg and start working my way backwards on my belly. Away from the trees, and the English, and the bullets. Keller starts doing the same. I don't mind fighting the English, but the road is simply a slaughterhouse.

Never has any snake crawled faster on his belly. Fear is a great motivator, but fear of dying is the supreme motivator.

My feet slide across grass on the far side of the road and I wriggle faster. The ground slopes away from the road here and I slither down gratefully. Just beyond the road weeds grow thick, the grass is tall, and only a few feet away is spotty hedge.

I am in the weeds and catch a glimpse of Keller coming after me. Across the road the firing sounds more intense than ever. I cannot hear the captain, as there are too many other curses, shouts, and screams. Screams are the worst. Among them are death screams. In war you learn to recognize those early.

I search for a gap in the hedge. When I find it, I shout at Keller, then head for it, half-expecting a bullet to smash my spine.

But no, I am through the hedge and running across an open field. Some farmer has cut hay here recently, and I pound through the stubble. Keller's footsteps thud dully behind me, but I do not look back.

The field slopes up to a ridgeline and I head for that. It is all open ground and we are perfect targets, but if we can reach the crest, the other side should offer shelter. I know the field cannot be huge, but it seems endless. However, I am moving again and the sounds of gunfire are beginning to fade.

Keller runs beside me as I make the crest.

"Which way?" he shouts.

I look to the left, then back to the right. The only promising cover is a stand of trees directly ahead. I point at them.

He nods then shouts, "We'd better hurry." I wonder why, but then he points, and I see British soldiers hurrying across the field and, working their way up the slope on our right and left. They are closing the net. Talk is useless so we run.

The trees are second growth, and the earth between them is full of wild hedge, vines, and brambles. I leap over a fallen log then stagger through a bush more substantial than it looks. I hear a crash behind me and whirl around. Keller has been tripped up by a vine and is stumbling to his feet. I start to call to him to hurry, but a sound stops me. Surely my ears are deceiving me. I hold my breath and listen with everything I have.

Yes, I was right. There are English voices, and they are close by in the woods. I come to a dead stop, then take a careful step and ease behind beech trees barely thick enough to hide my body. I look for Keller. He is hunkered down behind a gooseberry bush, looking at me, a question mark written across his face.

I cup one ear with a hand and nod toward the back of the woods. Keller nods; he is a quick study. I strain to hear, but the only sound is a light breeze worrying the leaves of the taller trees backed by the distant crackle of gunfire. Sweat trickles down the back of my neck and my left eye twitches. Then I hear the voices.

"Spread out. Cover this woods thoroughly."

"Whatever for? The fight's down along the road."

"Colonel Wilshire doesn't want any Germans escaping."

"Think this is the bunch that's been raising such a blood fuss?"

"Bet money on it."

"Hey, there goes one."

Sticks crack and leaves rustle. I stick my head out in an effort to see what's going on. Some poor soul is running toward the woods. He is too far away to recognize, but it is clear he is terrified. He has lost his rifle and as I watch, he pulls his helmet off and flings it away.

Rifles fire out and the man stops dead in his tracks. He is trying to determine where the shots came from. I want to scream at him, tell him to keep moving, zigzag as hard as he can back the way he came. But I can do nothing for already it is too late. Another German soldier's fate is sealed.

A shot rings out. Another. The man spins, driven by the force of the bullet. Another smashes into the center of his back. Both arms reach for the sky as he sinks to his knees. One final bullet delivers the *coup de gras*. The back of his head explodes and I look away. Death, death, death. All is death.

My stomach churns and my chest hurts. Ah, I have been holding my breath. I suck in air. A twig snaps, too close for comfort. On the back of my neck the hairs stand up. Moving by fractions of inches, I turn.

Only a few feet from Keller, a British soldier creeps forward. Keller's back is to the man and he stands no chance. The only chance is a shot, a shot that will bring down the English upon us, but what other choice is there? I do not even know if I have any bullets left. The Englishman has a knife in his hand. I lift my gun and squeeze the trigger.

Wham! The shot echoes among the trees. Keller's eyes go wide. If the English soldier makes a sound, I can't hear it. He merely looks quite surprised. Then he gazes down at the red flower blooming on his chest, a peculiar expression on this face. Then he sits down.

They are all around us—I can hear them crashing through the bushes. "Run!" I shout and take off, following my own advice, going as hard as I can, trusting my luck holds.

Keller vanishes between the trees. Maybe that is just as well. Perhaps one of us will escape to fight another battle.

The ground begins to slope downhill and in a few strides I am in a ravine. Off to my left there is much shouting followed by a volley of shots. Down in the ravine sound is distorted so that I can't tell where the shots came from. I trip, go down, then roll over and come up scrambling. The ravine bends left and I swing over a fallen tree and come face to face with an English soldier.

He's a rough looking sod, with a hooked nose and a three-day beard, and he goes at me with a damn nasty bayonet. I slip it and jam a shoulder into his chest, and, suddenly, we are both flying through the air. We smack the ground and most of the air goes out of me and I roll over on my back and try to suck in air.

He is on me. Heavier than he looks, and his muscles are like iron. Somehow the bastard has come up with a knife and the point is less than an inch from my right eye. My left hand encircles his right wrist. I am right-handed. The outcome is foreordained. Unless. Unless.

His left hand pins my right wrist. I buck like a wild horse and my right hand comes free. It still holds the revolver. I smash it against his ugly face. He moans and the knife falls away. I crawl out from under his body. My lungs gasp for air and sweat runs down my forehead and into my eyes. My heart pounds in my chest. My legs are trembly, but I force them to move, heading on down the ravine at a jog.

Trees overhang the ravine so that only a little light breaks through the canopy. Voices still penetrate, but they are distorted. The sound of the battle has grown faint. I refuse to think about the outcome, but I do wonder if Captain Goetz died cursing the enemy. He was no man for surrender, but a champion curser.

I wonder where Keller is. Now I am truly alone. It seems to me that I have not been this alone since that night in Belgium and then I was the hunter—not the hunted.

Almost imperceptibly, the ground has begun to slope upwards. More sunlight filters through the trees. I've caught a second wind and start to run faster. Some small animal—a hedgehog, I think—scurries away before me. I put my head down and run harder.

In a couple of minutes I can see the end of the ravine. Sunlight lies in a golden swath only meters away. Beyond the woods is a narrow stream, and beyond that a great open meadow where tall grasses and wildflowers bend in the wind. Muscles in my legs burn and my throat feels raw, but I press on.

The ground slopes more steeply and bends gently to the left. I jog up the slope, round the bend and enter a small flat glade at the edge of the woods. At the edge of the woods, no more than twenty meters away stands a British lieutenant, with his revolver drawn. I look left, then right. British soldiers line the glade. There must be twenty of them, every blasted one of them with a rifle.

I stop running and drop my revolver. I bend over and put my hands on my knees as I suck in air. Footsteps close in and I know how the hunted fox feels.

"Hands up, Jerry," the lieutenant says. "You've come to the end of your line."

Forty-one

Snow and Barbed-Wire

> *Bitter wind press hard*
> *out of the west,*
> *stirring the snowflakes,*
> *chilling the marrow in my bones,*
> *rattling the last leaf of the dying oak*

A black woodpecker is pounding on a decidedly ancient tree a few meters beyond the barbed wire. He has been hammering for some time. Hunting insects, I suppose. It certainly isn't the first time that particular tree has served breakfast to a woodpecker. The way the trunk is all pecked open reminds me of the way trees can look after a blast of machine gun fire smashes into them.

A gust of wind blows across the compound, and I shiver. What passes for my coat isn't thick enough to keep me warm and all winter I have been chilled. I finger the paper and pencil I have gathered. If it were not so cold, and if my mind were straight again, I would try for a poem. But this winter I am hollow, missing some essential element of life that I cannot name, a jigsaw puzzle missing a piece, a man profoundly incomplete.

Then, to my dismay, there is snow in the air, again. It has been a bad winter. No one big snow, but dozens of nasty middling ones. Cold and damp seem the operative words. Those and windswept. In all my life I have never seen such a windy period. And the wind is the dampish, pushing sort that chills a man's bones.

"Nasty sort of a day, eh?"

My muscles twitch. I hadn't heard footsteps. I turn to see a corporal I've chatted with before. His last name is Klostermann. I can never remember his first, although I recall he is from Berlin. Is his father a baker? Or is that the private with the weak chin?

"Yeah, another one."

"What day is it, anyway?"

"Who knows," I say. "Haven't seen a calendar since I got here."

"Well, it has to be March, and late March at that. Bruner has been marking the days off on a scrap of paper. You know Bruner? Short fellow over in Barracks C."

"Walks with a limp?"

"That's him."

"Know him to see him, that's all."

Klostermann rubs at the snowflake that landed on his nose. He has a long one, quite thin. Snow falls more thickly, swirling with the wind gusts. The good aspect of fresh snow is that it is clean and white and will cover the dirty snow. I shiver again. We keep the stoves in the barracks going night and day, coal when we can get it, wood or shavings, even rolled up hay when we can't. Most of the coal is of poor grade. German prisoners of war tend to be at the bottom of every pecking order.

"You're not much of a talker, are you?"

I look away from Klostermann, through the barbed wire, into the woods. Some nights I dream about escaping into those woods. In my dreams, there are always dogs chasing me. Always. Always right on my heels. If I don't dream of dogs chasing me, I dream of faces I have known. Faces of dead men. All winter I haven't had a good night's sleep.

"Not really," I say.

"Well, I'm a bit of a chatterbox. My old man used to call me that. Before the war, I mean. Chatterbox. 'Cause I used to talk all the time when I was a kid."

I give him a quick glance. His eyes have that faraway look—the one we all get.

He shrugs. "Suppose I still do talk a lot." Klostermann tilts his head and looks at me out of the corners of his eyes. "What else is a fellow supposed to do in here? Gaze at his navel all day?"

"There's not much to do," I say, looking to the woods again. Snow covers all the branches and is still falling. It is heavy, wet snow, and I have to admit there is a certain beauty to a woods in a falling snow. Snow covers up all the dead leaves, the fallen branches, the bare patches. I wonder if it is snowing in Belgium. Then I think about all my old friends, and my soldier brothers who lie in shallow graves on already forgotten battlefields in France. Such thinking does no good—it is not healthy. Prisoners of war have too much time for thinking about death—and graves—you only realize how much you have already lost forever.

I consider myself. My parents are dead. My brothers are dead, or as good as. All the men with whom I rode that first train are dead, or dead to me. Even Keller is simply a figure in my memory. For all I know he could be dead or dying. By now, he could be a prisoner, too. All this death, all this death. For what? As our British guards would say, "for bloody what?"

"You've got that look," Klostermann says, his voice jerking me back to the moment.

I let out air I didn't realize I was holding. "What look?"

"The faraway look. I know it. We all get it."

Snow falls on my eyelashes, and I blink. "I suppose we do," I say.

Klostermann nods. He looks like he wants to say something more, but he doesn't. Instead, he half turns and gazes out across the compound. Smoke rises from the chimneys, dark and dirty looking against the falling snow. A man wearing a watch cap sits on the steps outside Barracks D. Two men lean against Barracks H, seeking shelter from the wind and snow, smoking pipes—probably ones they carved themselves.

Without conscious thought, an image of the woods floats across my mind. Then I see Sanne's face and consider that perhaps I am going crazy. Before the war I read about men going insane inside prisons. I used to think they lacked discipline.

"Ever think about escaping?" I am startled by the sound of my own voice.

Klostermann's eyes spring open. He curls his neck as he gives me a strange look. He stares at my face, but does not speak. The wind pauses, and I can hear the woodpecker hammering.

"Not really," he says, after carefully considering his answer. I wonder if he thinks I have been bought. "Where would I go? I have no maps and doubt I know a dozen words of French." He coughs, turns his head, and spits in the snow. "France is a big county. I would be lost. Freeze to death, probably."

He shivers inside his coat. "You, on the other hand, know some French, don't you?"

"Yes," I say. "How did you know?"

Klostermann shrugs. "Heard it somewhere, I suppose. You know how it is in here."

I nod. He is right. There is little to do in here but talk. In such situations many men tell all they know, and maybe a bit more. I try to remember who I told that I could speak French.

"Where would you go? If you did escape, I mean?"

Suddenly I am reticent to say much about my plans. One never knows, one never knows. Still, I should answer him.

I make myself chuckle. To my ears the sound rings phony. "Hard to say. I don't have any maps either, so guess I'd try to make it back to our lines, or to Germany. Follow the sun, or a railroad line. Go cross country and stay off the roads. Too many French soldiers marching about, if you know what I mean?" That seems like a safe answer. I do not mention Belgium or Sanne. Certain matters are better kept secret.

The snow falls harder, covering the ground and the roofs of the barracks and Klostermann's watch cap and the forest and all the dead in France and Belgium and Russia and Hungary and Italy and Serbia, covering all the dead with a cold, pure, white shroud. All the dead. All the lousy dead.

Forty-two

Roust

Klostermann and I are sitting on the step that leads into the barracks drinking what passes for coffee in this place. They make it from acorns, but at least it is warm and has some flavor. Better than Swedes, at any rate. The morning is mild. Patches of snow still cover part of the ground, but the worst of winter seems to have passed.

Breakfast is just over—a hunk of day-old bread and a boiled potato—and we are about as full as we are likely to be today. Inside my mind I have drifted to that old barn in Belgium. At some deeper level, I know that it is pure foolishness, but I wonder, as I often do these days, if Sanne thinks of me. Strange things happen in war, you realize. Out of the blue, Klostermann elbows me.

"What?" I say, sounding a little put out, which I am, seeing how I was having such a nice fantasy.

Klostermann nods. "Take a look down toward the east gate. Lots of limeys and not a few Frenchies lining up."

I take a sip of my coffee and look. "So? Maybe they are getting ready for some sort of maneuvers."

"Nope," Klostermann says, "They are opening the gates. Must be some big inspection. Maybe the Red Cross has come at last."

A British officer is shouting out orders, but he is too far away for us to hear them clearly.

"Wonder what the buggers are up to?"

I shake my head. "Don't have a clue."

Klostermann sniffles. For a week he has had a cold. To tell the truth, it is a wonder we don't all have pneumonia. The winter has been long and hard—the barracks are drafty and cold and the blankets are thin and worn.

The British soldiers, with a few French sifted in, are moving from barracks to barracks. I can hear shouting and then some of our fellows are shouting back. The prisoners are pouring out of the barracks. Klostermann and I look at each other and shake our heads. Never have we seen anything quite like this.

A small squad of British soldiers advances on our barracks. The barrels of their rifles gleam in the sun. Their faces are round and they fill out their uniforms. My stomach growls as if in protest. A lousy crust of bread and one stinking boiled potato with no salt don't fill a man's stomach.

The British march smartly up to the front of our barracks. I sip coffee and watch them. Klostermann sneezes.

A lieutenant steps forward. He looks quite young and sports a mustache. He makes a sweeping gesture with one arm.

"Out of the barracks. Everyone must get out of the barracks. Now."

"Why should we?" Klostermann says in an aggrieved voice. "We just had a barracks inspection last week."

"No inspection today, Jerry. We're moving the lot of you down the road."

Before I realize what I am doing, I find myself on my feet. "Why are you doing that?"

"Spring is coming and command has plans for this area."

"Got a big offensive lined up, mate?" Klostermann wears a most serious look on his face.

"That's no concern of yours, Corporal."

I look at Klostermann. "Maybe they are having to retreat," I say.

The lieutenant takes a step forward. "That's enough. Now I suggest you and your companions get a move on before we have to use bayonets."

Klostermann gives the lieutenant a dirty look and blows his nose, loudly, into a filthy rag.

~ * ~

The day is mild, and the road is firm, and it feels good to be marching again. At least we are not burdened with rifles and iron rations. All we are carrying are our blankets and whatever few personal possessions we might have. I finger the chain around my neck. Every time I touch it, I am amazed that Sanne gave it to me, and that it has survived so long.

Without a calendar I have lost track of the days, so I cannot say whether spring has officially arrived or not, but the day certainly feels like spring. There is fresh greenness to the grass and the birds flit to and fro with speed and apparent purpose. Tiny white flowers bloom in a sunlit glade. If I squint hard enough, I can almost make myself believe that I am somewhere in Germany, say out for a hike with classmates. With the warm spring sun on the back of my neck and a mild, sweet breeze blowing across my face, it is almost possible to believe the war never happened, and never will. Life seems far too sweet to risk losing it over some foolishness in Serbia.

But then I open my eyes and see the scrawny neck of the soldier in front of me, and the glitter of the British bayonets and, between one heartbeat and the next, reality returns.

Off in the woods, a woodpecker hammers away and I recall the one who hammered so often just outside our prison camp. Why are they moving us? Do the British have some major spring offensive planned, or was my guess about a German push more on target than the British lieutenant would acknowledge?

Klostermann marches behind me and I can feel the heat of his breath on the back of my neck. "What do you think, Schiller?"

"Think about what?"

"Where they are taking us and why?"

"Who knows?" I say.

"My guess is they are taking us to some new camp further away from the fighting. You know we heard artillery just yesterday and I swear some of those guns were ours."

"Could be," I acknowledge. "Or maybe they need cheap labor somewhere."

"Yes, suppose that could be it. Someplace like a coal mine, maybe."

"Quiet in the ranks," orders a beefy British sergeant who has the face of a constipated bulldog.

I wonder why he is so aggravated over a little mumbling from a few prisoners. Our footsteps thud against the earth. A man coughs. Then I hear a different sound, a dull thud. I cock my head and listen harder. For several strides, I hear nothing except Klostermann's sniffling and low, off-key whistling from someone I can't see. Then I hear it again. Now I am sure.

Artillery so distant I can't tell if it is ours or the enemy's. A distant buzzing sound filters in, and we turn to search the sky. There, off to the west, fly two planes. Probably scouting. They bank, waggle their wings, and turn toward us.

"Into the woods," old bulldog shouts. "Into the trees."

As we start for the trees, I glance up. Yes, those are our planes, Fokker triplanes—the long rumored offensive must have begun. I throw up a hand as one of the guards pushes me along with the butt of his rifle.

They continue forcing us deeper into the trees. I guess this is because the trees do not grow so thickly here and they are looking for a heavier canopy. Even if the pilots were looking for us, I do not think they could see us. Still, it is satisfying to know that the German army is once again on the move. For well over a year, rumors have circulated that our high command was building up our reserves and planning an attack that would crack the British and French lines wide open. Rumors are only rumors; I know that. But oftentimes, embedded in a rumor is a grain of truth. Fokker motors throb overhead as Klostermann and I look at each other and grin.

~ * ~

For a day and night the shells have screamed overhead. Now and then one fell short or went long and smashed into the earth so close by that dirt clods rained down on us.

We are no longer in the trees hiding from German planes. That is, we are in a different sort of trees. You cannot call it a forest, as it is more an open field, with a few ancient oaks and soaring chestnuts scattered about like abandoned toys. Wide grassy spaces separate the trees, and during the day we saw a farmer plowing his field no more than half a kilometer to the south. We may still be in France, although I would not be surprised to learn that during our wanderings we have crossed over the Belgian border.

From the snatches of conversation I have overheard, the plan was to take us in another direction, more north and east, closer to Paris. However, from what I can glean, the German offensive has moved forward with such success that it cut the road they had planned for us to take. For three days we have wandered much like God's chosen people in the Bible, only in France, or perhaps Belgium, rather than the wilderness.

Klostermann and I, along with a dozen or more of our fellow prisoners, are hunkered down in a swale watching shells fly overhead through gaps in a twisty green hedge. Those that still have cigarettes smoke them. The rest of us have to be content with the aroma of burning tobacco. Thinking about smoking is better than thinking about our rumbling stomachs. Our offensive has thrown our captors' plans completely out of kilter. When we ran out of even tinned food yesterday afternoon it became clear they had expected to have us in a new camp much sooner. Even the guards have had nothing to eat since breakfast.

A shell screams and, like one giant head, we all turn toward the sound. The shell is coming in very high and it is clear the trajectory is off. It is going to fall short. All day long the shells have been passing overhead. This one is not going to make it. Already it has reached the apex of its flight and is turning its nose toward the earth. It screams as it begins its descent. We all cover our heads and press our faces to mother earth. If we knew which way to run, we would all be running.

One always wonders about incoming artillery. There is a degree of truth in the old saying that if you stay in the front lines long enough, one day there will be a shell with your name on it. I wonder if this one carries mine.

The air is filled with the scream of the shell and my bowels tighten and my legs twitch. Most assuredly, I do not want to die this day. Not that most men have a choice. Well, I suppose we do, but *mein Gott*, that is a hard one.

Somebody chokes back a sob and another prays aloud. The shell screams louder.

Suddenly the ground moves beneath us and then I am flying backwards. My right arm stings. I hear another scream and then a great blast of hot wind drives me to the earth. Pain explodes inside my head and the world goes black.

Forty-three

A Cold North Wind

Light comes first, then a throbbing pain at the base of my brain. Something heavy lies across my legs. I blink and my eyes come open. I am staring into Klostermann's ugly face.

"Ah, Sleeping Beauty has awakened at last."

I am lying flat on my back staring up at his nostrils. The sight is nauseating. I decide to sit up.

However, my body does not want to cooperate. My head spins and my brain aches and there is something heavy on my legs. A thousand black pinpricks swim before my eyes and I close them. I can still hear Klostermann talking, but his words are muffled as though I am hearing them through cotton. My face feels unusually warm and pain shoots up and down my right arm. I hear men moaning and then one cries out for his mother. I shake my head and force my eyes back open.

A man is lying across my legs. He is dead. I can tell because the right side of his face has gone missing in action. My stomach heaves and if I had eaten any lunch, I would have lost it. Grunting, I roll the fellow off my legs, then pull a splinter from my right arm.

We are sprawled at odd angles, in and out of the swale. A couple of the fellows are moving, but most are very still. Klostermann is sitting up, blinking like a besotted owl, a confused look on his face. A fellow I know only as Jocko holds his left arm with his right hand. The left arm dangles like a strand of soggy pasta. Another fellow, whose name may be Schultz, lies on his back. Blood trickles from one corner of his mouth. Just yesterday he told me he had a young son named Wilhelm. According to the bleeding man, Wilhelm was the champion speller of his entire school.

Another shell screams overhead and smashes to earth only fifty meters behind us. Someone is getting the range.

"Up, up, everybody up at once." The guards are moving among us, poking bodies and prodding the slow movers. "This is not a safe place. We must move, and now." Two or three of the English are bleeding. That is one thing about artillery. Shells do not discriminate.

Old Bulldog has survived the bombardment. I am not sure if I am pleased or disappointed. He is a real ass, but such a perfect type that I'm not sure I want him to be killed; however, I would love to see his face smashed a bit.

"All righty, you good little German boys," he growls, "time to get a move on. Your outfit is back to operating under the delusion that they still have a chance in this war. But this is their last shot. After they run out of steam and fresh troops, we'll roll them back to Berlin."

He nudges an unconscious man with the toe of his boot. "But you chaps won't have to worry; you'll be some place safe, behind barbed wire." He and a greasy haired corporal think that is so funny they bray with laughter, reminding me of jackasses.

"Come on now," he says, looking directly at me. "Everybody who can, get up. Then go help those who can't. We've got to get a move on. Mother Horton's boy has no intention of getting smashed by German artillery for the likes of you." As if to punctuate his last remark, another of our shells smashes into the ground no more than thirty meters in front of the little slope. I don't like the bastard, but this time he is right. I look at Klostermann, and he rolls his eyes, but I jerk my head and we struggle to our feet.

We know the need to move and I think we would hurry if it weren't for the wounded. No man wants to die unnecessarily. Wouldn't that be a lovely headline in the local paper—prisoner of war killed by own artillery.

We slice across a meadow with cattle huddled in one corner and white flowers blooming profusely. Larks fly up at our feet and something small, furry, and brown scuttles off through the tall grass. We step through a gap in another hedge, then stumble across a beet field before we hit another road. This one is narrower than the previous one, and I see a fistful of their officers standing around peering at a map. I'd give a lot for a quick glance.

Clouds are forming in the west and the wind has begun to worry our rags. I ease closer to Klostermann.

"Seem cooler to you?"

"A bit," he says. His eyes still look funny. I expect he is concussed. "Certainly the wind has a bite."

"Yes," I say, "and take a look at those clouds. Foul weather may be blowing in."

He groans. "Great, just what we need. First we get the living hell shelled out of us by our own artillery and then we get a good soaking."

"At least the damn British will get wet, too."

"*Ja*, that's something, I suppose."

Shadows dance across the ground and last year's leaves are blown before us like lost dreams and sent spinning down the road. We can still hear the artillery, but it is a distant sound, reminiscent of fading summer thunder.

The fellow in front of Klostermann turns around and makes a face. He is missing a couple of teeth. "Am I imagining things, or is it getting colder?"

"Getting colder," Klostermann says, "And doing it quickly, too."

The fellow turns his nose up and sniffs at the wind like a dog. "I smell rain coming." He taps his schnoz. "Never wrong. This beauty can smell water a kilometer off."

Wind whips at our hair and there is such a chill in that wind I long for my old overcoat. I wonder where I've lost it, as though that would make an iota of difference.

A British guard hustles by, looking more like a piece of string in a uniform than one of the king's own. "Hurry along now, you chaps." He jabs a bony finger at the western sky. "Lieutenant says a storm is blowing in. If we don't get a move on, we'll all get a good soaking. And I, for one, don't fancy that."

Suddenly a grin splits his face. "Still, I suppose a proper dousing will put an end to this offensive of yours, what?"

Klostermann gives him the evil eye, but the Englishman chuckles and moves on down the long line of bedraggled men, pushing here, prodding there, urging them on. I wonder if the British are worried about the oncoming storm or if our offensive is going better than they are letting on. Hope surges through me and I spend a pleasant moment imagining taking Old Bulldog prisoner. Wouldn't I make him jump over some fences?

We have left the farms and the road winds between a thick stand of oaks, beeches, and poplars. Their new leaves rustle and smaller branches bend before the wind. There's a nasty bite to that wind and a feeling of moisture in the air. Clouds fly across the sky and, as the sun ducks in behind a large dark one, the day goes instantly dim. I've caught a chill and start shivering.

"Damn, that wind's cutting me in two," Klostermann moans. For the first time, he looks frail to me. His uniform hangs on him like sacking, and I realize mine must, too.

"Yes," I say, "and there's a dampness to the air."

"With our luck, it will probably snow."

"Don't say that, even in jest." The winter has been long and spring is a sweet taste on the tongue. To snatch it away seems cruel beyond measure.

"Quiet in the ranks."

"Aw, stuff it," someone mumbles.

I don't say anything. By the minute, clouds grow darker and thicker. I sniff the air. Yes, there is moisture there. Somewhere off to the left, rifle fire breaks out. Trees on that side of the road block any hope of seeing what is going on beyond them. The road narrows further as it twists deeper into the woods and branches hang over the road until it is like walking under a canopy.

We come up on bodies lying in the shallow ditch that runs alongside the road. These men did not die yesterday. Birds and wild animals have been at their flesh and their uniforms have begun to rot away. Based on the swatches of blue flannel that still cling to their bones, I would guess them Frenchmen.

From some dark recess of my brain, the memory of that young Belgian soldier dying on that bridge as we crossed the border flashes like a meteor across my mind. He was achingly young. At the moment of his death I felt exhilaration, pride even. Now the only feeling I have toward him is regret, regret tinged with sadness.

But then I am filled with regret, regret for all the men I have killed and for all those I knew and loved who died so far from home in a strange land. They will never go home again, and those of us who do—assuming I make it—will never be the same again. War is nothing more, or less, than the greatest thief.

But who is to say who will survive? Perhaps none of us will. More rifle fire—off to the right this time. Beyond the trees, but not far beyond. This may be the end of the line for many. I shrug. What can I do about it?

Something cold and wet strikes the back of my neck and I lift my face. Rain falls, driven by the wind and mixing with something colder and harder. It stings. All around me men are cursing and hunching their shoulders, or tugging a hat down, or pulling a ragged sweater over the top of their heads. Even our guards look miserable.

A shell smashes into the woods on the far side of the road and trees fly apart. Splinters rain down upon us, and near the front of the line a man screams. A splinter has found his eye.

Another shell crashes into the middle of the road and we all run for the trees. Rain slashes against our faces. Every second it seems to rain harder. We run against a moving curtain of rain. Ice pellets are imbedded in the rain and they sting like frozen wasps.

"Damn!" Klostermann shouts above the deluge. "Are those raindrops or bullets?"

I don't answer because I am running too hard to have enough air to do more than pant. Shells fall about us without mercy. Between the rain and the wind and screams of wounded men, I cannot tell whose they are. French, English, German, it does not matter. Somebody has found the range.

Screams fill the air. Five meters away, a man groans, then falls face down at the edge of the road, blood gushing from his throat. Shrapnel has sliced his throat open the way a butcher cuts a hog's throat.

We are in the trees and branches slash at our faces. Klostermann shouts something, but I cannot understand his words. The earth trembles as another shell strikes the ditchline. A guard pitches face forward, a jagged piece of iron driven deep in his back. Rain smashes against our faces and the wind howls. Another shell hits the top of nearby trees and branches fly apart.

Now it is truly every man for himself. Guards and prisoners fall left and right. No one is watching us. The chance for escape has finally come. I look around for Klostermann, but I cannot see him.

Four of us run close together, three prisoners and Old Bulldog. For once he is not looking at me. Klostermann is nowhere to be seen and I can only hope he is safe among the trees. He is my last friend, and I would not like to lose him.

Machine gun fire breaks outs close by. Whoever is manning the gun is systematically firing up and down the line of trees. Do they not know they are surely killing some of their own men? A high shrieking whistle pierces the air and a projectile whirls toward us. I throw myself at the ground. Old Bulldog does the same. One of the other guards starts running, but the force of the shell catches him and spins him like a top. The last I see of him, his eyes are bulging out of his head and his lips have been sucked off by the vacuum created by the flying projectile. A fourth man has simply vanished.

I brush the dirt off my face as I sit up. The Bulldog is doing the same. For a second, our eyes lock. I try to read him, but it is like looking at polished brown stones. He could be feeling anger, hatred, or fear for all I know. I wonder what my eyes reveal.

Then we are both pushing up. As though by mutual agreement, we start running again, moving in the same direction. We come to an opening in the trees where a storm must have passed through years ago. There are no trees and the green spring grass looks soft and inviting. Another time.

We run hard across the open ground and leap across a slender brook masked by a row of cedars, panting for breath and ducking automatically when bullets whine by. I can see the last of the trees. There is a field beyond them and then another grove of trees. Machine gun bullets clip the branches like gardening shears. I glance over at the Bulldog and he gives me a hard look.

As I watch, his mouth goes open wide, and his eyes close as he collapses to the earth. His rifle flies out of his hands and lands a few meters away. A bullet rips through my jacket and then one burns along my forearm and I fling myself behind a beech tree so old it has gone hollow at the bottom. Blood runs down my forearm and I rip off a hunk of my shirt and wrap it tightly around the wound, which stings like nettles, but I do not think it is all that bad.

After a moment, the bullets move on and I crawl on my belly over to the Englishman. Rain pelts the back of my neck and baptizes me with its icy sanctity. Actually, the rain feels more like sleet and only the trees keep the wind from chilling me to the bone.

The Bulldog has been hit in the leg, below the knee. I examine the wound and see the bullet has seared through his calf muscle. The bleeding is steady, but it doesn't look as though an artery has been clipped. He moans low when I touch his leg.

His pack has fallen by his side, and I rummage through it. The lucky bastard actually has a packet of clean bandages. I don't know why I do it—I should let the arse bleed to death—but I wrap a tourniquet above the bleeding and cover the wound as best I can. If his men find him in the next few hours, he should live.

His eyes are open and he watches me like a wounded hawk. Does he think I would waste time bandaging him if I planned to slit his throat?

He coughs, grunts, and raises his head. "Figured you for tougher."

"What do you mean?" I jerk on the tourniquet, and he winces.

"I mean the second I got hit I said to myself, Jerry is going to do me."

"Do you with what? You know damn well I don't have a gun, or even a knife."

He screws his eyes shut and makes a face like he's just bitten into a rotten cucumber. He swallows the pain and gives me the evil eye. "You're a right bastard, you are. I've been watching you special 'cause I bet you've killed hundreds. Be no trouble for you to smash my brains out with a tree limb or a rock. Come right down to it, you'd choke the life out of me with your bare hands."

"Don't tempt me," I say. "You've been an arsehole since the first and I know more than one German soldier who's felt the butt of your rifle in their ribs."

He turns his head and spits. Guess he's showing me what he thinks of my little speech. Still, the bastard looks me right in the eye and doesn't give an inch. If I did try to kill him, he'd fight to his last breath.

"It's your lucky day, you bastard. I'm through with this war. There's been enough killing. And for what? For nothing, except the killing." I tie the final knot in the tourniquet and pull it tight. He sucks in air and his face goes pale, but the tightness is necessary. Does the fool want to bleed to death?

He shows me his teeth. As grins go, it's more of a grimace. Plus, his teeth are lousy. Most of them have a greenish cast and the ones that don't are blackened. I wonder when he last brushed his teeth.

He closes his eyes then opens them very wide. One hand slides down inside his coat and when it comes back out it is holding a nasty little pistol. The pistol looks like one a woman would carry in her handbag, but from two feet it will blow my brains out.

"Don't think we're quite done with the killing yet, Jerry. At least if you try anything." One eye blinks, or winks. I can't be sure which.

I let my head fall back and stare up at the mottled gray sky. Snowflakes are falling now, big and fat and white, feathering earthwards. Old Bulldog reminds me of something, or someone. The image hangs on the edge of my brain, hovering just below the surface. A snowflake drifts down and settles directly in the middle of my forehead. The image breaks through.

"You remind me of someone I read about when I was a boy," I say.

"Who?" he grunts.

"Ever read Robert Louis Stevenson?"

"What's he got to do with a bleeding thing?"

"He wrote a book called *Treasure Island.* Have you read it?"

The pistol wavers. The pain has to be fierce and he's lost a good deal of blood. "What if I have? That changes nothing. You're still my prisoner."

"One of the characters was an old pirate named Long John Silver. You remind me of him."

"Me, a pirate. You've lost your mind, mate. I'm one of the king's own, not some bloody pirate"

"Oh, I don't know. I feel a little like Doctor Livesey. He was always doctoring the pirates, knowing at any minute his life might be hanging by a thread." I give the Old Bulldog a big grin. "And now you know what I'm going to do?"

"No telling. You Jerries are all tricky bastards."

"I'm going to stand up and walk away, just like the good doctor in *Treasure Island.*"

"You try it and I'll shoot you right in the back." His eyes have narrowed to slits. Waves of pain wash across his face. I do admire him. In his own way, he is quite brave. Maybe in a different world, or at least a different time, I'd like him.

"No, you won't. As I said, there's been enough killing for this day. Besides, I've just saved your lousy life. The English are supposed to have a great sense of fair play, so it wouldn't be cricket if you shot me after I've saved your life. Now would it?"

Somehow, he summons the strength to raise up a bit. The gun wobbles then settles so that the round black hole is looking me right between the eyes. At this distance, Stevenson's blind beggar, Pew, couldn't miss. Suddenly I am very conscious of my heart beating, the tick in his left eye, and the falling snow. I consider making a grab for the gun but in the end, it just seems like too much trouble. If he wants to kill me so badly, he'll probably find a way. With an almost clinical air, I watch his finger tighten on the trigger. I suppose I could close my eyes, but I don't believe I will.

"Arrr," he groans and lowers the pistol. His hand is shaking. So are mine.

"Wish I could give you something for the pain, but I'm afraid I'm fresh out of medicines."

He lets his eyes close. They stay closed for a long time. Just as I am ready to get up, he says, "There's a bottle in my pack, if it isn't broken."

"Let's check." The pack is only a few feet away and I crawl over and drag it back, then rummage through the contents—mostly clothes, with a few rations and, to my surprise, a New Testament mixed in.

"My mum gave me that," he says as I hold it up.

"I was wondering. Ah, here's the bottle."

It is down in the bottom of the pack and it isn't broken. He's been at it, but there is still a half bottle of the good stuff. Real pain killer, Adolph would have said. I give a hell of a lot to share a glass with him now. But that's only a fool's daydream.

Old Bulldog grunts and I come back into the moment. "You ready for a little painkiller, old chap? Isn't that what you British say?"

"Among other things, you bloody German. Quit your blabbering and pass me the bottle. Somebody got me good this time."

"Yes, I'd say you've bought your ticket home. London?"

"No, Brighton."

I hand him the bottle and take a longer look at his leg. "You'll be out nine months or so, at a minimum, I'd say."

"Just like a bloody pregnancy, eh? Only I'm not having any baby." He twists the cap of the bottle and turns it up. I watch his throat work.

"Ah, that's the ticket. Good stuff. Burns all the way down me old gullet." He cocks his head and blinks his eyes at me. They are watering. For the sake of form, we'll blame it on the whiskey and not the pain.

"That nine months you were talking about..."

"Yes."

"Well, way I see it that means the end of the war for old Ted Horton." He gives me a crooked grin.

"What do you mean?"

"By then the war will be over, see. You birds are on your last legs now. Don't see how you last out the year."

"Our offensive is making strong advances. We are on the verge of a breakout, a big one. Paris is almost within our grasp."

"You're delusional, mate. Sure, for a few days your blokes were going great guns, but they've run out of steam and into a brick wall, namely our trenches and some French reserves Foch brought up. You might as well take it easy and surrender."

A wave of pain washes through him and I watch it slide across his face. He goes very still and the veins in his neck stand out as he works his way through it. Then it passes, and he breathes shallowly for a bit, the way a dog will when it's been running on a hot day.

"Tell you what, mate," he says, then pauses to nip at the bottle. "You help me get back to my outfit and I'll see that you live out the war in some quiet little camp. Not a lot of glory there, but you survive. Something to be said for that, eh?"

I look off across the field before me. Already the grass is lightly covered by the falling snow. A stand of pines grows tight along a fence row and the branches bend before the wind. I cannot see a single German soldier. Germany seems a long way off and, sad as it is, I doubt I will ever see my homeland again.

"Yes, there's something in what you say." I turn and look him in the eyes. His are hard and cold and remind me of marbles I had when I was a boy. "Only, I'm not interested, for a number of reasons. First of all, I'm a loyal German soldier, and there is no way I am going to surrender to a man who can't even stand and doesn't have a weapon. Second, I don't believe what you said about our advance. And third, I've got me a notion to see someone."

"And who might that be?"

"Just someone I knew briefly. Back in the early days."

"Of the war?"

"Yes."

"This friend back in Germany?"

"No, Belgium."

"Ah, ha. I see. You blokes really overran that little country, didn't you?"

"We needed the access. Going through Belgium was the only way for our offensive to succeed."

He laughs. "Right-o, the vaunted Von Schlieffen Plan. And how did that work out for you?"

"It was very nearly a success."

"Close only counts with hand grenades and on the dance floor, mate. And, anyway, that is no ruddy excuse for invading another country."

A chill runs through me. But it is anger, the cold kind, the deadly kind. I am suddenly very tired of the war in general and this mouthy British sergeant in particular. There is a comfortable feel to the weight of the rifle in my hands."

"You know I could kill you?"

He shrugs and plasters a grin on his ugly face. "Why don't you go ahead? At least that would put me out of my misery."

I can feel the trembling deep in my muscles and my arms swing the rifle up without any conscious thought. I close one eye and his face swims into focus. No one would know, I tell myself, no one would ever know.

Only of course, someone would. And I wouldn't care to live with that someone for the rest of my life. Despite the chilling wind, sweat covers my face. Nerves in my cheek jump and my right leg is all trembly.

"You're not worth wasting a bullet on," I say.

The Bulldog considers that for a moment and then he laughs out loud. "Guess you're right there, old chap." Voices come to us on the wind. They are shouting and there is some shooting mixed in. The voices are calling out in English. The wind plays tricks with the voices so that I can't tell where they are coming from. Then the wind falls away to a whisper and I realize the voices are coming from the road only a few dozen meters behind us.

The Bulldog looks me in the eye. "If you want to see that friend, you'd best be moving. That sounds like some of my bunch coming in behind us." He winches at a surge of pain. "Don't worry, you've done me a good turn and I won't spoil your chances."

We stare at each other through the falling snow. I wonder what he is thinking. Then the artillery starts up again, and I turn.

"Wait," he calls out. I turn around.

"Here," he says and holds out the bottle. "Better take this with you. Promises to be a long day and a cold night."

"But your leg..."

"No worries, my bunch will be along shortly and doctor me up."

I take the bottle from him. "Thanks."

"Don't mention it. There's also a couple of tins of beef and a loaf of bread in my kit bag. Just take it. I'll have plenty more when my companions come up."

I turn and rummage through his things. I take the tins and the bread and also a sweater. Spring suddenly seems more like winter. His rifle is beside his pack and I pick it up, too.

I turn back and study his face. Pain is writing its story across his ugly face. "Thanks," I say. He grimaces and nods. I turn to go.

"Hey," he calls out in a softer voice as though he is afraid of being overheard. "What's your name, mate?"

I glance back over my shoulder. "Why do you want to know that?"

He shrugs. "Let's just say I want to know the name of the man who saved my life. Like I said, mine's Ted Horton, First Sergeant Ted Horton of the Forty-third Yorkshires."

"Schiller," I say. "First Sergeant Karl Schiller of the Twenty-sixth Pioneers."

He nods. "Luck," he says and eases back to one elbow as the pain grabs him.

"Luck," I say, and then I am turning and running. Running through the falling snow. Running to Belgium. Running out of this lousy war.

Forty-four

One Very Long Walk

Raging fever
has soaked my skin
with sweat
and turned the words in my mind
to ice

I am not sure—has it been two days or three since I left the English bulldog? He'd told me his name, but I'm damned if I can remember it right now. That's what comes of combining almost no sleep with a fever. Can't say exactly when or where I'd come down with the fever; without notice, it was simply there. There as if it had been inside me all along and had taken advantage of an opportunity to float to the surface. All I knew for certain was that my brain felt like it was burning. My body wasn't so sure; one minute it was soaked in sweat and the next it was shivering with chills.

I try to count back, going by the nights. One night I slept out in the woods. I can clearly remember piling dead leaves over me. I remember thinking that if I did die during the night whoever found me wouldn't have to worry much about a shroud. Just scoop up a few more handfuls of leaves and scatter them over my corpse.

But what about the other night, or nights? At the fuzzy edges of my fevered brain it seems I slept in some sort of a shed one night. Not a barn and not a tool shed either, but rather a chicken coop, or an old stable where some farmer had kept a horse. Or had that been last year when we were trying to swing around the French flank? And had there been a night on a river bank? I seem to recall running water.

But then, does it matter whether it has been two or three days? I have been moving and that is good. What isn't so good, though, is that for a day and a half I have been lost. Ever since the fever got a good foothold, I've been walking around not knowing where I was, or where I was headed, or even what direction I was moving in.

All I know now is that I am tired, very tired. For what seems like hours, I have working my way up a slope through a forest of birches and I lean against one. The leaves are still small and new and I know it is spring. Still, I keep remembering falling snow and a cold driving wind.

The face of the Englishman who gave me his whiskey and bread is clear, but not much else. Where did our paths cross? Why have we separated? Nothing is clear at the moment. Lucidity comes only when the fever eases. Then I at least know who I am and where I am going.

I push off the tree I am leaning against and slog on up the slope. Not that I am at all sure what I'll see when I make it to the crest. Or even why I want to make it. The thing is to keep moving. One foot in front of the other. Up the slope. Up the slope.

~ * ~

I awaken with my head as clear as a glass tube. And as hollow. I sit up, with no idea of where I am, trying to get some grasp on reality. I look around, searching for clues. Reality seems to be a slick, squishy thing at the moment.

I cannot see the sky, only a roof of sorts. Only it's not of wood or straw, but of earth. On three sides it is cool and damp and dark.

Water drips and there are sounds of small animals scurrying. On the fourth side there is light. I crawl toward the light.

At the edge of the darkness, the earth falls away and I am gazing down a long slope. By pure chance, I must have stumbled on sort of a cave during the night and simply passed out. God, or my patron saint, must have been looking out for me. Or what is that saying about only the good die young?

The cave must be just below the crest of a hill. How I got here I do not know. Below is a valley with a stream running through it. Sunlight glitters off the surface of the water so that it hurts my eyes to look at it. The far side of the water is thick with trees and beyond the trees is a village. Roofs rise above the canopy and the spire of a church pokes at the clouds.

I have no idea of the time, but the air has the feel of early morning. My stomach rumbles and I realize I am hungry. I try to recall when I last ate, but that is a wasted effort. The fever had me in too tight a grip, I suppose. Only now, at least for a few minutes, it has lifted, and I know I must make good use of its absence. I push myself to my feet.

My legs are wobbly and my head wants to spin. If I focus very intently on a particular tree or rock, I am okay, but that makes maneuvering down the slope an interesting proposition. Still, I have seen many men who were wounded far worse than I am walk several hundred meters to an aid station. It is all a matter of keeping my eyes focused and placing my feet carefully. Part of my brain wonders where I am and whether the village below is French or Belgian.

But that doesn't matter. What matters is that I get some food. I may have to beg, or steal if need be, but I have to eat. Without nourishment, I cannot go much further. I run my fingers through my pockets, searching for coins. All I find is lint, one smooth round rock, and three or four bullets. As I have lost my rifle somewhere along the way, they are useless. Fingering Sanne's cross that hangs around my neck, I move down the slope, going slow, holding on to trees when the dizziness strikes.

~ * ~

The houses are scattered about as if they were toys of some giant who carelessly tossed them aside one afternoon when he tired of the game. Behind me, the little stream gurgles as I stand just inside the trees that line its bank. I am doing a bit of scouting. As long as the fever holds, I'm able to think a bit and one thing that is very clear is that I need to find different clothes. My uniform is dirty and ragged, but still it screams German soldier.

From where I stand, I can see the back of a few houses and several outbuildings, but not what I'm looking for. What I need, and rather quickly, is to find a clothesline with washing hanging on it. Ah, what I'd give for a good clean shirt and pants. A railway conductor's uniform would do, as would a milkman coat or a professor's suit. But there is nothing behind any of the houses I can see, so I step back into the trees and begin to work my way around to the south.

Several varieties of trees grow along the bank and there are often several meters between them. It is as though these trees are like people, in that they don't want to associate too closely with anyone unlike them.

In a way, that works well for me, as I can move through the trees quickly and can see enough to have a good idea of what is in front of me. The other side of that coin is that if I can see out easily, then someone looking at the woods from the road would have little trouble catching a glimpse of me. Still, I don't see what I can do except keep moving and trusting to luck.

I move from cedar to birch to oak to a thicket of willows. Beyond the willows the land begins to slope upwards and I bend low and go up the slope. Near the crest I go down on my stomach, then scoot forward. From the crest the view is excellent.

I am looking through wild grasses that bend in the breeze, while low growing bushes shield me from view of the houses on my left, and there is a mound of earth directly before me that would keep anyone except a very nosy person from seeing me. I am somewhat exposed on the right side, but all that is over there is a section of railroad track. I'll hear the train coming in plenty of time.

A road winds before me, going up and down the slopes of the land. On the other side of the road is what looks like a tavern. To the right appears to be an automobile repair shop. To the left is a three story building that might be a hotel.

The tavern won't do me much good, although maybe the occupants would be so drunk, they wouldn't notice my uniform. The auto repair shop offers possibilities. Mechanics usually wear uniforms, and if I could find an extra one lying about...

The building on the left might also be of value. Often hotels provide laundry services and I might well find a few shirts and trousers hanging on a line behind the building. Even a shirt would be a help. My uniform trousers don't stand out as much as my shirt.

As I watch, three men come out of the auto repair shop. One of them wears a suit; the other two wear just the sort of coveralls I need. The three men are talking. I can hear their voices, but too faintly to make out any words. Now they laugh and the man in the suit slaps one of the other chaps on the back. They start talking again and, as I watch, the fellow in the suit hands some money to the shorter of the mechanics, turns, and crosses a patch of gravel to where an automobile stands. I do not recognize the design. He opens the door and slides in behind the wheel while the mechanics head back inside the garage.

I am already moving, curling back down the slope and then going right along the curve of the land. After thirty, maybe forty meters, the trees thin, then give way to a field grown up in brambles and weeds. On the far side of the field are the railroad tracks.

The railroad bed is built up so there is a shallow ditch a few meters below the tracks. Crouching low, I go down the ditch as quickly as I can. Weeds tower above me, and I do not think anyone can see me. However, there is no use taking chances.

In any case, I'm not feeling lucky, for the fever is starting to rise again, and my muscles ache. My strength is waning and my steps feel awkward. A rabbit bounds up before me and I swear softly under my breath while my heart slows back to normal.

Now I am at the edge of the field. I have guessed well and have come out only approximately twenty-five meters south of the garage, which I can see clearly. The garage bay is open and I can hear voices, but I can't see the mechanics. In the center of the building there is a large glass window and my guess is that behind it is some sort of an office, or at least a room where people can place orders or pay for work that has been performed. Sunlight glares off the glass so I cannot see inside. Nothing left but to make my move. I cannot wait for darkness. Food and drink are what I need, and quickly, before the fever returns in full.

I rise, step out of a stand of horseweed, then trot across the road. Two automobiles stand between me and the garage. I assume they await repair, which is good for me, as they afford excellent cover. I duck behind one and hustle across the vacant lot, curling behind the garage.

Voices come clearly to me. Two men are talking about a bent wheel. A third voice chimes in. This man talks with a strong Parisian accent and concern runs through the voice. He is asking about prices. A cloud moves across the sky and its shadows bless me. A short distance away, a woman is singing in a clear, sweet voice. How long has it been since I have heard a woman sing?

Behind the garage, discarded metal and rusting automobile bodies are scattered about like forgotten toys. Scraps of paper blow about, and dirty rags flap from a sagging strand of rope. Smoke drifts skyward from a smoldering pit. Puddles of oil and pools of grease dot the ground. A few scraggly trees grow along what I assume is the property line. Dodging puddles, I cut across the ground and slip into the shade of the trees.

From there, I can see into the garage through the single dusty window set about midway along the back wall. A man is standing with his back to me. I can see his arms moving about and then I can only see his shadow on the wall. Then the shadow disappears.

The voices are clearer, but more distant, and I figure the men have moved outside. I glance around, then head for the back of the building, going in a low crouch, moving as quickly, yet quietly, as I can.

"The price is too high," I hear the man with the accent say. "I won't pay it."

"Suit yourself," says another voice, "only have someone haul your wreck of a machine away."

I stop and peer in through the window. It is hard to see much through all the dust. I remember an old joke my father used to tell, something about the dust that came over the Alps with Hannibal's elephants. One spot is a little cleaner and I shift my head and press one eye to the glass.

Ah, just what I am looking for—a mechanic's suit hanging on a nail directly above the insides of what looks like a truck motor. If I can only liberate it. My eyes search for a back door, but all I see are solid walls. My stomach growls and I would damn near sell my soul for a cool drink of water. I start working my way along the wall, moving toward the front of the building.

I cannot hear the voices, only a bird screeching from the top of a plane tree. More clouds are rolling in and the light keeps changing. I ease one eye around the corner of the building.

Two men are walking down the road. They are talking back and forth and their voices come to me faint and blurry. One of them looks like a businessman; the other could easily be a mechanic. I am sure I heard three voices. Where is the third man? I stretch my neck and peer down the front of the garage.

Tools I can see, and spare parts, and a lunch bucket, even an empty wine bottle, but no third man. Maybe he left a moment before the others. No, the garage bay door still stands open. I take one step. Two.

There it is—the mechanic's suit—only a few meters away. Where is that third man? I count to twenty, slowly, then listen as hard as I can. All I can hear is the faint hum of a truck motor in the distance and a fly buzzing about my head. Maybe the man has gone out back to take a smoke or answer the call of nature. I throw the dice.

Halfway there, I hear a sniff and press my back against the wall, wedging my body between inner tubes and wrenches. I reach for a wrench.

A foot scrapes across the floor. Then a shadow falls on the floor and I can smell tobacco burning. Seconds later, a man walks by me. A cigarette dangles from his mouth. He is looking at a page of newspaper. The wrench is heavy in my hand. Voices of children float on the air, happy voices, with undertones of laughter.

Somewhere on the edges of my mind, I sense that I should simply let the man be. Wait until he has left the room, then move on. But the fever is starting to build, and I am so hungry I cannot hold the wrench still. So there is no future in waiting. There are times when you simply have to rush the barricade, and this is one of them.

I take one step. Then another. I hold my breath. Despite my best efforts to move silently, one toe scrapes on the floor, and the man starts to turn. I swing the heavy wrench in a wide descending arc, smashing it against the crown of his head. The sound is that of a melon cracking open. His eyes roll toward the top of his head and his knees buckle. I catch him as he starts to fall.

His body is heavy, floppy, as if he were a sack of wheat. I am weak, as though I have undergone a long illness, and it takes all my strength to drag him behind a mound of tires. He groans, but I ignore the sound. I can only trust that no one else can hear. If they do, it is all up for me.

I step back around the tires and walk as quietly as I can to the opening of the garage. I risk a quick peek. I see no one, turn and head for the mechanic's coveralls, moving quickly, not worrying about the sound of my footfalls

I lift the coveralls off the nail, hoping they are not too small. Luck smiles on me, and the coveralls slip on easily over my dirty uniform. They aren't much cleaner than my uniform, but they are far less ragged. I button them up and start for the front of the garage

"Monsieur, what is wrong with this man?"

The voice startles me so that my entire body twitches. My throat goes instantly tight. I force my body to turn slowly.

Across the garage bay, a young boy looks at me. He appears to be about nine or ten years old, with a thin face and black hair that needs a good washing. He is staring at the man I knocked out with the wrench. I try to speak, but my voice doesn't seem to want to work.

I swallow and dab at the sheen of sweat that covers my forehead.

"What?" I say, hoping my French is passable.

"Why is this man asleep? He usually works on the motors."

"Ah, he is feeling poorly. I think he has a fever. Come away from him. He needs his sleep. Come on now, I need to close the shop."

A lock of hair has fallen across the boy's face, and he brushes it away with a hand. His eyes are fixed on my face.

"Who are you? I have not seen you before."

"My name is Aubier. I am the new mechanic."

"Ah, I see. My name is Pierre." He smiles at me. All I want to do is lie down on a soft bed and close my eyes, but I make myself smile at the boy. My legs are wobbly, so I lean against the workbench. As the boy walks by, I pat him on the head.

I watch the small fellow until he rounds a curve in the road and disappears. My brain feels hot and sweat is breaking out across my forehead. I summon up what strength remains and cross the garage floor.

The man has turned on his side and his breathing sounds better. I find it distasteful, but I push my hands into his pockets. One contains a pipe and a key that looks as though it would fit the lock on a door. The other contains a handful of coins. I take them all.

Spoils of war, I tell myself. And the Bible tells that the Romans hung a thief on the cross next to Jesus. Besides, I have killed many men. What can breaking one more commandment hurt?

Forty-five

In The Witchy Woods

Darkness is coming.

Darkness is coming, and I am deep in a woods I do not know.

Here the trees grow very close together and vines hang like snakes from the limbs. Even at noon, little sun would reach the forest floor. Although I do not think the hour is late, the air has gone purple, shot through with charcoal, and it is challenging to stay on the path, if it is even a path I am following.

Perhaps it is nothing more than a trail made by wild animals. It was the most promising I could find when I had to get off the road. An entire French division must have been moving down the road I was traveling. Although I was still in my mechanic's coveralls, I did not want to take a chance. Armies have been known to temporarily impress civilians into service, and my lack of skill as a mechanic would be readily apparent, my German soldier's uniform beneath the coveralls impossible to explain. So I tucked my loaf of bread under one arm, stepped off the road and started plodding up the trail like I was a French mechanic headed home. As the afternoon wore on, the trail narrowed until it is only inches wide.

I am walking through a stand of fir trees and the wind, which has come up in the last hour, sighs among the top branches. A coolness infuses the wind, and I feel certain I will soon wish for a coat.

The toe of one foot snags on an unseen vine, and I stumble forward, almost falling, only catching myself at the last moment by grabbing a sapling. The fever is back and, in spite of the cooling breeze, my face feels extraordinarily hot. Every bone in my body aches, and my throat feels as if it has been rubbed with sandpaper.

Off in the timber, an owl hoots. The last light lingers on a large white rock a few meters ahead, and I stumble forward and ease down on it. The chilling wind swirls about me as I rummage in the burlap sack I liberated from the village and pull out what is left of my bread and a bottle that was once full of good strong red wine. Now only a couple of swallows remain.

Bread and the wine are all the food I have. Earlier, I had an apple and a bar of chocolate, but I ate those hours ago. I tear off a chunk of bread and jam it in my mouth. As I chew, I try to figure out what to do.

Going on makes little sense, for in a few minutes all the light will be gone and I am traveling in a strange country. I swallow and my raw throat protests, so I sip wine to ease the pain.

I am very tired and what I really want is a good wash and a soft bed. The odds of finding either tonight fall somewhere between slim and none. The wind ratchets up and swirls down my neck and I shiver. I do not even have a blanket or any matches to build a fire. Spring is supposed to be in full bloom, but the wind bites at my nose and cheeks with a chilling ferocity.

Sitting on this rock is getting me nowhere. What I need to do is find a place to get out of the wind while the afterlight still glimmers, then try to hold on for daylight. Fever licks at my brain, and my eyes feel as though they are full of sand, but I push myself to my feet and stumble forward.

If I could find another cave, that would be ideal. A depression in the ground would not be too bad, especially if it was grass covered. Even a hollow tree would work if it were large enough. But all I can see are dark tree limbs and thick ropy looking vines. It is a spooky land, straight from the pages of a Grimm's fairy tale. Such is the power of suggestion that I pause and look about me for a lonely thatched cottage with a gurgling cauldron outside the door being stirred by a long-nosed witch in a pointy hat. But, of course, all I see are trees and vines. I tell myself to march on. What is it the French Legionnaires say? Ah yes, "March or die." In my chancy mood, that sentiment appeals to me.

There is the smell of rain in the air. A step later, the first drops strike me, hard and chilling, driven by the wind. I bow my neck and plod on.

Without notice, there is a break in the trees. In the poor light it looks as though a fire may have recently burned through this stretch of woods. In any case, enough light falls to allow me to see a cutaway in the bank. It is not a cave, but the overhang will keep the rain off and the earth itself will block the worst of the wind. As I step off what remains of the path and head toward the cut, I wonder if I will be able to find the path again in the morning. Then I wonder if I will live to welcome the morning. My body aches like it has been beaten with a dozen sound hickory sticks, while my brain feels like a fire smolders there. If I were still with my unit, I would have reported sick hours ago. Now I can only offer up feeble prayers and hope. Neither offers much comfort.

~ * ~

I come awake crying out a name. It has been a night of fever dreams. I call them dreams but in reality, they are more visions than dreams, perhaps more twisted memories than visions.

Dreams or visions or memories, they are so strange as to border on the bizarre. Faces belonging to one person suddenly appear on the body of another. The faces of my brothers, dead and missing, float in the air like lost balloons. Voices accompany the visions—I hear my mother calling me to "get up and rise and shine," and my father's comment that I must have heard a thousand times as a boy when I said I wanted something he didn't want me to have: "and people in Hell want ice water, too."

Sanne drifts through these dreams, as do M. Aubier, my aunt who showed me the patches of violets in yesterday's woods, along with Corporal Meister and dozens of men whom I have seen die. All seem to belong to another time, or to another man.

The night has grown chilly and the rain, pushed by the wind, is getting in under the overhang. I burrow deeper in the pile of last fall's leaves I pushed up last evening and rearrange the cedar boughs I latticed across the leaves. I pull my old burlap sack up around my ears. Temporarily, the fever has abated and I shiver in the chilly night.

The night is pitch black, and I have no idea of the time. Turning on my left side, I peer out into the night and, by craning my neck, I should be able to see at least a slice of sky, but no stars shine through the clouds and the glow of the moon is obscured.

Rain falls without ceasing. I can hear it pecking on leaves, and the sound reminds me of a long blast of machine gun fire heard from a great distance. I think about my old unit. Of all those men I rode off to war with on the train, there can be no more than a handful still fighting. The others are dead, or invalided out, or have simply vanished. Such a terrible waste, all those young lives destroyed. All the families who will never again see a father, a husband, a brother. It makes me sick to think about it. All that death...and for what? For lousy what? Why did I ever believe in the war? I curse my stupidity.

My stomach growls and I long for even a slice of day-old bread. Meat is beyond my imagination. Tonight I would even be happy to get a bowl of boiled Swedes. Ah, and wine, oh yes, wine. Or a good stein of beer. Since I can't have food, it seems to me that I should at least be able to have a cigarette. Smoking would calm my nerves and take my mind off food.

I roll over on my back and close my eyes. Sleep will not come and thinking about the dead and dying will do no one any good. So I think about what might be. What I would like to happen if this war ever ends. It might be pure foolishness on my part, but men who have lost everything else still cling to dreams. Call them fairy tales if you prefer. Mine is to see Sanne one more time, though she may not even speak to me. Maybe, in her anger over all that Germany has done to her, she will simply turn and pick up the rusty old shotgun she uses on foxes and wild dogs and pull the trigger.

I do not allow myself to hope for too much. Even to daydream about certain things is pure foolishness. I would settle for a sweet smile, accompanied by a few kind words. I would settle for one warm blanket. I would settle for a single cigarette. And to think I once thought I had to have wine and beef steak and boiled potatoes with butter and chocolate cake for dinner, followed by a good smoke from my pipe after.

I remember how I used to wear a shirt only once before washing and would buy a new coat on a whim, and I laugh at myself. The sound of my laughter does not belong in this rainy night and I choke it off, roll over, and bury my face in my hands. Rain falls against the earth, while the wind whines inside my mind like something alive. The fever is rising once more and my body shakes with chills. I doubt I will survive this night. Warm tears stream down my cheek.

I whisper her name to the night.

I have no one else.

Only Sanne and memories.

Only Sanne.

Forty-six

The Morning After

I come awake sensing something is missing. Sleeps still clouds my mind and I cannot figure out what has changed. Rubbing at my eyes, I sit up and look around. Night has given way and the first pale light of day covers the land. But that is the not the change that awoke me. For it is not light, but sound that has made the difference. The wind is down and the rain has stopped. The only sound is the dripping of water onto leaves, reminding me of a sound I have heard before. Only then it was blood dripping onto the decaying leaves of France.

I push leaves and branches off me and try to stand. My head feels high and hollow and my legs do not want to work properly. We have a little talk, and then I try again to stand.

This time I make it to my knees and crawl to the front of the overhang. On one side of the opening, rocks protrude, and I grab a smooth one and haul myself to a standing position. I feel my body swaying the way a sapling will in a strong wind. Before me lies the witchy forest, and I have no idea where the path is any longer, if it is even still a path. I try to recall maps I've seen and the marches I've made, but they all run together. What seems to stick out is that I need to walk north to get to Belgium. Unless I want to surrender to the French or the British, I had better head that way. Germany is not home for me anymore. My former homeland is a bridge burnt by this horrendous conflict, this war to end all wars.

I ease down the slope. Clouds still cover most of the sky, but there are enough cracks so that I can see a sliver of the rising sun. I maneuver around a fallen tree and the sun is on my right. My legs still don't want to cooperate, but I keep on putting one foot in front of the other.

Wet leaves are not the smoothest walking, and I slip and start to fall down a dozen times, only I'm able to grab a tree limb or stumble into a trunk. I pretend I am marching to meet my unit. I keep putting one foot in front of the other, just as they taught us in the early days when our leg muscles were as sore as boils and blisters dotted our feet. I know that is only a game of the mind, but there are moments when I almost feel young and healthy and happy again.

~ * ~

The sun stands directly overhead and the wind has eased until the day is as still as the altar of a church on Thursday afternoon. Perhaps it is only my imagination, but the trees do not seem to grow as close together as they did earlier. An hour ago I heard a train whistle. My sense of direction is not great, but the sound seemed to come from directly in front of me. If I can find the tracks I can follow them to a town.

I am standing on the top of a small hill and, for the first time all morning, I can see over the treetops. Off to the west is a field, and if there is a field there should be a farm. However, at the bottom of the hill a small stream flows, and I am almost beyond thirst. I push off the oak tree I've been resting against and start down the hill.

I can hear running water and, as if by their own accord, my legs break into a shambling run. I fling myself down along the bank and thrust my head into the water. Relief floods my mouth and rushes up my nose and presses against my closed eyes.

Spluttering and coughing, I jerk my head out of the water and shake my body like a wet dog. I lower it more slowly and let water run into my mouth. I drink until I can hold no more, then lift my head again. A train whistle screams, much closer this time, no more than a mile away. Reluctantly, I push away from the stream. Taking a nap on the soft grass is an enticing thought, but I need to keep moving while my thirst is slaked and the fever is down.

There is no bridge, but the stream is shallow and narrow, so I step in and splash across. Cool water feels good against my hot body and, as I clamber up the bank, I wonder if the fever will ever totally leave me.

I can hear the train rumbling down the track, and know I am close. All I have to do is follow the track and, eventually, I will arrive at a station. That is a wonderful thing about Europe—if a man is lost all he has to do is find a train track and follow it and somewhere down the line civilization will appear. If I catch a loaded freight train going up a steep incline, I might even steal a ride. Even a dirty freight car would beat walking.

The ground slopes upward again and I grab saplings and limbs and pull myself along. I am hurrying. A single train whistle has given me new energy. And though the fever is rising—my forehead feels hot again—I am still anxious to find the tracks. Amazing what even a teaspoon of hope will do for a man.

A small dark bird rises up out of a bush and wings its way before me. I follow the bird up the hill. Birds are often omens, and I hope this is a good one. I have had a long run of bad luck and am beyond ready for it to pass. The bird disappears among the trees and Sanne's face rises before me like a vagabond moon. The fever is rising once more and I can no longer think straight. All I can do is put one foot in front of the other and try to hold the vision of my Belgian. For all I know she may be dead, like thousands of others, but the remembrance of her face leads me on.

Forty-seven

Waiting for a Train

The sun seems to be amazingly close, at least the light seems extraordinarily intense. My body feels boiling hot, but that is surely due to the fever. Never have I had such a fever as this. What disease has found a home in my body, or what's left of it?

My brain throbs and even my bones ache. I cannot think straight. Why have I been sitting by a railroad track for what seems like hours? Surely I must be waiting for a train, but where am I going? All these questions make my brain ache. My eyes feel hot and full of dust. I rub at them.

A sound filters through the haze that covers my brain. Is a train coming? I force myself to listen more intently. No, it is not the faraway rumble of a train. The sound is closer. Just across the tracks on the other side of a hedge that borders a meadow. Through a gap in the hedge, dark shapes appear. Cattle moving along the fence row. Staring at the cattle, my head clears and I sense the fever is receding again. Now is the time for me to move. Who knows how long I have been sitting here waiting for a train that has not come? Or maybe it came while I slept a fevered sleep. I lick my lips and stand.

The ground seems to shimmer beneath my feet, and I wish for a stout walking stick to lean on, but I have nothing. Where have I left my rifle? Not that it matters. I am through with this war. My mind is made up, at least on this point. There is no point in fighting, or at least no point other than death. And death is something I have seen far too much of.

I look at the tracks, then lift my eyes to the sun. If I turn left, the tracks run to the northwest; right, and they flow toward the southeast. I wipe the fever sweat from my forehead and start walking northwest.

Walking along a railway is not easy because the crossties are spaced awkwardly, so that stepping from one to the next is too short a step for comfort and stepping on every other one is a step too long. Walking on the rail is a game for boys, so I plod along, stepping on the crossties as they fit my stride and on the cinders and gravel when they don't.

For the moment, the fever has abated, and I know I must make haste before it returns. My best estimate is that I have been walking for an hour. Even walking as slowly as I am, even with rest pauses, surely I will come to some village. Then I must trust to luck. However, trusting to luck beats a certain death.

For the last hundred meters the tracks have slanted up a faint rise, now they bend north, only to start down precipitously. My knees threaten to buckle, but I lean back and am all right, only I go slower, placing my feet with care. If I fall down, I am not sure I will be able to get back up. Dying of fever along a French railway line seems a particularly inglorious way to go.

A sharp staccato barking catches my ear, and I pause to listen. Yes, it is a dog. Dogs can run wild, but often they stay close to home. The barking sounds to me like it comes from a dog on a chain, though I cannot say why I think this, only that I would wager the dog is chained. And a chained dog means a house. I listen harder.

~ * ~

The house is nothing more than a cottage going to ruin. One corner of the roof needs patching and the entire structure leans east.

The grass in the yard is scraggly, but there is a smoothly worn path leading from the front door that turns and goes down a slope to a small barn that looks in better shape than the house. Three apple trees grow in the yard, and a garden plot has been plowed along one side of the house. Behind the house is a meadow. A small herd of cattle stand in the meadow, staring at me.

I step off the tracks, ease down an embankment, then cross over a ditch. On the far side of the ditch are a few scraggly trees and bramble bushes, but I push through them and come out into the yard. A brown and tan dog barks furiously, showing me his teeth, jumping off the ground a few inches every five or six barks. My hunch was correct—he is chained.

I walk around the chain, wondering as I do why the owners do not come to the door. No one could sleep through such a racket. Then it dawns on my slow working brain that they must not be at home. For a moment, I am unsure whether to be perturbed or pleased.

Just to be sure, I cry out "Hello, hello," in my best fever-encrusted French, but no one answers. Only the dog acknowledges my presence.

I pause to survey the landscape. Except for the dog, the cattle in the field, and a single bird soaring on the high winds, there is no sign of life. The dog guards the front door, so I walk around to one side of the house and press my face against the glass of the solitary window.

Inside is a bed covered with a comforter, a bedside table, a small dresser, and a single chair. A braided rug covers the floor beside the bed. On the dresser is a mirror. A blurry image appears in the mirror. It is the face of a decrepit ghost...it is my face.

Sunlight falls through the window glass, illuminating dust on the floor and on the dresser. Dead flies lie along the window sill. I count them. One, two, three—three dead flies. Three dead flies and a million dead men in France. The incongruity is hilarious. Before I can stop myself, I am giggling. For the sake of foolishness, I gently rap on the window with my knuckles. All reason seems to have fled my fevered mind.

My outburst seems to have done no harm. No face appears at the window, no voices call out, no shadows fall across my face. I turn from the window and walk to the back of the house. The day has gone quiet and, for a moment, that bothers me. Then I realize it is only that the stupid dog has quit barking.

Just as I supposed, there is a back door. I turn the knob and the door creaks open. I step into the kitchen. Like the bedroom, it is a simple, practical room. A small table is pushed against one wall and there are two straight-backed chairs, a stove, a counter, and a sink for washing up. There are no cupboards; however, a series of shelves is built into the far wall. Jars filled with pickles, corn, beans, and fruit sit on the shelves. Saliva fills my mouth.

Without hesitation, I pull a jar of peaches from a shelf and twist the lid off. I sniff at the contents, then, not bothering to hunt for a fork, I stick my fingers inside the jar.

Nothing has ever tasted sweeter to me. I jam peaches into my mouth until my cheeks protrude and it is difficult to breathe. Juice runs down my chin and I close my eyes. If I still believed in God, I would say a prayer of thanksgiving.

When all the peaches are gone, I take a moment to survey the kitchen. One of the first things I see is a bread box like my mother used. I step to it and lift the lid. Inside is the better part of a baguette. I pick it up. It is not more than a day or two old, the freshest bread I have held in my hands in weeks. Grunting like some animal, I sink my teeth into it.

~ * ~

Yap, yap, yap, the crazy dog is barking. He sounds excited, happy. When I was a boy, I had a dog. His name was Bruno and his hair was the color of freshly turned earth. I sense his name on my lips. Then I hear whistling and, because dogs do not whistle, I sit up.

I have been lying across the bed in the little cottage. I was only going to rest my eyes, but, as I glance out the window, I see that the light has changed. Shadows of afternoon stretch across the yard.

The whistling is louder, and the dog barks more shrilly. I roll off the bed and step to the window. My head has cleared and the aching in my bones has ceased, if only for the moment. I peer out the window and fear swirls in my mind.

A man is crossing the yard—a scythe hanging over one shoulder. As I watch, he bends down and unlocks the dog's chain. I am in a hell of a mess. Which door will he go to? The dog circles the man barking, yapping, and wagging his tail like something gone crazy. If I had been chained up all day, I'd be damn glad to get loose, too. They head for the back.

The instant they round the corner, I start tugging on the window. My plans had been to liberate a few more jars and two brown eggs I saw sitting in a basket, but to hell with that. My only thought is of slipping away before I am spotted. That scythe looked wicked.

The damn window is stuck. I close my eyes, take a deep breath, and push up with every bit of strength I have left. With a sharp pop it starts sliding up. Hoping the barking obscured the noise I made, I swing one leg over the sill.

My legs don't want to run, but I force them on. Halfway across the yard, I hear a change in the dog's barking. He is growling now, and I run faster, aiming for a line of scraggly trees only a few meters away.

Two strides from the tree I hear the dog growl again, then something heavy smashes against my right leg, and I am falling.

The dog and I roll together through the trees and into a bramble bush. His breath is hot and nasty against my face and his claws scratch at me like needles. I can hear myself cursing and then I get a grip on that miserable cur and shove him off me.

Before I can get to my feet, he is at me again. My right hand finds a fallen branch and I smash him across the face. The branch is rotten and flies apart without doing more than startling the dog.

That's enough for me to get back on my feet and I kick at him when he rushes in. Out of the corner of one eye, I see the man running toward us. He is shouting and waving the scythe. I cannot understand all the words over the dog's barking, but I do hear "Stop, thief." The dog lunges at me again and this time my boot finds its mark. The dog yelps and spins away, but I do not wait to see if it is hurt; already I am running down the embankment.

Something hard smashes into my shoulder and I stumble and almost go down, barely catching myself with my hands. Gravel rips at my palms and they sting.

I scramble up the far side of the ditch, glancing back over one shoulder just in time to see a rock whirling at my head. I duck and keep going, staying as low to the ground as I can. The earth is loose and I slip and start to slide back, but my hands find the thicker stalks of a bush and I pull myself up. Another rock strikes my leg, but the force is less and I keep moving.

I reach the tracks, turn and run north, leaping from crosstie to gravel to crosstie. I can hear the dog barking and the man cursing, but their voices grow faint. I put my head down and run, grateful that the man had a scythe and not a gun, hoping the fever will not return. I stumble, fall, and get back up again. My lungs gasp for air and I have a stitch in my side, but I run on. One thing war teaches a man early—he can do what he has to do. From far down the track, the train whistle blows and I jump off the track and slide halfway down the embankment. If my luck is right, the train will be loaded with freight. Not to be greedy, but I could use a patch of good luck.

Forty-eight

Trying For Belgium

She has been on my mind since the day I left her and I am determined to let nothing stand in my way. Yes, I suppose I am taking a wild chance, but what is war but chances, what is life?

In all likelihood I will never find her. Perhaps she has remarried, or moved, or died. Not to mention Belgium is no walk in the park, although I truly believe I can find the cross of stones, if it still stands.

Then, if I do find her, it is in no way certain that she will even speak to me. Were the situation reversed, I might not. But she has been a vision in my mind for so long her image has become imprinted on my brain.

It is early morning and the air is still cool. Fog silvers the air and sounds are magnified, yet distorted. I am lying on pine needles; I am lying very still.

Footsteps fall around me, making that solid, sullen sound that army boots make. *Gott in Himmel*, I know that sound—I must have heard it ten million times. As to whether they are French, or English, or even German I cannot say. Not that it matters, for I am through with the war and armies, all armies. I burrow deeper into the pine straw.

Above me, birds chirp and a squirrel chatters like he's gone mad. The bootfalls are closer, and I lower my head and place one side of my face against the fallen needles. Only one eye is open, so I can see only the first few inches above the ground. Mostly I see the trunks of pines, their low-hanging branches, and the sparse green shoots of grass thrusting up through the brown needles that cover the earth.

The marchers are so close I can smell their sweat, the oil on their rifles, and the onions in their knapsacks. I can smell fear, too, at least in my imagination, but that is surely my own.

The birds have fallen silent and the squirrel no long chatters.

A man coughs and brown blur catches my eye. I raise my head up one inch and see the dark object is a boot. Dirty gray uniform trousers hang just above the boot. The edges of the trousers are raggedy.

"Bloody foggy this morning, ain't it?" The voice is achingly young. English.

"Silence in the ranks. There are Jerries about, you fools."

And closer than you realize, I think. My fingers close around a bayonet I found along the railroad tracks. Once it had belonged to a French soldier, but the end has been honed to a fine point, sharp enough to poke a hole in a man's guts.

I try to breathe shallowly. If they weren't so close, I would deep into the pine needles like some frightened field mouse. But I have waited too late for that, so now all I can do is grip the bayonet and pray. Not that I am a believer in prayer. If there is a God, He has abandoned the world. At least the world I have been living in. My fever has finally left, and now this.

"Keep a sharp eye out." The voice has a Cockney twang, and I get a vivid image of a lean, leathery sergeant who has survived on wits and discipline. "Roust them out. Jab those bushes. We don't want Jerry slipping in our back door."

You don't have to worry about that, mate, I think. All this Jerry wants to do is slip over the border into Belgium. Unless you force my hand, my killing days are over.

Leaves rustle and a twig breaks inches from my face. My muscles tighten until they threaten to burst. My body is awash in a cold sweat, one eye twitches uncontrollably, and the urge to empty my bladder is strong. My lungs ache, and I realize I have been holding my breath. I let it out in a long low stream. Boots tromp past my hiding place as I wonder if the sergeant, or whatever rank he is, was right and there are more of my comrades in this wood. The war has turned against us—one must acknowledge that—and the weak and the weary will be striving to find the way home. I fall among the weary—that I freely admit—only I don't want to go home. I just want to slip away.

"Hey, I just saw something move."

"Where?"

"Down there, by that crooked fir."

"What did you see?"

I do not wait to hear the response. All about me men are running toward the voices which sound some distance down the slope. I am scooting my way backwards, out from under the bush. I suppose I could wait, but what if the English decide to set up camp, or if another, more vigilant, squad comes along? No, strike while the chance exists, for already the window may be closing.

I am out in the open, wriggling like some gigantic snake across a patch of grass. On the far side of the patch of grass are several large oaks. Lying on my belly in the presence of the enemy is abhorrent to me. Not that I am worried about being a coward—I freely admit I am afraid of dying—but I feel so helpless in that position.

I slither among another stand of trees, then rise up like some ancient creature springing forth from the earth. Pressing my back against rough bark, I listen for the voices. They sound farther away than before and I allow myself to begin to hope. I risk a look around the oak that hides me. All I see are more trees, so I step to the next one, moving away from the voices.

No alarms sound, and I move to the next tree, then the next. I am stepping more quickly, yet still exercising care where I place my feet. Dead branches and fallen leaves litter the ground, so I cannot move without caution.

The ground falls away, sloping down to a narrow ledge. I ease down the slope, turn, and start walking away from the voices. Three strides later I come to a dead stop.

Directly before me is a British soldier, squatting just where the ledge ends, answering a call of nature. His pants are down around his ankles, and he is looking at the ground. As I stare at him, his eyes rise to meet mine. Never have I seen a man look so startled.

His eyes flick to his rifle. It is propped against a tree a few paces away. His eyes swerve back to me, then back to the rifle.

I show him the bayonet and shake my head. His eyes grow very wide.

"Don't even think about it."

His mouth comes open.

"I will kill you," I say and jab the point of the bayonet at him.

He smiles at me, but his eyes flick to the rifle, then back to my face.

"Sure enough, mate. I know when I'm at a disadvantage. Why don't you go on your way and I'll say I was blinded by the light?"

Footsteps fall all around us. Just at the edge of my vision there are shadows, moving like wraiths. This man has many companions; thus he holds more cards than I do. But I hold the Ace of Spades—the bayonet. I show it to him again. A shard of sunlight glitters on the tip.

"How do I know I can trust you?"

As if by some ancient instinct, we both turn our heads ever so slightly toward the moving shadows.

The Britisher shows me his teeth. They are stained and one is missing. "Don't fancy that bayonet in my guts, no I don't." He nods toward his right shoulder. "Go on, mate, just go on. My lips are sealed. I'm as silent as the grave." To demonstrate, he presses his lips together in one firm hard line. He looks like certain German officers I have known.

A line from some play flickers through my brain, something along the lines of "Me thinks he doth protest too much." Is that Shakespeare? Does it matter? I take a step to my left and leaves crackle beneath my boots. The other man stays as still as the tree behind him. Only the lights in his eyes change, almost infinitesimally.

That tiny change worries me. My old grandmother used to say you could see another person's soul through their eyes. I've never known whether to believe that or not, but now there seems some truth to that old wives' tale. My brain is worried, or perhaps it is ancient instincts that arouse the fear. I ease another step left, glancing down for a second to make sure that my foot isn't going to slide into some hole or catch on a rouge tree root. At the very edge of vision, I see a flicker of movement.

I am almost too late. In that brief fragment of time, lasting hardly longer than it takes an eye to blink, my enemy has made a move to grab his rifle. The coppery taste of fear coats my tongue. I try to change direction and feel my feet slipping on leaves.

A cry rises in my throat, and I am falling. I catch myself with one hand and try to propel my body across the open ground. But the ground seems to give way beneath me, and for a half-naked man the British soldier moves with surprising quickness. The bayonet is still in my hand, and I twist my wrist.

No more than a half dozen meters separate us; blood sings in my ears as I gather myself for the leap.

The roar of the rifle is deafening. Fire burns along the ribs on my left side. As though caught in a great wind, I feel myself being lifted off my feet. Pain surges through me like electric current. I see a flash of light, so intense my eyes feel on fire. Then the world begins to spin and I am trapped in a powerful whirlpool, swirling down, down, down. I feel my body falling, falling, falling, and then it smashes against the earth and I am rolling, over and over and over, down a long slope of ground that seems to have no end.

Forty-nine

The Ant

The ant is very persistent. He is trying to get a crumb of some sort. It looks to be a fragment of a beetle shell curled over a twig that lies in the path he has chosen. He stands astraddle of the twig, well, as close to astraddle as an ant can. Getting over the twig is no problem for him. The challenge for the little chap is moving that fragment of beetle over the twig. Something on the fragment must be catching on the twig, keeping the ant from being able to pull it over.

The ant has been working away without pause for severak minutes. I have been watching him. Time has lost much of its meaning, at least for the two of us. We are out of the war, the two of us, yes, and time no longer matters, not as much as it did at any rate.

We do not have to answer the bugle any longer. We do not have to report to the mess tent at the designated hour. We do not need to worry about rising in the cold and dark to stand our watch. No, Monsieur Ant and I have left all that, along with our youth, behind.

Now we are only two simple creatures trying to survive. M. Ant is desperately struggling to bring food back to his queen. As for good old Sergeant Schiller, I am merely trying not to die.

My left ribcage burns and blood oozes down my side. I feel extremely weak, and if I lift my head, even a few degrees, the world spins. So I lie quietly and watch a lousy ant try to overcome a twig. A fine German soldier reduced to this—what a joke. Only the joke is on me.

The ant turns his finely carved head and seems to stare directly into my eyes. I give him a wink, then shut my eyes and gather my strength. Enough of this foolishness. Another hour of this and I will be dead. I will have bled to death after being shot by a bare-arsed Englishman. Hardly a fitting end for a solider such as myself. I open my eyes, and push off the ground with everything I have. This time I push through the pain that flashes through me like summer heat lightning.

I am upright, though my head swirls. Blood sings in my ears and, without conscious thought, I stumble forward. Twigs snap under my feet and as I lurch ahead, I realize I have killed the ant. Another death on my conscience.

My balance is bad and my legs are weak. Not a good combination. My vision keeps slipping out of focus. My left knee gives way and I collapse forward, spinning off a sapling, crashing through a bush, and fall face first into the trunk of a massive tree. My arms will not go all the way around this giant of the forest, but my fingers dig in and I keep my body erect.

It is a bad moment. The inside of my brain is like soup and the forest tilts first one way then another. I close my eyes and a thousand pinpricks of light flash before me. It is as watching the heavens come alive in an instant.

Gradually, the spinning slows and I open my eyes. I am not at all sure where I am, but I have the sense that I am on the floor of the forest. I hold my breath and listen. If the British soldiers are still around I must exercise the utmost care.

I think I hear voices, but no, that is merely the wind. A jay screeches off to my left and nearby, a creature rustles through fallen leaves. Filtered by the canopy above, the distorted light is tricky and directional findings are challenging.

All my thrashing around has done nothing to staunch the flow of blood. My uniform blouse is soaked with it and the thick cloying smell saturates my nostrils. Panic rises in my throat until it is difficult to breathe. I am bleeding to death and I have no real idea where I am or where I should go. Tears pool in my eyes. Weeping is unbecoming in a German soldier, but I don't feel particularly soldierly at the moment.

I blink back the tears and force myself to breathe normally, or as close to normally as possible. Gradually a thought coalesces in my battered brain—the bleeding must be stopped. I study my uniform until I find a fairly clean section. Luck is with me, for the fabric has ripped in a strategic place. I grip a corner firmly and give a jerk.

Pain races through me, but a longish section is loose. I grit my teeth and jerk again. The swatch comes free and I press it against the wound. I can't be sure, but it doesn't feel as though the bullet is still inside me. If it has passed through, I will need to keep both ends of the wound as clean as possible. More soldiers have died from unsanitary conditions than bullets. I work off the rest of my uniform blouse and tie it around me, pressing the fabric tighter against the wound. Then I start walking.

Fifty

Le Samaritan

A cool puff of wind in August may be a mercy
A sudden rain against the sands of the Sahar may be a mercy
A sudden death at a lonely crossroads may be a mercy
The loss of all life's memories may be a mercy
The end of a long and violent journey may be a mercy
The soft hand of a stranger against your face may be a mercy

Sunlight coats my face. My skin feels quite warm, the way the palms of your hands feel after you have been swinging an axe rapidly for several minutes.

I think about how my face feels. Then I begin to wonder where I am. The sense that I have lost several hours of my life keeps bubbling to the surface of my brain, and I open one eye.

All I can see is blue sky. I rotate my head, but cannot see a single cloud, only the great golden sun burning a hole in the lining of the sky. I open the other eye.

It seems I am lying on my back in a ditch along the side of a road. There does not appear to be a lot of traffic on the road, although I do hear a motor rumbling by every few minutes. My side aches like it has been smashed by a well-struck sledge hammer, and I remember the English soldier with his pants down and press my hand against the makeshift bandage. It comes back sticky, smelling of warm blood. My stomach rolls and I close my eyes.

~ * ~

Something is gently shaking me. I let myself float back to full consciousness. I can hear voices. They sound young. They are speaking French, but the accent is strange.

"I think he is dead."

"No, I tell you I heard him moan as we passed."

"Look at all that blood."

"That doesn't mean he's dead. A person can bleed for a long time before they die, unless one of those arteries is severed."

"You sound like a doctor."

"I should, my father is one."

"But he works on animals, horses and cows."

"Yes, but he can also treat humans. He set the broken arm of M. LeClaire last year."

"Was that after M. LeClaire's horse threw him?"

"Exactly. My father set his arm and now it is as good as new, maybe better. They say a broken bone heals stronger in the broken places."

I work my lips and try to speak. Only a guttural sound emerges.

"See, Jacob, I told you he was alive."

Hands press against me, shaking me. "Monsieur, monsieur, can you speak? Tell us how you are hurt."

It takes two tries, but I get one eye open.

"Ugh," is all I can say. Faces swim before me like the faces of fish just below the surface of the water.

"Monsieur, do not worry, we are here to help you. My father is a doctor. I do not think you should be moved, at least not much. Until he sees you, that is. So my friend, Jacob, is going to help me carry you under the shade of those trees." The boy's blurry face swings to the right. "Do you understand?"

My throat feels as though it has been packed with cotton. I swallow. "Yes," I mumble. My voice sounds strange to my ears, as though it is coming from far away.

"*Bon*. Now my friend and I are going to carry you to the shade." He pats my head, very gently, as if I am an old dog. "There will be some pain, but you must grit your teeth and endure. It will not last long. *Oui*?"

"*Oui*," I say as hands grasp me and I feel my body rising. The boys mean well, but I am heavy, a dead weight, and they grunt with the effort. For a moment, I swing loosely in the air. Then they have me firmly in their grasp and there is the sensation that I am flying. Then one of them stumbles and pain jolts through me like heat lighting. My blood sings in my ears and the world whirls black.

~ * ~

The initial sensation is that of smell. Onions, I can smell onions, onions being cooked. Meat, too. Beef, I think, and pepper and garlic and other spices I cannot name.

Next comes feel. I am lying on something far softer than mother earth. My fingers reach out and what they feel is wonderfully soft. Linen? I stretch out an arm and allow my fingers to slide across the glorious smoothness, until they can find only air. I open my eyes.

I am lying on a chaise-lounge in a small room with a single window. The curtains are drawn and the only light comes from an oil lamp flickering on a small table a few feet away. More light, and voices, filter in from an adjoining room. One of the voices sounds vaguely familiar, although to be sure I have absolutely no idea where I am.

I start to sit up. "Ah," I cry. What a mistake: My side is on fire.

With great tenderness my fingers explore. Someone has bandaged my wound. The bandages are soft, neat, smooth. Ah, a professional touch. I hear footsteps plodding toward me. They belong to a short man with gray hair and a luxurious mustache.

"You are awake, monsieur?"

"Seem to be," I say.

He smiles. It is a rather sideways smile as though he finds me amusing in the way a child or a dog can be amusing.

"You have been, shall we say, asleep for some time."

Vestiges of that sleep still linger in my brain. Thinking clearly is beyond me for the present. "How long?"

"For several hours, monsieur. You were asleep, or to be more accurate, unconscious, when my son and his friend carried you into the house."

My fingers press ever so gently against the clean bandages. "I vaguely recall hearing someone say something about a doctor. And now I have been expertly bandaged. Am I correct in assuming that you are that doctor?

The man inclines his head. "*Oui*, of a sort. My name is Grisand. I am a veterinarian, a doctor of the animals. Still, I know how to dress a wound." He cocks his head to one side and looks at me from under bushy eyebrows that put me in mind of caterpillars.

"You were shot, monsieur. No, no, do not say anything. I am a doctor, so I recognize a gunshot wound when I see it. Yours was not the first such wound I have treated over the past few years. Since the fighting began, soldiers have wandered into this town, or been abandoned during retreat. Doctor Belmonde and I have treated dozens." He smiles at me. "You are a solider, no?"

I shrug. "I used to be."

"But you are no more?"

"No, I am no longer a part of the war."

"You have been invalided out?"

I look at his face. His is not an easy one to read. But what difference does it make? I will not fight again. Honesty is said to liberate the soul. "It is more that I have resigned from it."

"Ah, that is a good way to express yourself. I understand." He smiles. "You see, I, too, have resigned from this war. Never have I been fond of war and to fight for so little purpose seems to me to be beyond foolishness. After all the excitement died, I began to wonder why all the countries had gone to war in the first place." He looks away for a moment, then looks back and stares into my eyes.

"Do you ever wonder about such things?"

Again I shrug. "Don't all men wonder about the reasons behind war?"

It is the doctor's turn to shrug. "*Mon ami*, I am not sure they do. In fact, I am almost certain some men do not concern themselves in the least as to why wars start. Unless it is to figure out to start another. You see, I am convinced that some men live for war. And not only soldiers. There are men who are infatuated with words like glory and honor."

My savior snorts. "What is sad, or sick, depending on how you look at it, is that most such men are not, nor never have been soldiers."

A hundred images flash in my mind. "Yes," I say, "it is easy to ask other men to die."

The doctor nods. "Agreed, and I, for one, am not going to fight another man's battles, no matter who the man."

At that, he turns and gazes across the room. Only I do not think he is seeing anything in that room, or even the house for that matter. I wonder what measures of death the doctor has seen, for it seems clear he is a man who abhors violence. No longer do I worry about being turned over to the authorities, whoever that might be.

Thinking about the authorities makes me wonder. I glance around the room, but see no clues. I clear my throat.

"Excuse me, Herr Grisand, but tell me what country I am in."

His head turns slowly. I note the grey in his hair and the crow's feet around his eyes. Those eyes are blue, a faded blue, a blue that leads me somehow to believe that they were once a more vibrant shade but have somehow lost much of their intensity over the years. They gaze at me without blinking.

"And what country would you like to be in, monsieur?"

The question strikes me as a peculiar one and my calm is shaken. As though by instinct, my fingers flutter across my bandages.

"My desire is to reach Belgium."

The doctor smiles. He smiles a small smile.

"Then your wish has been granted." He rubs the palm of one hand along his jawline. I can hear the rasping of his stubble. "If you don't mind, monsieur, will you tell me why you wanted to get to Belgium? You do not strike me as a Belgian."

"No," I say, "I am not from Belgium." I take a deep breath. There is nothing more I have to add, but I feel I owe this man something. After all, he surely saved my life. Without his care, I would almost certainly have bled to death. Still, I do not have to say anymore. Yet I feel obliged.

"I am a German, you see."

The doctor nods. "I thought as much."

Suddenly, I feel weak and ease down until I am flat on my back, staring at the ceiling. My blood sings in my ears. "Earlier in the war, I met this woman. And..."

"And you would like to find her again?'

"Yes."

"Does she want to see you again? Not all wartime meetings are, shall we say, mutually friendly."

"That is a good question, Herr Grisand. Time, I suppose, will tell."

He rubs at his blue eyes, then yawns. I feel sleepy myself.

"And where was this earlier meeting?"

"The name of the town escapes me." I make a face. "My mind has been battered about a good deal of late. However, just outside of this town there is, or at least there was, this huge cross made from white stones. It stood at a crossroads, and you could see it for miles. Perhaps you know it?"

"Ah," says the doctor. "Yes, I know the place. The cross is quite a famous landmark and, yes, it stands outside a small village." He rubs at his head. "Now, what is the name of that town? Curses, it is on the tip of my tongue. It is...it is? Ah, it is Hasstend. Yes, that is it, Hasstend."

"Hasstend," I say as I close my eyes. "Hasstend." Darkness covers me like a soft warm quilt and I drift gently into a realm of dreams.

Fifty-one

A Field of Violets

I glance at the sky. No longer is the sun directly overhead. Instead, it has drifted far to the west, and all around me purple shadows have flung themselves upon the ground and bled out until their colors have mingled in the green grass. A field of wildflowers and violets flows like a river of earth beside the road and, on this late afternoon, Belgium, is very beautiful. For as far back as I have memory, I have loved violets. When my mind is more settled I must write a poem about them, about violets.

A fragment floats through my brain:

In the spring,
violets will thrust through
the hard shell of Mother Earth
and bloom again,
the purple glory shimmering
through the alabaster skulls
of the dead,
the dead who lie in woods and fields

and on mountain sides, unburied,
forgotten by all,
except,
perhaps,
God.
Markers of war
and waste
their hollow mouths open,
yet silenced forever.

My legs are tired, and now and then I felt a jab of pain in my side. However, the pain is manageable, and in all other aspects I feel good. For a horse doctor, Herr Grisand is a fine physician. His bandages are smooth and clean, and for over two days there has been no obvious bleeding. For more than a week, I have had no fever, and my stomach is full of the doctor's good soup, and dumplings, and brown bread. Speaking of bread, I carry half a loaf in the pack on my back, along with a bottle of the doctor's homemade wine.

Since daylight, I have been on the road. That is when I reached the end of the railway line that runs in the direction of Hasstend. All day I have hoped for a ride from some farmer or lorry driver, but luck has not been with me. I have no complaints, however. A couple of weeks ago, I was convinced I was going to bleed to death. Now it seems I will have an opportunity to plead my case.

How many kilometers have I come this day? That is not an easy question to answer. First, because I have not walked at a steady pace. When I have felt strong, my pace has been good. However, there have been moments when waves of weakness washed over me just as waves from the sea wash over the sands of the shore.

Second, my strength has not yet fully returned, and I have been forced on occasion to seek the soft grass in the shade of a tree and rest for several minutes. Once, at noon, after my midday bread and cheese and wine, I felt my eyelids grow heavy and I lay on my back with my eyes closed and welcomed sleep.

At the moment, however, I feel life flowing through me like a rising stream, and I swing along almost like in the old days. Almost, I say, because I am not the same man I was in those younger days. Aches and pains visit frequently, and scars cover my aging hide like the designs of some lunatic artist. My mind no longer drifts to family and friends, except to recall their passing, or a brief pleasant interlude from the sepia-tinted past. No, these days I think only of Sanne, and leaving the war, and how I can find my way to the cross of stones.

Before me the road gently bends to the west. As it bends it rises, and I'm panting as I come up the slope. Clearly, I have not fully recovered from my wound, and I wonder if I ever will regain the strength of my youth.

Part of me longs to step off the road and stretch out in the grass that grows alongside. Shadows cover much of it and it looks thick and soft, and I think about resting, think about it long and hard. But I have come so far it would seem a shame to stop when surely I am so close.

At the crest I pause. A large birch tree grows close to the road and I lean against it and shut my eyes. But only briefly. I have made a promise to myself, one that I shall keep.

Faces swim out of the darkness and float before me. I see my parents, my brothers, and dozens of my comrades. For a few seconds, I see the face of that Belgian boy on the bridge—the first one we killed.

He was so young.

I was so young.

The world was so young.

The call of a lark lacerates the moment, and I open my eyes and step back out on the road. My legs ache, there is a throbbing in my temples, and if I move my head too quickly, the earth gently spins. However, I must soldier on, for night is coming. Already the trees are wrapped in purple dusk, and soon it will be dark. But the road flows open and white before me and I slog forward. Shadows dance along the road while a bird trills at me from the gloaming.

A breeze springs up and kisses my face. I bow my head in gratitude. War has taught me to be grateful for even small things, especially small things. My feet move on their own, automatic pistons churning without conscious direction.

I am climbing up another, longer slope and earth flows beneath me like a brown river. Without notice, I reach the crest, slightly out of breath, and I pause to survey the land unfurling before me. In the distance, just at the edge of vision, is a white blur. Could it be stones? I urge my tired legs to action.

The mass of white is maybe two hundred meters away. Suddenly new life surges through my tired legs. For the first time in weeks I break into a trot. Trees and bushes are a blur, my heart pounds wildly, and my lungs ache for air.

Yes, yes, yes, it is the cross of stones. I am almost home. Funny to think of it that way, but that is what throbs in my mind. I wonder what Sanne will think when she sees my face. Perhaps she will not remember. It seems as though lifetimes have passed since our night and, for all she knows, I am dead. The odds are good for that. Or she could be dead. These have not been kind years to many.

The shadow of the cross falls across my face as I pause and run my fingers along the cool stones. Now I know the way. In my dreamings I have made this journey a thousand times. I draw in a lungful or air and hurry forward.

I trot down the lane, the house and barn rising up before me out of the dusk. Yes, that barn. Memories flame up in my mind as if they were kerosene set afire.

A lamp glows in the window of the house, and I sense my feet slowing. Fear rises in my throat. How long has it been? A year? No, two, at least, perhaps three. The war has been long, and I am tired, and at times my mind plays tricks on me.

What if she does not want me? What will I do? Perhaps I will shoot myself. In certain ways I feel guilty for surviving, especially as so many have not. What if she no longer lives in the house that stands before me? What if she no longer lives?

Some things cannot be considered, not if a man wishes to hang on to whatever sanity he retains after being so long in such a horrific war.

I stand as still as the cross of stones and listen to the coming night. I can hear the lowing of cattle and, from a neighboring farm, voices call to one another. But there is another sound. For a second, I cannot place it. Then it comes to me—it is the sound of a barn door screeching open.

Two figures step out from the barn, one much larger than the other. They do not see me standing in the shadows. In the distance, a dog howls. A brain aberration reminds me that dog is only God spelled backwards. Whatever the hell that means.

The very ground is shaking. No, it is only my legs quivering. Quivering as though I am about to go over the top again. Just as in the trenches, I am terribly afraid. Part of me wants to step out of the shadows into the light, while another part wants only to watch and wait. My heart pounds wildly and I tremble.

The taller figure turns, her head cocked as though she has heard an unusual sound. Has a word escaped my lips unknowingly?

Barn swallows do barrel-rolls in the purpling sky. The air is redolent with the scent of hay and dust and freshly turned earth. The taller figure takes the smaller one by the hand and they start walking in my direction. If I am to flee, I must go now. But it has been a long journey and I am tired to my very bones.

I am ready, too. Ready for an end of some sort to the madness. Yes or No—the question must be answered. A whisper of wind brushes my face.

The figures step out from the shadows thrown by the barn into the afterglow of evening and in that instant I am sure. She lives and I smile, knowing that part of my prayer has been answered.

"Sanne," I whisper.

"Sanne?"

"Who's there?" she calls out. "I know you are there. I see you lurking in the shadows, you coward. Step out and show your face or leave."

My legs have turned to stone and I am as fixed to the ground as the cross of white stones.

"Come out and show yourself. Show yourself or I will shoot." Sanne reaches into the basket hanging from her arm and pulls out a French officer's pistol. It shakes in her hand, but the black hole still speaks of death. I wonder where she obtained it.

"Step out or I'll shoot." Sanne takes a step closer. "At this range I cannot miss."

I am not certain if she even knows how to pull the trigger, but that does not matter. Just as it did in the war, the fear has passed, and I draw breath deep into my lungs and step boldly into the last light of day.

I watch with small hope as her face rearranges itself. At the very edge of vision, I see the smaller figure move. It appears to be a small child. Boy or girl I cannot be sure.

"Who are you?" Sanne gasps, her voice a throaty whisper that somehow sounds like the voice of a Colonel Vandermeer I knew once in another time. That is, it sounded as his voice sounded after he had been gassed by the British.

"Who are you?"

I lick my lips. My mouth is full of cotton.

"Is that you, Sanne?" I say. My voice is pitched soft and low, but in the still of evening it sounds harsh and strident.

"Who are you?" she asks again. "Tell me your name." She lurches forward a step. The pistol has dropped to her side. "Are you man or ghost?"

"I am both, and neither." I start to walk slowly toward the woman I have dreamed of for all these months. "In another life, I was Sergeant Karl Schiller."

Her eyes grow so wide they seem to cover her face.

"In what seems a lifetime ago we spent a special night in that old barn behind you."

"No," she whispers. "No, it cannot be."

"Ah, but I speak only truths these days," I say as I come to a stop before her. "I have left the war, and it no longer has power over my soul." I can see her face clearly. Lines are there that I do not remember, and in her hair threads of silver among the brown. Time bypasses no one.

"How can it be?"

"God has been kind."

"Has He?"

"Ah," I say, "I understand."

"No," she says, a harshness running through her voice now. "You cannot understand. You and I share one night of drunken passion and then you march off to other women and greater glory, leaving me to deal with the consequences." She pauses and turns to the smaller figure.

My eyes follow hers. A small child, a boy, stands before me. He looks as if he might be about two years old. His hair is blond, the same shade as mine, and in the chancy light his eyes appear green—the same green that looks back at me from the mirror.

My mind whirls. Can it be? Is it possible?

I open my mouth, but no words come out.

"Yes," Sanne says, "he is yours. At least he is yours if you truly are my German of the long night."

My heart flutters wildly in my chest. My hands tremble as I lift them to my shirt and unbutton the top button. The thin silver chain is cool against my fingers. I lift it off my chest and the metal catches a final shaft of light and the cross glitters.

Sanne's eyes are fixed on the tiny piece of silver. The mosaics of her face change, and her lower lip begins to tremble. "I thought you must be dead," she whispers. "A hundred nights I dreamed you were dead."

She wipes her eyes with the back of a hand. Swallows swoop and call out to one another in the sky above us while out of the corner of one eye I see the child watching me.

"What is his name?" My voice sounds funny as though my throat has suddenly thickened.

"His name is Karl. I named him after his father."

With my right hand I reach out and touch the boy's hair. It feels like silk. My left hand finds Sanne's face. My fingers trace love songs across her lips.

"Can it be?" I say. "Can it truly be?"

Without speaking, she steps into my arms and presses her lips against mine. Her tears wet our faces. Or perhaps those are my tears.

Only a good German soldier is not supposed to cry. But then, I am no longer a good German soldier. The war belongs to another man, to another place, another time.

I pull her so tightly against me that I fear she might break. The little one scratches at my leg and I bend and pick him up and press him against us both. "My son," I say, "my son."

Sanne kisses my cheek. "Shall we go into the house?" she asks. "It is past time for his supper and I know you must be tired."

She smiles. "Besides, the light is going, and I want to get a good look at my German soldier. See if he is as handsome as in my dreams."

I cannot speak. Instead, I take her hand and we walk as one through the gathering night toward the deeper, welcoming shadows of the house. My son's fingers caress my check.

My son, my son, I say to myself in a litany of wonder.

As we walk, I feel as though a hundred ghosts walk with me. Brothers and friends and enemies. One by one, they drift away into the shadows of the night until I am alone with the woman I have dreamed of through a thousand lonely nights.

Just my foolish self and Sanne and our son.

They are enough.

No, they are more than enough for this tired, battered, lonely German soldier who has left the war to find his family, the woman he loves, his very soul. I bow my head and count my blessings.

Meet Chris Helvey

Chris Helvey's short stories have been published by numerous reviews and journals, and he is the author of the novels *Yard Man* and *Dancing on the Rim (Wings ePress), Snapshot, and Whose Name I Did Not Know, plus the short story collections One More Round and Claw Hammer*. He currently serves as Editor in Chief of *Trajectory Journal.*

Other Works From The Pen Of
Chris Helvey

Yard Man - Judas Cain, a lonely man simply trying to survive finds a job he doesn't want, a woman who doesn't love him and incurs the wrath of the most dangerous man in Mississippi.

Dancing on the Rim - A rich American goes to Mexico looking for a good time but instead discovers a drug cartel, a private prison, and that his wife is trying to kill him.

Letter to Our Readers

Enjoy this book?

You can make a difference

As an independent publisher, Wings ePress, Inc. does not have the financial clout of the large New York Publishers. We can't afford large magazine spreads or subway posters to tell people about our quality books.

But, we do have something much more effective and powerful than ads. We have a large base of loyal readers.

Honest Reviews help bring the attention of new readers to our books.

If you enjoyed this book, we would appreciate it if you would spend a few minutes posting a review on the site where you purchased this book or on the Wings ePress, Inc. webpages at: https://wingsepress.com/

Visit Our Website

For The Full Inventory

Of Quality Books:

Wings ePress.Inc
https://wingsepress.com/

Quality trade paperbacks and downloads

in multiple formats,

in genres ranging from light romantic comedy

to general fiction and horror.

Wings has something for every reader's taste.

Visit the website, then bookmark it.

We add new titles each month!

Wings ePress Inc.

3000 N. Rock Road

Newton, KS 67114

CPSIA information can be obtained
at www.ICGtesting.com
Printed in the USA
BVHW040825181121
621921BV00012B/214

9 781613 095706